False Pretences

by

Rosemary Morris

Books We Love
A quality publisher of genre fiction.
Airdrie Alberta

Print ISBN 978-1-77299-181-9

Copyright 2nd Edition 2016 Rosemary Morris
Cover Art 2016 by Michelle Lee

All rights reserved. Without limiting the rights under copyright reserved above, no part of this publication may be reproduced, stored in or introduced into a retrieval system, or transmitted, in any form, or by any means (electronic, mechanical, photocopying, recording, or otherwise) without the prior written permission of both the copyright owner and the publisher of this book.

Dedication

*With love and gratitude to my identical twin
sons, Chirag and Lalit,
gentlemen who I am very proud of.*

Chapter One

1815

"I have good news for you, Annabelle," said Miss Chalfont, the well-educated head mistress and owner of The Beeches, an exclusive school for young ladies.

Seated on a straight-backed chair opposite Miss Chalfont's walnut desk, Annabelle clasped her hands tightly on her lap. "Has my guardian told you who my parents are?" she asked in a voice quivering with excitement.

Regret flickered across Miss Chalfont's face before she shook her head. "No, I am very sorry, he has not. For your sake, I wish he had. In fact, I do not know who he is. I receive instructions from a lawyer in Dover. To be honest, for no particular reason, I have always assumed your guardian's identity is that of a man, but it could be that of a woman."

Dover! Annabelle thought. The town where she had lived with her nurse before a nameless elegant lady, with a French accent, brought her to The Beeches. Time and time again, she had wondered if the lady was her guardian, or whether she was a stranger ordered to bring her here. She had no way of knowing, for the lady had not answered any of her questions.

Annabelle looked into Miss Chalfont's eyes. "Who is the lawyer, ma'am?"

"I do not know, for he does not identify himself. He merely arranges for your…er…upkeep, and sends me your guardian's instructions."

No clue to the mystery of my own identity, Annabelle thought and gazed down to conceal her disappointment. "Has the lawyer given you permission to tell me who my guardian is?" she asked, despite her suspicion that he had not.

Miss Chalfont looked down at a letter. "No, your guardian, whom I have no doubt has your welfare at heart, still wishes to remain anonymous. However, my dear child, you are fortunate. Your guardian has arranged for you to marry Monsieur le Baron de Beauchamp."

Annabelle looked up with a mixture of astonishment, disbelief, and intense indignation at the arrangement that took no heed of her wishes. "I am to marry a man I have never met?"

With restless fingers, Miss Chalfont adjusted her frilled mobcap. "Yes, your guardian has arranged for you to marry Monsieur le Baron tomorrow."

Annabelle stared at her kind teacher as though she had turned into a monster. "*Mon dieu*!" she raged, reverting to the French she spoke when she was a small child. "My God! Tomorrow? My guardian expects me to marry a

Frenchman tomorrow. "Miss Chalfont, surely you do not approve of such haste."

"Do not take the Lord's name in vain." Miss Chalfont tapped her fingers on her desk. "My approval or disapproval is of no consequence. Your guardian wishes you to marry immediately, so there is little more to be said. A special licence has been procured and the vicar has been informed." Miss Chalfont smiled at her. "You have nothing to fear. This letter informs me that Monsieur speaks English and lives in this country."

Annabelle scowled. Her hands trembled. For the first time, she defied her head mistress. "Nothing to fear? My life is to be put in the hands of a husband with the right to…beat me…or…starve me, and you say I have nothing to fear, Miss Chalfont? Please believe me when I say that *nothing* will persuade me to marry in such haste."

Not the least display of emotion crossed the head teacher's face. "You should not allow your imagination to agitate your sensibilities. For all you know, the monsieur is charming and will be a good, kind husband."

"On the other hand, he might be a monster," Annabelle said.

Miss Chalfont ignored the interruption and continued. "At eighteen, you are the oldest girl in the school. It is time for you to leave the nest and establish one of your own."

"Twaddle," Annabelle muttered. "My education is almost complete and I suspect you wish to be rid of me."

Miss Chalfont smoothed the skirt of her steel-grey woollen gown and looked at Annabelle with a cold expression in her eyes. "I beg your pardon? Did I hear you say *'twaddle'*? As for wishing to be rid of you, child, that is not true. However, I will admit that in recent months I have worried about your guardian's future plans for you. Nevertheless, I need not have worried. As a happy bride, I daresay you will go to London where those pretty blue eyes and long lashes of yours will be so much admired that Monsieur le Baron will be proud of you."

At any other time Miss Chalfont's rare compliment would have pleased her. On this occasion, it only served to increase the fury she tried to conceal. Losing her temper would be pointless. Before Annabelle spoke, she took a deep breath to calm herself. "It is unreasonable to order me to marry the man without allowing me time to become acquainted with him."

"Do not refer to your bridegroom as *'the man'*. I have told you his name is de Beauchamp."

Rebellion flamed in Annabelle's stomach. "What do you know of my…er…bridegroom-to-be, ma'am?"

Miss Chalfont looked down at the letter. "He is described as a handsome gentleman of mature years."

"One would think the description is of a piece of mature cheese or a bottle of vintage wine."

Miss Chalfont frowned. "Do not be impertinent, Annabelle, you are not too old to be punished."

"I beg your pardon, ma'am, but please tell me how mature he is," Annabelle said, her eyes wide open and her entire body taut with apprehension.

"Monsieur le Baron is some forty-years-old."

"How mature?" Annabelle persisted with her usual bluntness.

"He is forty-two-years-old."

Annabelle stood, bent forward, and drummed her fingers on the edge of the desk. "Please be kind enough to inform my guardian that I will not play Guinevere to an aging Arthur. I would prefer to build my nest with a young Lancelot."

Miss Chalfont's shoulders heaved as though she was trying not to laugh. "Regardless of your preference, you must marry according to your guardian's wish."

"Dear ma'am, you and your mother have always been kind to me. I cannot believe you approve of—"

"As I have already said, my approval or disapproval is of no importance. Your duty is to obey."

Annabelle's anger boiled and she felt sick in the stomach. Now that she was old enough to leave the seminary, it seemed that unless she refused to co-operate, she really would be disposed of without the slightest consideration for her personal wishes. Simultaneously afraid to obey her guardian and furious because not even Miss Chalfont seemed to care about her dilemma, Annabelle straightened up. She looked around the cosy parlour, with its thick oriental rugs, pretty figurines on the mantelpiece, and a number of gilt-framed pictures on the wall, one of which she had painted. "I will consider the marriage." Annabelle looked down again, in case rebellion revealed itself on her face. However, she had not lied. She would consider the marriage proposal, but not in the manner Miss Chalfont expected, for she would find a way to reject the elderly baron.

Miss Chalfont stood, walked round her desk, and patted Annabelle's shoulder before resting her hand on it. "My dear child, there is little for you to consider. I dread to think of the consequences if you disobey your guardian. You could be cast penniless from here with only the clothes on your back. After all, your guardian does have complete power over you."

Annabelle wanted to jerk away from her uncaring teacher's hand but forced herself to remain passive. She did not want the woman to suspect the nature of her rebellious thoughts and have her closely watched. Inwardly, she seethed and decided that whatever the cost, she would escape the fate in store for her. An image of her former nurse, with whom she corresponded, flashed through her mind. With it came a sense of security and purpose.

Chapter Two

Still outraged about the marriage that had been arranged for her with such high-handedness, Annabelle joined her bosom friend, Viscount Hampton's stepsister, Fanny Greenwood.

"What did Chally want?" Fanny demanded, using their soubriquet for Miss Chalfont.

Annabelle groaned and flung herself onto the well-padded sofa. "To tell me my guardian has arranged my marriage."

Fanny perched on the edge of the sofa without pausing to smooth her white muslin gown to prevent it from creasing. The omission indicated intense excitement, since Fanny never neglected her appearance. "Wonderful," Fanny breathed.

"Don't be such a goose. If your brother ordered you to marry a man you had never met, would you obey him?"

As theatrical as ever, Fanny clasped her hands against her bosom. "No, I don't think so, but I would give almost anything to escape from this dungeon."

"A remarkably comfortable dungeon," Annabelle murmured, her sense of humour coming to the fore.

"Why are you laughing, and who is your prospective bridegroom?"

"I am laughing because you are so dramatic, and to answer your other question, Monsieur le Baron de Beauchamp, is a Frenchman, many years my senior," she explained, indignation in every syllable.

"Not de Beauchamp?" Fanny gasped. "I cannot believe anyone in their right mind would expect you to marry that rakehell."

Although Annabelle was not sure of the exact meaning of the word, she knew it was a term for a dishonourable man. *Rakehell!* She was expected to marry a baron with a shocking reputation. Her cheeks burned with indignation.

Fanny twirled one of her fat, flaxen ringlets round the forefinger of her right hand. "It is said Monsieur le Baron kisses the maids and ogles all the unmarried girls." Fanny pressed her hands to her cheeks and looked into the shadows as though someone, who would overhear her, might be lurking there. "It is even said that he is the father of more than one unfortunate babe born out of wedlock."

Annabelle quivered with wrath from head to toe at the thought of being expected to marry a man with such wicked ways. The voice of reason sounded in her brain. Surely her guardian would not have decided on her marriage to such a man. "Fanny, are you sure about this?"

Fanny nodded vehemently. "Everyone knows it."

As usual, Annabelle refused such vagueness. "How do they know?"

"Do you never listen to the other boarders gossiping when they return from vacation?" Fanny sighed dramatically. "No, I suppose you don't. You spend most of your leisure either reading or sketching."

"Fanny do you think—?" Annabelle began, her heart beating faster than normal.

"What?" Fanny looked at her curiously.

"Why should de Beauchamp agree to marry me? Do you think he knows who I am?" She looked down, yearning as ever to know who her parents and guardian were.

"I should think so. I mean, de Beauchamp would not marry you if— Well, you know what I mean," Fanny said, her embarrassment obvious, her nervous fingers toying with her handkerchief.

Yes, Annabelle did know what Fanny meant. Her friend thought she might be base born, but was too polite to say so. When they were children, they made up many stories about her unknown father and mother. They had imagined she was either a foreign princess or an orphan whose guardian stole her fortune. Perhaps, they had speculated, she was kidnapped, and one day, her parents would receive a demand for ransom, which they would willingly pay to have their beloved daughter returned. However, she and Fanny were no longer children and she must face the possibility of an unwelcome truth.

Annabelle sighed more deeply than before. Perhaps there would never be a happy outcome. Maybe, as the vulgar saying went, 'she was born on the wrong side of the blanket'.

Oh, the humiliation and misery she had suffered. Most of the well-born pupils were proud of their noble birth. They would not speak to her because she did not know anything about her family and was probably a commoner. She smiled and glanced at her friend. Dear Fanny had never ostracised her or voiced an unkind word on the subject. Not only that, Fanny always defended her from any malicious comments or unkind taunts.

Her friend patted her hand. "Perhaps there is a simple explanation to the mystery which surrounds you."

Annabelle sniffed and shrugged.

"If we are to be parted by your marriage," Fanny began, "I hope you will have happy memories of our schooldays. After all, your guardian is very generous. Your gowns rival those of any other pupil, your shoes and gloves are of the finest quality, and no other girl in the school has such generous pin money as you do. If you were not my dearest friend, I would envy you. Indeed, I am jealous of you for having your own horse and extra riding lessons as well as extra drawing and painting lessons."

Annabelle gazed absent-mindedly at Fanny. When she arrived at school at the age of five,

Miss Chalfont had said, "My dear child, please think of The Beeches as your home. Instead of sleeping in a dormitory, you shall share a bedroom with another little girl. The two of you will also share a parlour, because the greater part of your vacations will be spent at school."

Wondering about the identity of the elegantly dressed lady who brought her here and refused to answer questions; missing her nurse, who had taken care of her single-handedly for so long; and bewildered by the change in her circumstances, Annabelle had stared at Miss Chalfont.

"Now, now, I hope you will not cry, child," Miss Chalfont had said. "You will be happy with us. You shall have your own pony and enjoy many of the pretty rides near here. Moreover, you will learn to read, write, and figure, besides many other things."

Her eyes full of what were presumably sympathetic tears, Fanny leaned forward and patted Annabelle's hand again. "Don't look so sad, dearest. Miss Chalfont treats you like a favourite niece, and I know that you are not entirely unhappy here. And…and I was wrong to call our school a dungeon. I only meant that I want to see more of the world."

Yes, Annabelle mused, she was well provided for, and Miss Chalfont had been all that was kind, but she would gladly exchange all her privileges for an affectionate family.

"I wish Hampton would provide as well for me as your guardian provides for you,

Annabelle." Like an actress, Fanny clasped her hands together. "Oh, it is tragic to be an orphan at the mercy of an ogre such as my stepbrother. Even if you find out that you are also an orphan, Annabelle, your lot could not be unhappier than mine."

"Yes, it could. Your position in society is assured and mine is uncertain."

Fanny blushed and looked away from her with palpable embarrassment. "I meant that now I am seventeen-years-old, it is outrageous of Hampton to leave me to languish here instead of arranging for me to have a London Season."

Annabelle genuinely sympathised with Fanny's impatience to take her place among the ton. "Don't fret. Now that your stepbrother has returned to England, I daresay he will visit you and make suitable arrangements for your future. Compared to my situation, you fare better than you think. For what am I to do? I will not marry a forty-two year old man, even if he is a nobleman. These are not the days when knights were bold and cruel parents or guardians could force unfortunate maidens into marriage. Rather than marry the baron, I shall run away."

Fanny's eyes became rounder. "Of course you won't run away. Please do not speak so wildly. As you said, Hampton is sure to visit me soon. Since his return, he has been busy...." Fanny hesitated and pulled a loose thread from the lace edging her handkerchief. "Perhaps Hampton would help you."

Annabelle took the ruined handkerchief from Fanny and ruthlessly crumpled it in her hand. "Why should your stepbrother assist me? You have always said he is heartless."

Fanny rolled her eyes and babbled her excuses for Hampton. "I have said many foolish things about him. When all is said and done, it is not Hampton's fault that his father died when Hampton was only twelve-years-old. And he is not to blame for our mamma marrying again, and then becoming my guardian after she and my papa died while Hampton served under Wellington, both in the Peninsula and at Waterloo."

Very generous of Fanny, Annabelle thought wryly, already conversant with Fanny's family history.

"But I do wish Hampton had allowed me to stay at home instead of arranging for me to be educated here," Fanny continued. "Oh, I should not complain. After all, this school is not so very bad. You know it is not, Annabelle."

How dramatic Fanny was. Only a few moments ago she referred to The Beeches as a dungeon.

"Fanny, whatever the circumstances after we leave here, I doubt your brother will allow you to remain friends with a girl of unknown parentage. Anyway, I would not wish to be beholden to him."

"Beholden! What strange words you use," Fanny teased.

A teacher entered the parlour. "Young ladies, you should be ready for bed by now."

Annabelle glanced out of the window at the night sky.

The teacher drew the curtains, shutting away the absolute darkness caused by dense clouds veiling the quarter moon. "I will return soon to ensure you are in bed."

"You can't be serious about running away," Fanny said, when they were again alone together. "Where could you go? What would you do?" she asked, as they took off their short woollen jackets, muslin gowns, and cambric petticoats worn over warm, red flannel ones.

Annabelle shrugged.

"I shall pray for you," said Fanny, who always said her prayers.

"Thank you," murmured Annabelle, with the guilty knowledge that she often neglected hers. She did not see why she should recite them because she neither believed God had any more time to care about her than anyone else, nor did she wish to trouble Him.

A little later, her devotions completed, Fanny clambered into bed. "Goodnight, Annabelle, sleep well."

"Good night and God bless you, dear, dear Fanny," Annabelle replied, with such heartfelt emotion that Fanny looked puzzled.

Annabelle hesitated for a second and wondered if she and Fanny would ever see each other again.

Chapter Three

Annabelle's mind teemed with doubts, questions, and uncertainties. Why had her guardian's identity never been revealed? She frowned. Her nostrils flared. Why should a French baron, who had never met her, agree to marry her?

Under no circumstances would she wed a man of Baron de Beauchamp's years. For the last thirteen years, she had only left The Beeches when she attended church with her teachers and the rest of the schoolgirls, or when she rode in the company of others. Before she married, she needed to spread her wings beyond the confines of her school. She longed to know what the world beyond the high brick walls around The Beeches was like, to meet people outside those walls and see different places.

She sighed, bewildered and confused by the proposed change from schoolgirl to married lady. It seemed her guardian was not short of funds. Instead of the high-handed order for her to marry, a London Season could have been arranged. She caught her lower lip between her teeth and winced. Did her birth preclude her from being introduced to the ton? She must face facts. Perhaps she was a commoner whose birth would never permit her to enter polite society unless she married into it and, even if she did, there would be those who looked askance at her. Whatever her true circumstances, she shared Fanny's wish to discover what life was like outside Miss Chalfont's establishment. Her hands trembled. What did she really want? She knew the answer to her question. More than anything else, she wanted to discover the truth about her past and find out who her parents were. She needed to know and understand her place in the world.

Annabelle snuffed out the candles and lay still. In deep thought, she reviewed her plans to run away before the kitchen maid came downstairs to the kitchen to rake out the ashes and light the fire for the cook.

Certain that she had enough money to carry out her plan, Annabelle considered every detail. She should be able to complete her journey in a little over twenty-four hours. It was a simple matter to ride to the post house, arrange for her horse to be returned to The Beeches, and to purchase a ticket on the stage. Surely, she would not come to harm. There must be other young girls who travelled alone and reached their destinations without mishap. Of course, most girls were protected by a companion, but protected from what? From rakehells such as the baron? But surely, she would be unlikely to encounter one of his ilk. Annabelle wished she was not so ignorant about life outside school, but if she was cautious and did not engage in conversation with strangers, she doubted anything bad would happen to her.

Of course, if she was honest, the thought of leaving the school, which had been her home for thirteen years, was daunting; but who knew what her guardian might do if she refused to marry the baron. As Miss Chalfont had said, he might turn her out into the world with no more than the clothes she wore.

Annabelle tried to remain calm and weigh the odds. Even if other travellers met adversity, why should she? After all, if she did not run away she might suffer worse misfortune. She might fall down the stairs and break a limb or be thrown off her horse and be severely injured.

As soon as Fanny fell asleep, Annabelle crept out of bed and chose a change of clothes that would fit into a saddlebag. Having completed her preparations, she dressed in her new, forest green riding habit. In the parlour she shared with Fanny, she set out her riding hat, trimmed with a jaunty cream plume. She laid her leather gloves beside it and together with money saved from her allowance, put her gold chain, cross, and earrings, as well as a cameo brooch, into her reticule, which she then placed in the pocket of her voluminous cloak.

She feared she would fall asleep if she lay down and sank into the comfort of her goose feather mattress, so she sat on a wing chair and watched the clock tick the minutes away while planning her journey.

If only she possessed a pistol, but even if she did, she would not know how to fire it.

During the vacations, when all the other pupils returned to their homes, Miss Chalfont had been eccentric enough to allow her to fish and swim in the lake, but not eccentric enough to allow her to learn to handle a firearm. As for her secret desire to learn the art of fencing, she had not so much as hinted at it, for she knew Miss Chalfont would throw up her hands in horror at the idea of any of her pupils learning so masculine a skill. She smiled optimistically. Who knew what her future held? Perhaps there would be an opportunity to learn to shoot and fence, as well as other more feminine accomplishments such as her love of drawing and painting.

She should not let her mind wander. How long would it take to reach her destination? The main road was good. Should she use it? *No*, for the first part of her journey, it would be prudent to take the less frequented track across the downs. The main road was the obvious route, but the most dangerous one, on which she had heard highwaymen and footpads, posed a threat. Besides, a young lady travelling alone on horseback along a main highway would arouse other travellers' curiosity, something she must avoid as much as possible so that she would not be traced.

In spite of her good intentions, Annabelle yawned, her eyelids drooped, and she dozed.

When she woke, she shivered with cold after sitting for so long in front of the dying fire. She panicked and jumped up. Was it too late to leave undetected? Her limbs stiff, she staggered.

Annabelle lit a candle and peered at the clock on the mantelpiece. What was the time? A half hour after four. Time to leave. Should she leave a note? No, later on, she would write to Miss Chalfont and Fanny to set their minds at rest about her welfare.

Annabelle opened the bedroom door to make sure her friend slept. "Fanny, dearest," she whispered, her eyes moist, "I hope we will meet again in happy circumstances. I also hope Hampton will arrange your London Season before much longer. If he does, I am sure you will be the toast of the town and break all the handsome young bachelors' hearts. I pray you will marry someone splendid who deserves you."

Fanny stirred. Annabelle closed the door without making any noise and put on her hat, gloves, and cloak. She picked up the bundle containing her spare clothes, went out into the dark, silent corridor and crept along it.

After each squeak of a floorboard, she paused in the expectation of waking even one of the fifty boarders or one of the dozen teachers who slept in the east wing of the refurbished Elizabethan manor house. She tiptoed down two flights of stairs and across the uneven, red-tiled hall to a side door.

Annabelle tugged back the bolts. Fortunately, they were too well oiled to squeak. She lifted the latch, pushed open the heavy oak door, and stepped out into the chilly but invigorating night air, which drove away all traces of sleepiness. Mercifully, the clouds had sailed past the sickle moon that now shed enough light for her to see her way. She kept to the shadows of the shrubs, which edged one side of the path, and skirted a pair of well-manicured lawns until she reached tall wrought iron, double gates. Annabelle held her breath and looked back at the front of the manor.

Not a thread of light shone from the west wing where Chally and her mother lived. With the hope that no sleepless person observed her from the dark bulk of the central wing, which contained classrooms, a dining parlour, and a communal parlour, she opened one of the gates and stepped into the cobbled stable yard.

She must be very quiet to avoid waking up either the grooms, who slept above the stables, or the head groom, whose single storey, thatched roofed cottage faced them.

Annabelle opened the upper and lower sections of a loosebox door and went through them. Her mare, Empress, opened dark eyes and whickered.

"Shush," Annabelle soothed, patting Empress on the neck before she went toward a door on the other side of the loosebox. Beyond it, a narrow corridor led to the large tack room.

"Who's there?" demanded a sleepy voice when she opened the door to the tack room.

"Annabelle Allan. Who are you?" she replied, startled.

"Dan."

"The boy they say is too forward. What are you doing here? Why are you not in your bed?"

"I could ask the same of you, miss."

"Don't be impertinent," she said in imitation of Miss Chalfont at her haughtiest.

"I be here because t'other lads tease me till me flesh and blood can't put up with it. The horses be better company than them."

The victim of more than her fair share of teasing from many of the boarders and a few of the day pupils, she pitied the boy who could be no more than thirteen or fourteen years old. "Ignore them," she advised.

"That's what me ma says. Now, tell me, miss, what be you doing here?"

"I am going for a ride." She hoped he would not try to prevent her.

"At this time in the morning?"

"Yes, it is refreshing to ride at dawn."

"But it ain't dawn yet."

"Yes…. Well, since you are here, you might as well make yourself useful. Please saddle Empress and do not forget to fetch a saddle bag."

Dan lit a pair of lanterns and hung them up. "No, miss, I won't forget. That is, I wouldn't forget if I saddled up for you. Orders are for none of the young ladies to take a horse without Miss Chalfont or the head groom's say so."

She glared at the lad, and then her lips twitched, but she repressed her laughter at his ill-fitting buff breeches and the ludicrous blue coat that hung loose to his knees.

"I will pay you."

Dan ignored her offer while he buttoned his canary yellow waistcoat, worn over a clean but faded shirt, washed until the material wore thin.

"Will you not answer me, boy?"

He bent to adjust his wrinkled stockings before he spoke. "I'll not deny that money's always useful, miss. I'll saddle up Empress and another horse for me. 'Tisn't right for you to ride alone."

Surprised by the suggestion, she stared at him. Miss Chalfont would say she should not ride alone, but the sight of a well-dressed young lady and a scruffy attendant might arouse curiosity. Nevertheless, in case she was thrown—although that was unlikely because she had never been thrown from a horse before—or Empress cast a shoe or some other mishap occurred, it would be good to have a companion, even if it was only this boy. "Very well, you may accompany me, but you might lose your position here for doing so."

"Doesn't matter, miss. I love the horses but am unhappy here. I want to find work in another stable."

Dan fetched a saddlebag—which she filled quickly while he collected the tack—and entered Empress's stall where he worked fast and skilfully, making little noise.

After he saddled both horses, he bent and picked up one of Empress's feet.

She tried to conceal her impatience. "What are you doing?"

"I be tying cloths round their feet so they'll not clatter on the cobbles and wake anyone." He peered out into the yard. "Come on, miss. I'll lead the horses till we reach the drive."

Birdsong filled the air, silver streaks on the horizon heralded dawn's arrival, and a gleam of golden light shone in the head groom's cottage

"Old man gets up early. Hurry up. He'll thrash me if he catches us."

* * *

Annabelle did not need Dan to urge her on. Apprehension about her guardian's reaction to her flight bolstered her resolve, and it diminished her regret over being forced out of the school where she had been happy. She tilted her chin. Even if Fanny's brother agreed to help her, she did not want to be under an obligation to a stranger.

They reached the drive and Dan removed the cloths from the horses' hooves.

"Mount up, miss." He bent, cupped her foot in his hands, and helped her up onto her sidesaddle.

She held out a coin taken from her reticule. "Take this if you have changed your mind about leaving here. It is unnecessary for you to accompany me."

"No, miss, I be running away with you. I reckons we can look after each other. For now, you can pay me way and I'll protect you."

So, Dan possessed more intelligence than he appeared to. "It seems I have no choice other than to take you with me," she said.

He nodded. "My mother will understand why I'm leaving here. Which road be we taking?"

"The one leading away from The Beeches to the junction, where, instead of turning onto the new highway, we will cut across the downs along the old road."

"Walk on," Dan ordered the sturdy gelding.

At the beginning of the old road, which led through folds of downs cropped by sheep and dotted with gorse bushes, Dan reined in his horse. "Where be we going when we reach the end of the road?"

Annabelle sighed. After they left this road, she knew she should not ride on a public highway. Her reputation would be ruined if they encountered anyone from the school or church who might recognise her and gossip.

"Miss?"

Annabelle looked up and down the winding road. "We are going to Dover."

Dan held the reins with one hand and combed his spiky, sandy hair with the other. He wrinkled his snub nose. "Horses won't make it."

"I know. They will be returned to The Beeches and we will travel on the Mail." She patted Empress's glossy neck, sad at the thought of parting with her. Maybe, she would be able to send for her in the future.

Dan's forehead creased. "Will you send a message telling them where you're going, miss? They'll be worried about you."

Presumably, he meant Miss Chalfont and the other teachers. "Not now, but one day I will let Miss Chalfont know we are safe and well."

"What be you going to do in Dover?"

"You will see when we arrive."

Dan heaved a sigh. "Be you hungry, miss."

"Is it time to breakfast?"

Dan looked at the sun still low in a dawn sky streaked with red, salmon pink and gold. "No, but I reckons it will soon be time to eat. Anyways, me stomach's growling."

"So is mine, the fresh air has given me an appetite," she admitted. "Dan, I think it will be a nice day. Something tells me that spring is in the air."

"Maybe, but you knows the old saying. *'Red sky at morn, shepherds warn.'* I reckons it'll rain later. Best be on our way."

"Yes, of course, you are right." She looked up at the fiery streaks across the sky with trepidation. It was becoming sultry and she feared a thunderstorm. With no wish to be drenched by rain, she straightened her back and patted Empress's neck again. She gathered the reins. "Walk on."

Dan's horse trotted alongside Empress. "I knows this road. If I'm not wrong, we're a half-mile or so from an inn where the gentry changed their horses before the new road was laid. We could have our breakfast there. Happen they'll serve steak and eggs and mugs of beer."

"Happen they will and you'll be having some," she teased.

Dan grinned and blushed and then they rode on in silence, their horses trotting abreast until the road narrowed and fringes of native woodland replaced the rolling downs.

Annabelle looked up at the branches, which formed a canopy hazed with green leaves. She was about to say it was very quiet when a masked man burst out of the shadows. His bedraggled appearance offered no threat but the pair of pistols he brandished did. "Stand and deliver," he shouted.

Empress whinnied a startled protest. Annabelle screamed before she looked up and down the road in search of assistance.

"Damnation!" Dan swore.

"Dismount," the footpad ordered.

Terrified, Annabelle recoiled when the man thrust the muzzle of a pistol in her face. Outrage replaced fear. She scowled and opened her mouth to protest.

"For Gawd's sake, do as he says, miss." His face pale with palpable apprehension, Dan slid down from his saddle, held onto the reins of his horse, and caught hold of Empress's bridle.

"Let go, I can control her," Annabelle snapped.

"If you don't do as you're told, it'll be the worse for you. I'll shoot," the masked man threatened.

Her heart pumped wildly and her hands grew damp but she straightened her back, and tried not to reveal her increasing fear, coupled with indignation. "It will be the worse for you if you harm us," she said, annoyed by the wobble in her voice.

"I'll harm you if you don't dismount now," the footpad snarled.

Knees shaking, she obeyed and stared at the man's round-toed, scuffed shoes, wrinkled grey stockings, and stained brown breeches.

While watching Dan, the footpad grabbed her shoulder and held a pistol to the side of her head before he turned his attention from Dan to her.

Appalled by her situation, and at that moment regretting her precipitous flight from safety at The Beeches, she stared at him and gagged at the stench of his unwashed body, and at the blood dripping from the pocket of his threadbare olive green coat where a hare's hind feet protruded.

"Didn't yer ma tell you it's rude to stare?" the horrible man asked.

She shook her head in spite of the pistol.

"Well, you'll be dead to yer ma if that lad doesn't throw that saddlebag to the ground."

"I have no mother. I am an orphan." She hoped her words would incline him to mercy.

"Now, missy, give me your pretties."

She did not doubt that he would shoot her if she did not obey. Seething with indignation, tinged with escalating fear, Annabelle realized she had no choice in the matter. She prayed he would not ask for her cloak with the purse of gold coins in the pocket. If he did, she would be destitute and forced to return to The Beeches. With reluctance, she removed her coral and gold earrings and her gold ring. "Why don't you seek employment instead of robbing innocent travellers?"

"I'm jobless 'cause I was turned off without a reference, and nobody will take a fellow on without one." He glared at Dan. "You there, take missy's pretties and put them in the saddle bag."

Although Dan's hands trembled and his knees shook, he obeyed.

"Take your cloak off, missy, and—" he broke off. "What's that noise?"

Like a trio of wary birds, they tilted their heads and listened to the sound of a fast approaching vehicle.

"M….more than likely someone's on the way to The Beeches," Dan stammered.

The footpad pushed Annabelle to the ground and hit Dan so hard with the pistol butt that he rendered him unconscious.

"Scoundrel!" Annabelle exclaimed. She raised her face from the dirt with no thought for her safety.

The thief struck the gelding, which reared, whinnied, turned, and galloped down the road toward The Beeches. He then mounted Empress and rode away.

A chaise thundered toward Annabelle. Her heart pounding, she scrambled to her feet and tried to pull Dan out of its path. In spite of his small stature, he was muscular and too heavy for her to drag off the road.

Chapter Four

The chaise came to a halt no more than two yards from Annabelle and Dan.

Annabelle swallowed the bitter bile, which rushed into her throat in response to her brush with near death from horse's hooves and deadly wheels, and all her limbs trembled.

A groom alighted from the back of the chaise and opened the door nearest to her.

"Why the devil have we stopped?" a crisp male voice demanded.

The groom scrambled down from his seat next to the coachman, lowered the steps, and mumbled something before a tall gentleman descended.

Annabelle glanced at the coat of arms on the chaise and assumed they must be those of her would-be-bridegroom, for who else would travel along this shortcut to The Beeches so early in the morning? Besides, her mind was too preoccupied with Dan to consider other alternatives. "Monsieur le Baron de Beauchamp, I presume. Your arrival is more than welcome, monsieur." She pointed at Dan, who lay limp on the road. "We need help. A footpad held us up. You cannot imagine a dirtier, scruffier, more impertinent person…"

"Indeed," the gentleman murmured, his eyebrows lowered.

She stared up at Monsieur le Baron. Some six feet tall, dressed in a beautifully cut dark green coat, cream-coloured unmentionables almost moulded to his powerful legs, a dark grey coat with as many as twelve capes and a snow white, intricately tied cravat at his throat, her artist's eyes approved of him. Her eyes also approved of his short black hair, which curled at the ends, a pair of large brown eyes with golden depths, and a well-shaped, clearly defined mouth that had deep, endearing dimples on either side of it, softening the effect of his square jaw and cleft chin.

The baron picked up her hat, dusted it with gloved fingers, and inclined his head. "I regret I have no comb in hand for you to tidy your curls."

She sighed, well able to imagine the small, unruly curls that often escaped and clustered round her face, despite her best efforts to subdue them.

"You are trembling. Allow me to help you to stand and I shall return your hat to you," he said, his eyes troubled and his expression thoughtful.

She stood without his help and he handed the hat to her. "Thank you." Made ill at ease by his scrutiny, she tried to smooth those annoying little curls before she replaced her hat. "Monsieur, a footpad took my saddlebags, knocked Dan down, and stole my mare."

"Good God! Did he harm you?" The gentleman stepped forward to clasp her hands.

His touch sent fire up her arms. She pulled herself free from him, and then tried to shake the dirt from her skirts. "I am uninjured but, as you see, poor Dan is unconscious." She knelt next to the stable boy. "He is so pale."

"So would you be if you had been knocked senseless. Do stand up again. Rest assured that I will not leave the lad here. My groom shall put him on the floor of the chaise. That will not leave much room for our feet but we shall contrive until we reach the next village."

Annabelle hesitated. She was not ignorant of the ways of the world, and knew she should not travel in his chaise without a chaperone, but realised she had no choice. It would be folly to reject his offer and either wait for help or walk to the inn, prey to any other footpad lurking in the woods. She stood and pointed in the opposite direction to the one from which the chaise had approached. "Dan said there is an inn not far from here."

The baron beckoned to his groom. "Put the lad in the chaise," he ordered.

When the muscular groom picked Dan up without the slightest difficulty, Dan did not stir.

"Gently," the baron ordered and watched his groom settle the young man inside the chaise. The baron nodded at his coachman. "Turn the chaise round." He turned to Annabelle and offered her his arm. Without pause for prudent hesitation, she put her hand on his smooth broadcloth sleeve, surprised by the sudden tingling in her fingertips.

Annabelle permitted him to lead her far enough down the road to make way for the chaise to turn.

"Good, you have stopped trembling." The baron smiled. His dimples deepened. Her heart lurched and continued to when the baron scrutinised her face as they waited to get into the chaise. "May I ask how you know my name, Miss—?"

She removed her hand from his arm and looked down at the tips of her dusty riding boots. "I am Miss Allan. We were expecting you. That is, Miss Chalfont told me, oh dear, this is so awkward, monsieur. I am sorry to disappoint you, but I must be honest. Nothing would persuade me to marry you, for although your eyes do not bulge like a frog's and you are handsome, you are too old for me." Nervous, she moistened her lips with the tip of her tongue.

"Thank you for your compliment, I am relieved to hear my looks do not displease you," the gentleman said dryly.

"Don't try to persuade me to change my mind." Her cheeks burned. She should not have been outspoken and rude. Yet she ran away because she did not want to marry at her guardian's command, and she still believed she had no other choice despite Monsieur le Baron's handsome appearance and charm. She peered up at him before resuming her contemplation of the tips of her boots.

Le monsieur's mouth twitched. His eyes laughed at her. "Please be good enough to tell me why you are here with an unconscious ragamuffin."

"I like to ride early in the morning."

"Ah." His eyes still laughed at her, their golden flecks deepening. "As soon as we reach the inn, I will send someone to notify the authorities of the crime."

"Do you think my mare will be recovered?" She looked up at the seemingly harmless man whom Fanny had described as one overly fond of women. Thank God, he was not ogling her. Even Miss Chalfont could not have objected to his manners. She looked away from his expressive eyes, fringed with sooty black lashes, long enough to make any young lady envious.

Oh, she understood his success with the fair sex. Not only did he possess an attractive personality but he had broad shoulders and a slim waist, and those muscular thighs beneath the tight fitting unmentionables she had already noticed.

"Do you like what you see?"

She focused on the verge, sprinkled with clumps of bright green dandelion leaves. His question was outrageous. Her cheeks felt so hot that a wave of colour must have spread to the roots of her hair. She glanced up at him, embarrassed as always, by her uncontrollable blushes. With a wave of her hand, she indicated the woodland beyond the verge. "Some people think this part of the country is not without charm."

His beautifully moulded lips parted in a smile, and he stared into the depths of her eyes. "Those who live here are not without beauty and charm, Miss Allan, I have rarely seen eyes as blue as yours."

How many people did he know here in Surrey? How many maids had he ogled and kissed? She shuddered, tried to quell her imagination, and failed. What would his kiss be like? How would the touch of his lips feel on hers?

"Come, the chaise awaits us," the baron said.

Inside the chaise, she took off her cloak, rolled it up, and put it under Dan's head. "Should we lift him onto the seat? I can sit on the floor."

"He is better off where he is," the gentleman replied after a moment or two, during which time he seemed to be deep in thought.

Annabelle sat down. "Why?"

"He might roll off the seat and sustain another injury." He raised a hand. "If you are about to argue, please refrain. Arguments weary me. Now, Miss Allan, please be honest. Enlighten me, where were you going when you were held up?"

"Going?" she squeaked. "Nowhere in particular, as I told you, I like to ride early in the day."

A mischievous gleam appeared in his eyes. "How fortunate," he said, in an affected drawl.

"What do you mean?"

He chuckled. "I also like to ride early. We have something common. However, I take my fences, I do not run away."

She pressed her gloved hands to her hot cheeks.

"Were you running away because you do not want to get married?"

The baron gazed at her intently. Transfixed, she could not look away. Annabelle clasped her hands so tightly that her nails dug into her gloves. She forced her eyes to look away from his compelling stare. "You will not take me back to The Beeches, will you?"

"The Beeches!" the rascal exclaimed, as though he had never heard of it. "I cannot abandon you in your present circumstances, but I do think it would be best if you returned."

She glared at him. "Indeed, Monsieur, you are mistaken if you think I will remain there and be coerced into marriage. I would run away again before allowing it."

"How dramatic you are. Am I to understand you fear being dragged to the altar and whipped until you make your matrimonial vows?"

Indignant, she glared at him. How dare he mock her when he was the cause of her dilemma?

He chuckled once more and touched a spotless handkerchief to his lips. "I believe you would run away again, but I should take you back and, by the way, you deserve to be locked in your room and fed on bread and water. Respectable young ladies do not run away from their academies."

Unable to conceal her curiosity, she eyed him. Miss Chalfont said the baron was forty-two-years-old. He looked much younger. But what did she know of men other than the vicar at the church she attended, the gentlemen she saw there, and the elderly teachers who taught art, dance, music, and riding at The Beeches?

He stared boldly at her. "I hope you like what you see."

Before she could respond with appropriate indignation, the chaise turned into a stable yard. The groom lowered the steps. With utmost gentleness, she removed her cloak from beneath Dan's head. Thank God, the footpad had not stolen it together with the money and jewellery in the placket pocket. She stood and wrapped herself in the cloak's warm folds.

De Beauchamp stepped out onto the cobbled stable yard and turned to offer her his hand.

The innkeeper and his wife bustled out to greet them and shook their heads when they saw Dan and Annabelle's untidy state.

"Have you a room for the lad?" the baron asked.

"Yes, my lord," they chorused.

"Good, my groom will see to him."

Annabelle's anxiety increased when she looked at Dan's unnaturally pale face. "Please send for a doctor."

"Very good, miss," the obliging couple replied.

"A private parlour for us," the baron ordered.

Their host bowed low. "Yes sir."

With the baron at her side, Annabelle followed the innkeeper into the clean, low-ceilinged building. It smelled of fragrant beeswax, which did not eradicate all the odours of the cooked food, dogs, the taproom, and tobacco.

"Ale for me, coffee for the lady, and breakfast as soon as you can serve it," Monsieur le Baron ordered.

"Yes sir." The innkeeper withdrew.

Annabelle took off her hat and gloves and sat on the window seat with her wrinkled cloak swirled round her.

The baron flicked the lid of his green enamelled snuffbox open. "You are very pale, Miss Allan."

"Am I?"

"Yes, you do not look 'the thing.'"

"You would be dishevelled and furious if you had been held up by a smelly ruffian, pushed to the ground, and seen your companion knocked unconscious. Moreover, you would not look 'the thing' if you had been forced to run away because a lecher like yourself wants to marry you." Oh no, yet again she had spoken before she thought, one of her greatest faults for which Miss Chalfont had scolded her times without number.

The gentleman's shoulders shook. He spread his arms wide. "Do I look like a lecher?" He seemed amused.

With great dignity, she looked at him reproachfully. "It is not funny. And as for your question, I do not know whether or not you look like one, for this is the first time I have met a wicked man."

He gesticulated with a long-fingered, slightly tanned hand, indicating he sometimes failed to wear gloves when outdoors. It was something else she seemed to like about him as it proved he might be a nonpareil, not a dandy, even if his morals were appalling.

"My dear child, I am only interested in your accusation of lechery. Do you accuse me of being—?"

"Yes," she interrupted, nodding, "Fanny told me—"she broke off and caught her lower lip between her teeth. No well-brought-up young lady should speak thus to a gentleman, even if he was a reprobate. She must stop being so free with her words.

"Fanny?"

"Yes, my lord, Fanny is my best friend. Poor creature, she is shockingly neglected by her half-brother, Viscount Hampton."

"Neglected," he inquired—his eyes alert—in a silky tone, with no trace of his affected drawl. She nodded once more, this time to emphasise her statement. "Fanny has not seen the wretch for years. Would you believe he is home from war and has neither removed her from school nor arranged for her to be presented at court?"

"I believe you, but do you not think the viscount may have his reasons for acting as he has? Perchance he thinks his sister—"

"Half-sister."

He laughed. "I beg your pardon. Perchance he thinks of his half-sister as a child."

"Why are you laughing at me?" The gentleman's amusement made her cross, very cross indeed.

"Because, my dear Miss Allan, you are adorable and brave."

His compliment shocked and unnerved her. "If you try to seduce me, I shall scream."

"Upon my word, what a thing to accuse a gentleman of, and what, do I dare to ask, does a schoolroom miss know about seduction?"

"More than you might think for—" she broke off, hot flushes flooding her cheeks.

"No, do not tell me, I can guess. Fanny told you."

"Yes, she did. What is more, she warned me that you ogle all the unmarried girls and kiss the maids."

He stretched his hands out toward her. "Miss Allan, I must protest."

The plump innkeeper's wife, all smiles and curtsies, bustled in with a neatly dressed maidservant. De Beauchamp turned aside to look out of the window and Annabelle hid her cheeks with her hands to conceal more burning blushes.

Within a few minutes, the maidservant had laid the table and the host had brought a platter of steak.

"Oh!" Annabelle exclaimed and pressed her hands to her mouth.

"What is it, miss?" the woman asked.

"N–nothing, forgive me, I am sure everything is delicious, but I feel sick."

The baron cupped her elbow with a firm hand. "Sit down. Strong, hot coffee will set you to rights."

"No, I could not drink it," she protested, and for the first time in her life wished she had some smelling salts.

The landlady bustled to the door. "Sir, miss, I shall fetch the coffee."

"My poor child," de Beauchamp began, with sufficient concern in his voice for her to widen her eyes as she peered up at him. "I am not surprised by your feeling unwell. You have suffered a dreadful ordeal. Most ladies of my acquaintance would have succumbed to a hysterical fit. You are to be congratulated for not doing so. Have no fears. I am not a rake and I promise you are safe with me."

She looked into the depth of his eyes; the golden flecks seemed subdued. "I am?"

"Yes."

Annabelle wanted to believe him. She smiled. Her stomach settled. In spite of Fanny's warning, she trusted him and relaxed.

"The coffee," he said unnecessarily, as the landlady returned to the room. "Thank you Mrs…?"

"Fuller, sir."

"Thank you, Mrs Fuller. The young lady needs to rest for an hour or more, can you provide a bedchamber for her?"

"Yes sir."

"Good, now please tell me how the lad is."

"He's woken up. Doctor's looking at him now, sir."

Annabelle sipped some coffee. "No, I cannot drink any more and I do not want anything to eat."

"Come with me, miss, you'll feel better after a nap," Mrs Fuller said with motherly concern.

Chapter Five

Annabelle woke to the tune of wind moaning in the chimney and rain beating a tattoo against the lattice windows. She opened her eyes. A fire glowed in the grate. Her riding habit and cloak hung from a wooden peg on the wall. What time was it? How long had she slept? She got out of bed. A few short steps took her to the window. She wiped condensation off a small pane and peered through the glass. Outside the grass glowed emerald green in stark contrast to the gunmetal grey sky indicating more rain would fall.

Someone tapped on the door and did not wait for her to call, "Do not come in."

The door began to open. Annabelle seized her cloak from the chair and, conscious of her state of undress, wrapped it round her just before her rescuer stepped into the bedchamber.

The baron did not look away, and his breath seemed to come faster than usual. "I beg your pardon, Miss Allan. When you did not answer I assumed you were still modestly tucked up in bed."

In so small a room, Annabelle supposed he could not avoid being so close to her that she could smell his invigorating scent of spice mingled with lemon and a faint hint of horses.

With suspicion, she noted the gold gleaming in his eyes beneath heavy lids. What did it signify? "Please leave, Monsieur. You should not be here."

He ignored her expostulation and sat on the edge of her bed but averted his eyes from her. "Dan is awake. The doctor says the lump and bruise on his temple are painful but not a cause for concern."

She clasped the edges of her cloak together at her neck and wished its folds hid all of her chemise and petticoat. "Thank you for telling me. You may go." Nervousness caused her to address him as though he were a servant.

His raised eyebrow slanted even further toward his temple, giving his face a satanic appearance. "I also came to tell you I did not mention your name when I made my report to the constable. I stated Dan was returning the horses to The Beeches."

"Why?" she asked, frowning at him.

"Miss Allan, do you want every Tom, Dick, and Harry to know your business?"

She shook her head.

"No one will be able to trace Dan and obtain news of your movements. He has agreed to recover at my house in the country where he will be employed in the stables when he is fit enough to work."

Annabelle smiled. "That is good of you. The other grooms at The Beeches bullied him."

De Beauchamp inclined his head. "We must consider what you will do next."

"Please do not concern yourself with me." She had spoken faster than she intended. A hearty gust of wind drove smoke down the chimney. "I shall spend the night here and continue my journey tomorrow," she said, thankful for the gold coins in her cloak pocket.

"What am I to do with you?" he mused as though she had not spoken.

"Nothing, I am not your concern."

Le monsieur stood and remained motionless, the expression in his eyes thoughtful. "Circumstance has made you my concern. Although it is most improper, it seems I must take charge of you. After all, what would the Fullers think of me if I abandoned you?"

"It is improper of you to be here in my bedchamber." A harsh laugh escaped her. "And I cannot believe you care so much as a snap of my fingers for the Fuller's opinion of you."

"True."

"I shall not allow you to trick me into returning to the academy."

The baron laughed. "Ridiculous child, do not clutch your cloak as though I will ravish you if it slips. Of course, you are charming in your cloak, chemise, and petticoats, and I would enjoy ravishing you. But it is not my habit to take advantage of innocent schoolgirls."

She glared. "No gentleman would speak to me so boldly." Was she flushing again? She feared she was. It was difficult to appear dignified with red cheeks and dishevelled hair, while only partially clad.

"Am I a gentleman? Didn't Fanny claim that I am not one? But gentleman or not, I insist on accompanying you to your destination. Don't think you can escape from me. I shall give orders you are not to hire a horse or vehicle, and if you try to run away, I shall follow you. Be sensible and remember it is a long walk to the next village. Alone you would be at risk. Even on horseback, accompanied by a groom, you were held up."

Well aware of the enormity of travelling with a gentleman to whom she was not closely related, she shifted from one foot to the other, her nostrils flaring.

"Trust me, child."

"Why should I?"

The baron's eyes flashed. A warning? She shrugged. So far he had given her little cause for alarm other than remaining in her bedchamber while she was not fully clad, something no gentleman should do. On the other hand, he was not likely to kiss her in an inn where a scream would bring someone to her assistance. She clasped her hands tightly together to stop them trembling. Her cloak fell farther apart. The baron's eyes widened as he looked at her. It seemed that for now she could not escape him. "Very well," she agreed sulkily, "it seems I have no choice. But I am not a child."

He cocked his head to one side and surveyed her from top to toe, his breath again coming faster than usual. "I agree, but your behaviour is that of a thoughtless child, although you may not look like one."

"How dare you accuse me of being both thoughtless and a child," she stated, her words sounding weak in her own ears.

"You cannot be forced to marry against your will. It was unnecessary to run away and put yourself and that lad in danger. Be glad he did not die and you were not assaulted."

Unexpected shyness prevented her from speaking.

He stood, crossed the space between them, and then stroked her cheek with his forefinger. "Trust me to see no harm befalls you, Belle."

"B-belle?" she stammered.

"Your name is Anna Belle. The translation is beautiful Anna, is it not? With your permission, I shall address you as Belle in private."

She nodded, wondering how and why he had rendered her speechless.

His eyes mocked her, as though he could read her muddled thoughts. "I am trustworthy. Elderly ladies like me, children enjoy playing with me, old gentlemen invite me to offer my opinion, and dogs do not bark at me. Another point in my favour is that I do not bite."

"'Pon my word you do think well of yourself," she managed to reply, although rendered almost speechless by his undeniable charm. But, she imagined, a lecher needs it in order to claim his victims. For, although bosoms heaved, and wicked men seized hold of fair ladies in the novels smuggled into school, she could not imagine what followed.

The baron laughed and bowed. "Are you hungry, Miss Allan?"

"Yes, I am. What time is it?" she asked, aware of a hollow sensation in her stomach.

Le monsieur consulted his fob watch. "It lacks a few minutes to four of the clock."

"So late? I have no excuse for being a slug-a-bed by day other than that of not having slept last night."

"Worn to the bone with worry about your suitor?" the baron murmured. She giggled before he continued. "Belle, I hope you have a hearty appetite. Mrs Fuller assures me her fare is plain but good. We are to have soup, roast chicken, and apple pie served with cream, and I do not know what else."

Her mouth watered. \"I look forward to the pleasure of your company in the parlour."

Chapter Six

Annabelle no longer completely believed in the truth of Fanny's description of Baron de Beauchamp. Nothing in his behaviour indicated a rakehell. She did not accept that, as Fanny had said, "He would kiss the maids and ogle all the unmarried ladies until they squirmed with embarrassment." As for herself, she did not object to the monsieur calling her adorable, although she wished she had been fully clad at the time.

A thrill ran down her spine. The baron was not as she had imagined him. He really did seem much younger than forty-two.

Although Annabelle had always been protected and had little knowledge of the ways of the world, for once, an inner voice cautioned her. In spite of the fact she had run away—convinced it was the only alternative to being persuaded into marriage with a stranger—she felt she should exercise caution. She must be sensible and resist his lordship's delightful dimples.

If she could find a way to escape from the baron, should she spend the night here instead of continuing her journey? Annabelle looked out of the window at the rain lashing the trees and flattening plants. Yes, she should put up here until morning. No one would fancy travelling on such a night. If she did, she might catch a severe chill and possibly die. Her shoulders heaved. If she died, only Fanny would mourn her. Not for her the grief of a loving family.

She set her mouth in a resolute line, and made up her mind to find an opportunity to run away from Monsieur le Baron on the following day.

A clock struck. After she smoothed the crumpled muslin gown she had taken from her saddlebag, Annabelle left her room, and hurried along the narrow corridor and down the stairs.

* * *

The meal was tastier than he had anticipated. He spoke little to Annabelle while they ate with obvious enjoyment, glad to be snug and dry while the wind moaned and lashed torrents of rain against the exterior shutters.

After eating until he was too full to partake of another morsel, de Beauchamp dabbed his mouth with a table napkin before looking at his companion. "Belle, I think you are still fatigued and, as the weather grows worse, we must put up here for the night."

Annabelle showed no sign of alarm as she looked at him with large eyes, fringed by long lashes beneath perfectly arched eyebrows. Without doubt, Miss Allan—with her fair complexion unmarked by the pimples that often plagued young ladies, glossy brown hair, high cheekbones, small mouth with luscious full lips, a youthful figure with curves in the right places, and a small waist—was a very beautiful young lady. All the more reason to offer her his protection. Although he knew the risks to her reputation, if it became known that she had travelled with him without a chaperone in his chaise, that he had entered her bedchamber—not to mention she had been partially dressed at the time, thus revealing more of her charms than it was proper to see—and had spent the night under the same roof. Curse the weather, which made it impossible to journey on and make more suitable arrangements.

"I suppose we must stay here for the night," Annabelle said, her voice breaking into his thoughts.

He looked at her. Was she really such an innocent that she did not understand the gravity of her situation? "I am glad you do not object to my suggestion. We shall stay here because I neither wish to risk the chaise getting stuck in mud nor being held up in the dark by a highwayman."

Annabelle smiled although her hands trembled. "My poor horse."

He leaned forward, reached across the table, and held her long-fingered, soft hand. "She might escape and make her way back to the stable."

Although Annabelle did not return the pressure of his hand, she did not seem discomposed by his touch.

"So, is it agreed, we shall put up here for the night?" He released her hand.

Annabelle nodded her agreement without hesitation.

The corners of his lips twitched. "I am glad you are not an argumentative female. I cannot abide ladies who brangle."

"My teachers would be quick to disagree, for they complained I argued the point too often."

He smiled and rang a hand bell.

After a short delay, Mrs Fuller answered the summons. She bobbed a curtsey and wiped her hands on her apron. "I'm right sorry for keeping you waiting. A gentleman kept me busy. No sooner did his carriage turn off the main highway—his coachman having mistaken the way in the storm—than a wheel came off. He has booked a room for the night and ordered a meal. He wanted—"

While the landlady spoke, de Beauchamp covered his mouth with his hand to conceal a yawn. "Be good enough to light a candle for the lady and see her to her bedchamber," he said to bring an end to her flood of explanations.

"I'm sorry, sir, I shouldn't rattle on. Come, miss," Mrs Fuller replied, her expression sheepish.

"A moment, Mrs Fuller. Have you a serving girl who can sleep on a truckle bed in this young lady's room?"

She beamed at him with palpable approval. "Yes, sir, there's my daughter, Molly, as good a girl as ever lived."

"I don't want to share my room," Annabelle objected.

Everything she said, every reaction, confirmed his opinion that the young lady had been educated with little knowledge of the ways of the world. "Miss Allan, have I not told you I do not care for females who brangle. Goodnight, sleep well."

"Goodnight." Annabelle turned to leave the room. At the door, she looked back and smiled at him. "Monsieur, I am very grateful to you for rescuing me and bringing me here, but that does not mean I shall marry you."

After the door closed behind Annabelle, the baron took a deep breath. She appeared oblivious to her effect on him. It could not be good for the state of his heart.

He raised his eyebrows. Annabelle might be ignorant of the proprieties but he was not. For fear of gossip claiming he had passed the night in her bed, it would not do for her to sleep alone. Even in such a remote place, who knew what the consequences of a bachelor, in the role of protector to a well-bred young lady, might be? In addition, even though this inn was off the beaten track, he might be recognised. If he were, what would the consequences be for Annabelle? Gossip spread as fast as fire in polite society. Members of the ton would put the worst possible construction on the situation.

Chapter Seven

By morning, the storm had ended and the sun shone in a cloudless blue sky. Annabelle opened the window, leaned out, and savoured the scent of the earth perfumed by rain.

A large gentleman, whose high collar and elaborate neck cloth made it impossible for him to look either right or left, came round the corner of the inn, and looked up. He smirked when he saw her and made an elaborate bow.

"Bonjour," the stranger called.

From behind her, Molly peered out of the window. "Do you know him, miss?"

Annabelle shook her head.

"Then come away from here, miss. It isn't fitting for the likes of you to lean out of your bedchamber window and talk to a gentleman you don't know."

Annabelle hesitated, reluctant to be rude by not replying to the stranger but suspecting Molly was right. If only she had a mother to advise her.

She frowned at the dandy dressed in a blue coat with shiny silver buttons. He looked as though he had been forced into it like sausage meat into a skin. Thank goodness, Monsieur le Baron de Beauchamp was nothing like this gentleman. Her sense of humour reasserted itself and she withdrew her head. "Molly, that gentleman bowed so stiffly, I swear he wears stays."

Molly spluttered with laughter as her mother entered the bedchamber. "The gentleman's waiting for you in the parlour, miss. Begging your pardon, you're to hurry up and have your breakfast. He's given orders for his chaise to be brought round within the half hour and does not want to keep his horses waiting."

"Please tell him that I will join him immediately," Annabelle replied. "I daresay," she muttered too low to be overheard, "that the baron not only abominates ladies who brangle but he also abominates those who are tardy."

Annabelle left Molly to set the bedroom to rights and went down the shallow stairs to the ground floor. She turned right to enter the private parlour where they dined the previous evening.

A side door on her left opened. She turned and saw the gentleman she had viewed from her bedchamber window enter. As he bowed, he creaked.

Annabelle suppressed a giggle. Her supposition had been right. He must be wearing stays.

The gentleman's eyes, the colour and shape of bulging ripe gooseberries, ogled her.

"Good morning to you. I trust you will not ignore me again," he simpered.

With Molly's warning fresh in her mind, Annabelle took no notice of the gentleman and would have passed him by had he not caught hold of her arm.

"Not so fast, my pretty." He clutched her arm more tightly.

She surprised herself by crying out, not because she was cowardly but because his impertinence startled her and his grip hurt.

The parlour door opened. Baron de Beauchamp stepped into the corridor and the gentleman released her.

"I might have known you would turn up here," said Monsieur le Baron, the expression on his face murderous. "Be good enough to allow me to say you are as unwelcome as false coin!"

His stays creaking, the rude fop retreated and de Beauchamp led her into the parlour.

"Who is that toad?" she demanded.

"Toad?"

She nodded vehemently. "Toad. His eyes bulged at me and his mouth spread as wide as a toad's."

"How dare he offend a lady under my protection? Shall I challenge him to a duel? No, I cannot for fear of your good name being dragged through the mud," de Beauchamp fumed, the expression in his eyes ferocious.

"Thank God." Annabelle tilted her chin.

Monsieur raised his eyebrows. "Thank God for what?"

"For your decision not to duel with the toad," she said, unable to keep a tremor from her voice.

He drew close and looked down into her eyes. "Do you care so much for me?"

Yes, she did care for him. She not only cared, but she liked him very much. "Although I have lived at the academy in the company of females nearly all my life, even I know that duels are illegal. Monsieur, I would not see you arrested for participating in one. And although I am sure you would be better with either sword or pistols than Mr Toad, I do not want you to risk an injury or…er…a fatal wound."

"Thank you for your crumbs of praise." He raised her hand to his mouth and kissed it with warm, silky lips.

The baron raised his head. His face was very close to hers. She stared at his lips and shivered with…. She knew not what. She trembled and tried to decide what to do. "Monsieur, you said that you fear my name being dragged through the mud. Why should it be?"

"Do you really not know?"

She shook her head. "Why should it be? Apart from running away—and it will make Miss Chalfont very cross with me—I have done nothing wrong. After all, you took me up in your chaise out of the kindness of your heart and although I know I should not be alone with you, surely there is no cause for gossip because I have done nothing wrong."

Judging by the crease between those slanted eyebrows of his, the monsieur was worried, but before he could answer, Mrs Fuller served a substantial breakfast.

Annabelle sat down, murmured grace, and helped herself to bread still warm from the oven. She spread it with pale, creamy butter before she spoke again. "Mrs Fuller, how is Dan this morning? Has he regained consciousness?"

The woman adjusted her apron. "Did you not know that the lad left on the stage soon after dawn?"

Surprised, Annabelle stared at her. She should have said goodbye to him. Why did no one tell her he was leaving? "From where did Dan get the fare?"

"I made the arrangements," de Beauchamp said. "I have already sent him to my country estate, where he can recover until he is ready to work in the stables."

"How good you are, Monsieur."

The baron smiled at her and speared a piece of ham with his fork.

"I hope you enjoy your meal," said their garrulous landlady, who then smiled and withdrew with the serving girl.

"Eat up, Belle. We must be on our way."

Annabelle obeyed, for she also wanted to depart as soon as possible. She did not doubt that by now Miss Chalfont had sent out a search party. Before long, someone would make inquiries at this remote inn.

* * *

After breakfast, the baron escorted her to the chaise and handed her into it.

The groom raised the steps and took his place on the dicky. "Ready," he called to the coachman.

"Will you change horses at a posting inn?" Annabelle inquired.

"Why do you ask?"

"To continue my journey, I must hire a vehicle or catch The Mail."

"No need, as you said, you ran away to avoid an arranged marriage. I take the blame for your current predicament and will not allow you to travel alone in case harm comes to you."

"I shall not be alone in a public conveyance," she said, determined to continue her journey—at the end of which she might receive answers to her questions about her parentage.

The monsieur raised his eyebrows, as he might in response to a naughty child. "True, but, in my opinion, no lady should travel on The Mail."

Annabelle caught her lower lip between her teeth. What did she know about de Beauchamp? "Where are you going, Monsieur?"

"I am taking you to my grandmamma's house near Guildford."

The word grandmamma reassured her. It conjured up an image of a respectable old lady. Nevertheless, he had surprised her. "Why are you taking me there?"

"You don't want to return to The Beeches and even if you did want to go there, I could not return you with a ruined reputation."

"Ruined? Nonsense! Pray tell me how I am ruined?"

"You ran away and spent the night at an inn under the protection of a gentleman to whom you are not related."

"And that has ruined my reputation, although you treated me as though you are…are my brother? Besides, apart from *the Toad,* no one knows about it."

Annabelle wondered why he frowned as though her words displeased him.

"It is not so simple. *The Toad*, might be a problem."

"Then the sooner we part, the better." She straightened her back. "Please allow me to continue my journey alone. My affairs are no concern of yours."

The baron shook his head and chuckled. "I have made them my concern."

"Very well, if you will not respect my wishes, please take me to my guardian."

"Who is your guardian?"

"I do not know, but you do, monsieur."

"Why should I know?"

"Please do not play that game with me. You know because my guardian arranged our marriage."

A gentle snore answered her. De Beauchamp's eyes had closed and his chin now nestled on his neck cloth.

From the corner of her eye, she thought he peered at her through the fringe of his eyelashes, but when she turned her head to look at him, his eyes were shut.

"Well, Monsieur le Baron," she muttered, "although you don't match Fanny's description, I will not marry you because you have a shocking reputation."

Annabelle pressed her lips together and ordered her heart not to trust the delightful stranger.

The monsieur did not open his eyes until the chaise halted on a gravel drive that encircled a horseshoe shaped lawn. He smiled at her. "Ah, we have arrived at Merrow House."

De Beauchamp alighted and supported her arm to help her descend without tripping over the hem of her wrinkled gown. She sighed, ashamed of the sorry sight she presented.

As soon as Annabelle's feet touched the gravel drive, she looked at the square mansion, with its mansard roof and double flights of semi-circular steps leading up to a portico with white Ionic columns.

Before the groom had time to knock to announce their arrival, a short plump lady came round the side of the house. De Beauchamp's grandmother, Annabelle assumed, eyeing the lady dressed in black with numerous keys hanging from a chatelaine. "If you'd told us you were coming, my lord, you'd have saved yourself a journey. Mrs Eames has gone to

Bath," the round-faced woman said and curtsied.

"To Bath! I've never known Grandmother to go there. Why has she gone?"

"For the same reason that most people do, to take the waters, for the sake of her health, my lord. No, no, don't look so worried. You know she has been liverish these past few months and even thought she was dying."

"I take it her health is not yet fully restored?"

The woman rolled her lively dark eyes and nodded.

"Damnation," de Beauchamp breathed. "My apologies, Miss Allan, I should not swear in front of you. He pressed her hand onto his muscular arm, so unlike the flabby arm of the vulgar gentleman who accosted her at the inn. "This good lady is Mrs Herries."

The housekeeper looked Annabelle up and down, the expression in her eyes hardening as she did so. Conscious of her crumpled riding habit and her battered shako, Annabelle fidgeted.

"Mrs Herries, please admit us," Monsieur le baron said.

The housekeeper pursed her lips and continued to scrutinise Annabelle before she stepped aside

"Come, Miss Allan." De Beauchamp guided her through a hall with a parquet floor and up a flight of broad stairs, on the walls of which hung portraits of gentlemen mounted on fiery horses, ladies dressed in glistening silk, and family groups.

De Beauchamp opened a door. "In here, Miss Allan."

Annabelle stepped into a drawing room. The door closed behind her. Alone, she observed the furniture's extraordinary imitation crocodile feet that, more than likely, had replaced a collection of mismatching sofas, tables, chairs, and other items, which Fanny had told her were to be found in many country houses. She sank onto the nearest chair. What was she going to do? Relief rushed through her. Perhaps the baron, whom she liked very much, would tell her who her parents were.

* * *

In the hall, Mrs Herries glared at de Beauchamp. "Upon my word, never did I expect you to darken Madam's doorstep with such a creature as that girl and—"

"Stuff and nonsense!" he said, with the manner of a gentleman much annoyed and aggrieved. "Shame on you. Do you think I would bring the sort of female you are thinking of here to meet my grandmother? How could I have known Grandmamma would take it into her head to restore herself with those evil tasting waters served in the Pump Room at Bath?"

He sighed. A week ago, his grandmamma had summoned him, and lain abed as though the doors of death were opened wide to receive her.

"Oh," Grandmamma had whispered after they greeted each other, "you are the last in the direct male line of succession and I dread going to my grave before you have fathered an heir."

He had sat on the edge of the bed, much alarmed by the breath rattling in her throat. "Very well, Grandmamma, to please you, I promise to marry as soon as possible, but I have no intention of marrying either a spoiled beauty or a simpering bread-and-butter Miss primed by her mamma to land the largest possible fish in her net."

Upon hearing those words, his grandmamma had revived enough to touch her handkerchief to her lips. "Don't be vulgar," she had protested, with a force remarkable in one who claimed to be at the end of her life.

Now, still with the air of a man much aggrieved, he frowned at Mrs Herries. Alarmed she took a step backward. "No need to act like a startled hare, I hoped Grandmamma would take Miss Allan under her wing."

Mrs Herries's eyes rounded and she raised her eyebrows, seeming amazed at the idea of her mistress taking anyone under her wing.

He smiled at her. "During Grandmamma's absence, is it too much to hope that you will keep an eye on my protégée? She is in my care because a footpad attacked her while she was out riding with a stable lad. As far as I can make out, the experience addled her brains. She thinks I am Baron de Beauchamp." He paused in the hope that God would forgive him for his lies.

"The scoundrel who made free with that motherless heiress, what was her name? Ah, yes, Miss Foster—" Mrs Herries began, her expression as hard as the face of a granite cliff.

"Yes, the very same man. Do you not find the notion of Miss Allan marrying him shocking?" he asked, knowing how good-hearted Mrs Herries was.

"Indeed I do, but why does the young lady think you're Baron de Beauchamp?" she asked, her eyes sharp with suspicion. "What mischief are you up to?"

Like an actor, he placed his hand over his heart. "As I have explained, her encounter with a rough footpad addled her brain." He held his hands out. "Mrs Herries, although I plagued you when I was a boy, have you ever known me not to tell the truth?"

The housekeeper heaved a sigh. "No, but I've known you to bend it," she said tartly. "And by allowing the poor young lady to believe you're Baron de Beauchamp, you're bending it again."

He returned his hands to his side. "Mrs Herries, there is no need to be suspicious of me. Miss Allan is a gentlewoman in distress. Please extend every civility to her until I can make proper arrangements."

"Arrangements? Why should you make arrangements for her?" she asked, her face set in disapproving lines.

"She is delightful, Herry, but you must not tell her I said so."

At the use of his childhood name for her, Mrs Herries's face softened.

"I will go to my grandmother and tell her about Miss Allan. In the meantime, while I am absent, please look after her and do not allow her to run away," he wheedled.

"Why should she run away if your intentions are honourable?"

"She wants to travel on The Mail and that would not be appropriate for a young lady."

"Of course it would not, but why didn't you tell her you're not Baron de Beauchamp?"

He sighed. The trouble with servants—who had spanked one as a child for some childish misdemeanour such as sneaking into the pantry and spooning up preserved fruits and conserves—was that even after one grew up they spoke their minds. At least Mrs Herries did, and she had always treated him with such kindness that he could not bring himself to reprimand her.

"Why?" repeated Mrs Herries.

"To tell you the truth, I allowed her to think I am the baron so—"

"So, telling the truth will embarrass you?"

"Y-yes," he replied, disconcerted by her directness. "But Herry, my intentions are good." He hesitated, unable to tell her his real reason, for not even his grandmother knew what he was up to in the line of duty to his king and country. "Please oblige me. Can you imagine what her situation would be as de Beauchamp's wife? I brought her here for fear that if I returned her to school she would be forced to marry the…er…*Toad*." He smiled wryly at the memory of Belle's description of the baron.

Mrs Herries's face softened even more. "Very well, I will take care of her."

He grinned. "Thank you. Warn all the servants to refer to me and to address me as Baron de Beauchamp."

She opened her mouth with, he assumed, the intention of making some protest or other.

"Herry, we are famished and would like to eat as soon as possible," he said to forestall her.

Chapter Eight

The pseudo-baron caught his breath when he entered the drawing room. Where was Annabelle? Had his charming but impetuous young protégée, who did not hesitate to speak her mind, run away from him? If so, he must find her for her own safety. She was not worldly-wise enough to travel alone. If she were, she would not have agreed to travel with him. As for himself, he knew he should not have befriended a schoolroom miss. To the contrary, he should have returned her to The Beeches, but when her beautiful eyes pleaded with him and she mentioned the unspeakable de Beauchamp, he had found himself unable to do so. He smiled ruefully, suspecting he would find it difficult to deny her anything. He looked around the room. Ah, there she was, asleep, curled up on a chair in the farthest corner of the room. How innocent she looked.

He should not have concealed his identity. How would she react when he told her the truth? "Wake up, Belle," he said softly to avoid alarming her. He gazed down at her lovely face, the temptation to kiss her smooth forehead irresistible.

"Where am I?" Annabelle murmured, half asleep. "I dreamt someone kissed me." Her eyes opened with a startled expression.

"Hush. There is no cause for anxiety. I took the liberty of kissing your forehead."

Her cheeks rosy from sleep, she smiled before she spoke. "Should you have taken such a liberty, monsieur?"

"No, please forgive me."

"Very well."

She did not seem displeased, which made him want to kiss her once more, this time on her pretty lips, as unblemished and unknowing as a dewy rosebud's petals.

"As for where you are, don't you remember? You are in my Grandmamma's house."

Annabelle sat up straight. "Forgive me, I was wool gathering."

He smiled at her. "Did you collect much wool?"

Her sleepy face with delicately flushed cheeks, brightened. "You are teasing me."

"Guilty as charged," he replied. Still he could not bring himself to reveal his identity for fear she would not forgive him for his deceit. "Forgive me for bringing you here, I thought Grandmamma would look after you, but in her absence I must make other arrangements. While I do so, promise me that you will not run away."

"Please don't leave me. What will I do here without you?" she asked, her voice rising as she spoke.

Surprised by her passionate tone, his heart seemed to beat a little faster. "Have I come to mean so much to you in so short a time?"

"Yes, I mean no—that is, I don't want to stay here with strangers."

"But *I* am a stranger."

Annabelle looked into the depths of his eyes. "Y-yes, but I am getting to know you."

His heart seemed to do peculiar things and his breath definitely came faster than usual. "You are blushing."

She stood. "Am I?" she whispered, as though his slightest utterance was of the greatest importance.

Flattered, he moved closer to her, tilted her chin with one finger, and withdrew it as though he had been burned. "God forgive me, I was about to kiss you, Belle, and I have not the right to do so."

"I forgive you," she said, the expression on her face demure as she looked down.

Although her words encouraged him, he controlled himself instead of taking her into his arms as he wanted to. "As soon as we have eaten, I must leave. So, please give me your promise not to run away."

"Very well, on my word of honour, which I never break, I promise to wait here until you return." She looked up at him. "How long will you be away?"

"I hope to return within three or four days."

Annabelle glanced down at her crumpled skirts. "I don't know how I will contrive."

He frowned. "What do you mean?"

"Doubtless you can choose from a dozen coats or more but I cannot choose from a dozen gowns."

"Mrs Herries will refurbish your wardrobe." His strong desire to solve all of his delightful protégées problems took him by surprise. "Now, please excuse me. I have matters to attend to."

* * *

Alone, Annabelle remained where she was and wished his lordship had kissed her, for although she knew a respectable lady's kisses were only for her husband, she was shamefully eager to experience her first one.

Embarrassed by her thoughts, she looked across the room toward the door, which opened as the housekeeper bustled in.

"Miss Allan, if it isn't like his lordship to arrive unannounced and stir up the household," Mrs Herries grumbled. "Cook's gone to Bath with her ladyship and the under-cook is in a state, thinking there's nothing fit to be served."

How ungracious the woman was. "I am sorry for the inconvenience," Annabelle apologised, although the problems were not of her making. After all, she had not asked the baron to bring her here, and he had not known his grandmother would not be at home.

"I beg your pardon, miss, I shouldn't be complaining to you. Indeed not. Truth to tell, I'm glad to have something to do. That's not to say there's not too much to do when her ladyship's in residence, but when she's away I'm dull. Oh dear, what am I thinking of? I shouldn't be so talkative. Please follow me."

* * *

On the second floor, Mrs Herries led her to a luxurious bedroom furnished with pale green curtains, a soft-hued Aubusson carpet, and well-polished furniture. "What a beautiful room."

Mrs Herries pointed to a tester bed large enough to accommodate three people. "You'll be comfortable here. The feather mattress is new. And in case you wake up in the night and need something, I'll have a bed put in here for a maid."

"That will not be necessary."

"I know what's fitting, Miss Allan. Although you and his lordship have no chaperone, nothing will take place in this house that will cause malicious gossip."

"I see," Annabelle murmured, although she did not understand what could cause malicious gossip. After all it was not as though she and his lordship were alone at the inn where he had entered her bedchamber and seen her partially clad. Surely he would not do such a thing under his grandmother's roof.

"I'm not sure you do understand my meaning, miss. You seem very young and you're not the sort of female I thought you were when I first set eyes on you."

"What sort of female did you think I was?"

"Shame on you for asking such a thing, miss," Mrs Herries said. "Mind you, I'll not have the servants gossiping and saying his lordship visits your room at night."

Really, the servant was too garrulous, but Annabelle could not resist the temptation to probe. "But please tell me what sort of female you thought I am?"

Mrs Herries's face assumed a severe expression. "That's only for me to know, miss."

"If you want a maid to sleep in my bedchamber because his lordship may visit me, there is no need. He is going away."

"But he'll be back," the housekeeper said and pressed her lips into a firm, thin line. "Although I doubt he would do anything improper under Madam's roof."

Before Annabelle could put forth more interesting questions to which she really wanted answers, a maid carrying an armful of clothing entered the room.

"Ah, there you are, Jane. You took your time about coming." Mrs Herries looked at Annabelle. "Miss Allan, Jane is the sewing maid." Mrs Herries waved her hands at Jane. "Put those clothes on the bed."

After Jane did so, Mrs Herries examined the gowns and other garments. "A good choice, Jane, the mistress never wears any of these. When you have altered them, they will do very well for Miss Allan."

Annabelle stared at the gowns. Judging by the styles and fabrics, the baron's grandmother dressed girlishly instead of in a manner appropriate to her advanced years. On the other hand, perhaps she did not, for the housekeeper said the lady never wore any of the gowns Jane had laid out on the bed. Maybe Jane's mistress realised they were unsuitable after she purchased them.

Jane picked up a cream silk gown with a low neck, puffed sleeves, and several frills. "Please try this on, miss."

* * *

The clock struck five when Annabelle joined the baron in a small, south facing parlour. He bowed and then straightened. "Come," he said and led her to a circular table set before a fire that took the chill from the room.

"The dining room is so large we prefer to eat here when there are no more than four people," he explained.

Annabelle sat and admired the starched tablecloth, solid silverware, and fine china, hand painted with a design of summer flowers.

"If we'd known your lordship was coming, there'd be a better spread. The under-cook is mortified. She says the meal doesn't do justice to her skills," Mrs Herries explained, while, under her supervision, maids placed tureens and platters on the table.

The monsieur looked at the soup, bread, butter, a cold joint, a dish of preserved plums and a jug of thick cream, as well as other culinary offerings. "You may go. We will serve ourselves. Please convey my compliments to the under-cook and her assistants. There is more than enough to satisfy us."

When they were alone he smiled. "If I may say so, Belle, that gown looks well on you, very well indeed."

Annabelle fingered the knot of hair on the crown of her head and ran a finger through one of the ringlets falling from it. This was the first time her hair was not tied back at the nape of her neck in the style suitable for schoolroom misses. The result pleased her. In her opinion, it gave her dignity and added to her height.

"You have beautiful hair, Belle," Monsieur le Baron said.

"Thank you," she replied, conscious of blushing while she observed the perfect cut and fit of his black coat. "You look very handsome, monsieur."

He ladled some chicken soup from the tureen "Kind of you, but you must not be thinking I am a dandy."

"No, no, I do not," she said, and then burst out. "I do not want you to leave me here. Please take me with you. How will I manage without you?"

"I would like you to accompany me, but will not put your good name at further risk. The…er…*Toad* has already caught sight of you and I don't want you to be seen in my company outside this house. Mrs Herries will look after you very well, so please be patient until my return."

What would she do if he abandoned her? Annabelle realised she should not have run away with so little thought of how she would accomplish her plan. Yet, somehow or other she must carry it out and reach her destination. However, her rash flight from The Beeches now seemed an impractical folly. "Y-you are not tricking me, are you? You will return," she faltered.

For the time being, perhaps she should return to school. If she did, would Miss Chalfont and her guardian be very angry with her? If she agreed to marry Monsieur le Baron perhaps they would be so pleased they would not scold her. Indecisive, she caught her teeth between her lips. She liked the baron, but did she like him enough to marry him?

"Of course I will return—gentleman's word of honour. Now, please allow me to enjoy my soup before it grows cold."

Although Annabelle still did not want to be separated from him for even a few days, she smiled and nodded. While they partook of soup, she appreciated his consistent politeness—the courtesy of a true gentleman. No, that was not quite so. She suppressed a giggle. He should not have entered her bedchamber at the inn and remained while she wore no more than her chemise and petticoats. Yet, to herself,

Annabelle admitted, she was always at ease with him and would miss him very much during his absence.

* * *

Several days after Monsieur le Baron's departure, Annabelle sat in the parlour scrutinising a fashion plate in *La Belle Assemble* when the door opened. "You may put the tea tray on the table."

"I have not brought a tea tray," a deep voice replied.

The periodical tumbled to the ground. The baron smiled and she scrambled to her feet.

"Monsieur, you have returned."

"An unnecessary remark, but, yes, as you can see, your humble servant kept his promise and even has a surprise for you."

A giggle escaped her. She would never use the word humble to describe the baron. She looked at him. If his smile was anything to judge by, her delighted response to his arrival gratified him.

"Begging your pardon," a maid said.

Le monsieur moved aside to allow the girl to bring in a tea tray and put it on a low table in front of Annabelle.

"Some tea, monsieur?"

"Yes, please," he replied and sat down on the sofa next to her.

The maid left the room and Annabelle poured tea into two cups.

"I have a confession to make," the baron said without the least sign of repentance.

Annabelle put the cups on the table and looked down at the toes of her dainty satin slippers. "You are not accountable to me, monsieur."

"In this case, I am." He reached out and clasped her right hand in his strong ones as though he feared she would run away. "How beautiful you are," he breathed.

Surprised, but not alarmed by his firm hold, she smiled at him. "No, I am not beautiful. Fanny is beautiful."

"You are mistaken. Do I not call you Belle?"

She moistened her lips with the tip of her tongue.

"Look at me," he urged.

Despite her sudden shyness, she gazed at his handsome face.

He released her hand. "Belle, I think we should marry."

"Why?" she asked, although she knew it was her guardian's wish.

Flames flickered in the depths of his dark eyes. "There is no easy way to tell you this. I am not Baron de Beauchamp—"

"What!"

"The man you met at the inn, whom you nicknamed Toad, is de Beauchamp."

She could scarcely make sense of his words. "The Toad is the baron?"

"Yes," he confirmed, his voice calm although his eyes belied that calmness.

His hold on her hand tightened. Alarmed, she pulled it out of his grasp, stood, and stared at him in dismay. It was one thing to have entrusted herself to a man whom she thought her guardian wanted her to marry; it was another to have trusted a man she knew nothing about. As for marriage, why should she marry him? Annabelle gathered her scattered wits. "Why did you say you were de Beauchamp?"

"I did not. You assumed I was the baron. Please trust me when I say I had an excellent reason for not telling you."

"You tricked me into believing you were the man my guardian wants me to marry." She shuddered at the thought of the Toad. "Although, now that I have seen the creature, nothing would persuade me to marry him. But you should not have lied to me."

"I did not introduce myself as de Beauchamp. You assumed I was."

"It was ill done of you to allow me to think you were Monsieur le Baron."

"You are not going to rail at me?"

She shook her head. "What good would that do?"

No matter who he was, she still liked him, but his deception infuriated her.

"Good, but I confess your generosity makes me feel guiltier than I would if you lost your temper with me."

"But what of Mrs Herries and the servants. Do they—?"

"Mrs Herries knows the baron has a bad reputation, so she agreed to conceal my true identity from you for a few days."

"The servants must be laughing at me behind my back." Annabelle seized a valuable Canton rose vase from the top of a cabinet and flung it at him. "How dare you make a fool of me by tricking me?"

The gentleman lunged forward and caught the vase. "I thought you were not going to rail at me."

"I will not, but I am furious." She snatched the clock from the mantelpiece.

"Put it down. Grandmamma will be furious if you break it."

Annabelle raised it with the intention of hurling it onto the parquet floor. "What is your name?" she demanded.

"Roland, Major Sarrat, at your service," the false baron said and seized the clock.

"Why should I believe you?" Annabelle eyed one of a pair of dainty figurines on either side of the mantelpiece.

"No, Belle, don't even think of smashing them. If this were my house, I would not mind but it is not. We are guests here. It would be devilish bad manners to destroy Grandmamma's ornaments. As for believing me, ask Mrs Herries who I am. She's known me since I was born. If I ask her to, she will vouch for me on the Bible."

Annabelle pleated and re-pleated a fold of her gown with nervous fingers. "The only fact I know about you is your rank and your real surname."

His eyes laughed into hers. "You know much more, for your heart tells you to trust me."

Annabelle looked down, smiled, and peered up at him through her long lashes. "How can a trickster such as you know what my heart says?"

"I learned how to judge others during my years abroad."

"Did you fight the French?"

"Yes, until I was wounded at Waterloo. By the time I recovered my health, the French king was on the throne."

Her heart lurched at the thought of his injury. Thank God his handsome face had not been scarred and he had not lost a limb. But had he hesitated before he replied? And if he had, why did he do so?

"So, your grandmother is Mrs Sarrat?"

"No, her name is Eames. After my paternal grandfather died, she remarried and is to be pitied for being widowed for the second time."

Why did the names Sarrat and Eames seem familiar? She could not remember. Perhaps one of the girls at school had mentioned them. She pushed tendrils of hair back from her forehead and looked thoughtfully at the major.

He took her hand in his again. "My dear, you should marry me to save your reputation."

"Why should my good name be ruined?"

"Sometimes I wonder if you are really as ignorant as you seem. Oh, I am sorry, I did not mean to be unkind it is merely that you appear ignorant of—"

"Ignorant!" she seized the figurine of a lady with a hunting dog at its feet.

"Belle, no, please put it back. Mr Eames bought it for Grandmamma. She treasures it."

Annabelle passed the figurine from one hand to another. "I am not ignorant. I had a very good education. I speak French as though it is my mother tongue, as well as Italian and—"

"You misunderstand. I meant you seem to have no knowledge of society and its expectations. Now, please hand me the ornament." Her lower lip caught between her teeth as she handed it to him. "Thank you, Belle." He replaced it and sat on a chair on one side of the hearth. "Please sit down, and allow me to explain. De Beauchamp knows me. If he gossips, it is enough to damn you in the eyes of the world. In addition, believe me when I say he will be outraged that you do not wish to marry him despite your guardian's order. I have no doubt he will take his revenge by speaking of you in damning terms."

She sank onto the sofa and hesitated. Fanny had told her it was common for young ladies to marry gentlemen they did not know well. In fact, not only was it acceptable, "It was usual," Fanny had said and added with feeling. "I hope that will not be my fate."

Major Sarrat's face hardened. "Are you wondering if I can support a wife and make proper provision for her?"

"N-no," she replied, much shocked by his mentioning pecuniary matters at such a moment.

His face relaxed, making him seem younger and even more handsome. "Nevertheless, I will arrange for a settlement for you in the event of my death."

She pressed a hand over her heart. "Don't mention death, I am sure it is unlucky." She cleared her throat. "Your proposal is ridiculous. I know so little about you." The major, scrutinised her face.

"What do you want to know about me, Belle?"

"How old are you?"

"Twenty-eight."

She toyed nervously with a loose curl. "Ten years older than I."

"Does it matter? De Beauchamp is more than twenty years your senior."

"I am very sorry, Major."

"Why?"

"You must feel trapped. If I had not run away and you had not helped me, we would not be in this coil."

"I assure you I do not feel trapped," he replied, amusement in his eyes. "Without a doubt, fate provided you with another prospective suitor."

What should she do? Oh, she liked the major, liked him very much, but to marry so precipitously.

"Belle, what would you say if I asked you to marry me immediately?"

She stared at him. "Surely that is not possible."

"I busied myself while I was away. I have a licence in my pocket and a parson waiting in the gold salon." He raised her limp hands to his cool lips and kissed them. "If you marry me, I will protect you for so long as I live and try to make you happy."

"A marriage licence! Are they so easily obtained?"

"There are ways and means, and the chaplain of my former regiment was very helpful. He persuaded his uncle, who is a bishop, to grant a common licence." He cleared his throat. "Although, in order to obtain it, the chaplain and I...er...added some years to your age. Do not look so worried, if you agree to wed, the chaplain assured me that our marriage will be legal."

Perplexed, she pressed her lips together. Would he help her find out who her parents were? Would she be able to carry out her plan? Apart from those considerations, why should she trust so untruthful a gentleman? Yet, in spite of common sense, instinct urged her to depend on him.

"B-but where would we live? What will you do?" She frowned—a foolish question, for the fine cut of his clothes, his gold ring, and the diamond pin in his cravat all indicated he was a gentleman of means.

"We shall live at my manor, where I will devote myself to you."

Her eyebrows drew together.

He chuckled. "I shall be a gentleman farmer and—"

Annabelle giggled. "Somehow, I don't believe you know anything about farming."

"It is true I know very little, but I am sure I can learn to be an agreeable husband."

An adroit reply. Annabelle took a deep breath. Did she want to marry him? And if she did, *why* did she want to? She looked down to conceal a smile. If she was honest, her heart knew the answer. "Major Sarrat, are you sure you want to marry a girl who does not know who her parents are?"

"Yes," he said without a second's delay.

She did not doubt his sincerity and allowed him to turn her hand over and kiss its palm. At the touch of his lips, her skin tingled in the most curious manner.

Her hands trembled, but this time she did not pull them away.

"Never fear me."

"Indeed, I am not afraid of you. At least, I do not think I am."

"Belle?" he queried, his eyes scrutinising hers.

"Yes," she replied, almost unable to speak for the excitement that was bubbling up within her.

"If you will trust me, I believe I can make you happy," he repeated. "Oh, I admit I have not been a saint where your fair sex is concerned, but I will never give you cause to suffer the embarrassment you would experience if you married de Beauchamp. And, believe me, he is worse, far worse, than Fanny said he is."

"Do you mean you will not keep a mistress if I marry you?"

"Belle! Whatever were you taught at school?"

"I listened occasionally to a few of the young ladies gossiping about gentlemen. And Fanny—"

"Ah, your informative friend who seems to know more than is good for her," he said, his face set in severe lines, although his eyes regarded her kindly. "Well, allow me to reassure you, I do not have a mistress, and please do not raise such an improper subject again. Now, Miss Allan—may I say *adorable* Annabelle Allan—please tell me if you want me to kneel, and ask you to give me the pleasure, no, the honour, of your hand in marriage?"

How should she reply?

"You will not marry me?" he asked wistfully.

His voice touched her heart, convincing her he was really being truthful. Her mind raced. What had she to lose? She might never find the answer to the questions she burned to know, and the likelihood of ever receiving another proposal of marriage from a handsome man with means, whom she liked as much, was remote. She took a deep breath. "Yes, Major, I will marry you."

He stood, drew her to her feet, and held her close to him, muttering an endearment she could not make out before he kissed her.

The sensations his lips evoked in the very pit of her stomach surprised and thrilled her. Her first experience of passion vanquished any remaining doubts as to whether or not she really wanted to marry him.

Major Sarrat released her. "Belle," he began, in a husky voice, "you have entrusted your life and person to me and I swear I will not do anything you do not wish me to." He slipped a diamond and emerald ring onto her finger. "My mother's betrothal ring. I hope you will be as happy with me as she was with my father."

Her lips quivered. "What a lovely thing to say. In return I hope I will make you happy, b-but—"

"What is amiss?"

Annabelle looked down. "I wish I knew who my parents were. I fear you will regret marrying me."

Her mouth quivered and he kissed her again until her toes curled and she wanted him to kiss her like that for as long as she lived. When it ended, she looked at him as if bemused by passion, and then buried her face in her hands.

Very gently, the major drew them into his. "I hoped you would agree to marry me and I have instructed Mrs Herries to prepare for our wedding." He smiled at her. "You are sure? It is not too late to say no."

Her senses afire, Annabelle nodded. She had agreed and would not retract her promise.

"Good." His eyes blazed before he held out his hand. She placed the tips of her fingers on it and allowed him to lead her to a salon furnished in gold and yellow, decorated with flowers and greenery.

"I wish you happiness, Miss Allan," Mrs Herries said as she handed Annabelle a posy of fragrant hothouse flowers.

Annabelle had never imagined being married in a borrowed gown, but it was of no consequence when she stood next to her husband-to-be in front of a table, serving as an altar.

"Dearly beloved, we are gathered here together in the presence of God and in the face of this congregation to witness this man and this woman being joined in Holy Matrimony, which is an honourable estate…" began the clergyman.

Annabelle made her responses in a low clear tone, awed by the enormity of her decision. She accepted the clergyman's congratulations after the ceremony. With a steady hand, she signed the register after her bridegroom penned his name. "Come," he said and led her to the hall where Mrs Herries put a cloak around Annabelle's shoulders.

"Come," her husband repeated and led her to his chaise.

Chapter Nine

Darkness enveloped Annabelle during the brief time it took to reach her bridegroom's manor. The chaise drew to a halt. Roland sprang out of it and held his arms out to her. Nervous, she set her foot on the top step of the chaise. Instead of allowing her to alight, the major reached up and swept her into his arms.

From every one of the many windows in the large, foursquare building, candlelight shone out into the dark night and illuminated his face. Her major carried her into the manor, and continued past a dozen or more servants—whose figures she only had time to glimpse—and up a flight of stairs to a large bedchamber.

After he put her down, his lips parted in a broad smile. "Welcome to your home, Belle. Please allow me to help you to take off your cloak before we sit by the fire and enjoy some wine." His smile was so boyish that it eliminated any embarrassment she might have experienced.

Yet how strange it was to be in a bedroom full of old furniture and sombre curtains at the window with a man whom she had known for so short a time. Suddenly ill-at-ease, and wondering why she agreed to marry him in such haste, Annabelle sat while her bridegroom filled two glasses with sparkling wine and handed her one. She sipped and wrinkled her nose.

"If it is not to your taste, I will order something else."

"No, please don't trouble yourself. This is the first time I have drunk wine."

"I want everything in your life to be to your taste." The major's face lit with his disarming smile.

"Thank you."

"You cannot imagine how busy I have been. I obtained the marriage licence and told Mrs Knowles, my housekeeper, to employ more staff because the house has been mostly unoccupied during my years in the Peninsula. I also purchased a wardrobe for you."

"A wardrobe?" she queried with a sense of unreality.

"Yes, I ordered gowns and pelisses from a *modiste* and purchased reticules and fans—and whatever else is deemed necessary for a lady of fashion. Of course, you need more and in the near future, I will take you to London to buy whatever else you require. For now, if the clothes do not fit, they can be altered."

"You are very kind. How did you manage to do so much in so short a time?"

"I am used to campaigning. Half the battle is organisation. Mind you, I could not guess your shoe size, so I bought four different sizes. If none of them fit, they can be returned and you may go to Guildford to see what you can find."

Annabelle's stomach lurched. From now on, she would need her husband's permission for everything she did. Oh, how she hoped she had made the right decision. No matter how much she liked him, he was still a stranger to her heart.

The major clasped her upper arms and drew her to her feet. "Why do you look so dismayed?"

She could not voice her doubts to him. "I am tired," she said truthfully. "At school we went to bed at nine of the clock."

Her bridegroom released her. "I will tell the dresser I have employed for you to attend you."

"Thank you. Goodnight."

"Not goodnight!" He raised her hand to his lips and pressed a kiss onto it. "I shall join you soon."

"Join me?"

"Although you have lived with females for so many years, surely you know that married people sometimes share a bed."

At the thought of the major getting into her bed, her eyes widened. "Y…yes, I suppose they do. I had not considered the matter. You must think I am stupid. You were right to call me ignorant."

"Ah, does that disturb you? Please accept my further apologies. I only meant that you are unfamiliar with society. Now, I suspect that, as you have no mother to advise you, perhaps you know little about marriage." He raised her hand to his lips again. "From now on, when we are in private, please call me Roland."

"Roland," she mouthed, still apprehensive because she had always slept alone.

"Do not look so worried, Belle, you will enjoy sharing your bed with me."

Would she?

Alone, Annabelle pressed her hands to her hot cheeks. She removed them when a tall, thin woman with black hair partially covered by a starched, white lace cap entered the bedchamber.

The woman's dark, almond shaped eyes surveyed Annabelle for a moment before she curtsied. "I'm Deacon, your dresser, Madam."

Her alarm at the prospect of Roland sharing her bed uppermost in her mind, Annabelle acknowledged Deacon with a nod.

"I shall leave you in Deacon's capable hands," Roland said and went through a door that led not into the corridor but into another room.

"Will you bathe, Madam?"

"Yes, but my husband—"

Deacon smirked. "Don't worry about him, Madam, I'm sure he's a gentleman who won't return until you are in bed."

Maids brought a portable bathtub and brass cans of hot and cold water. In silence, Deacon attended to Annabelle and when she finished her ablutions, would have dried her if she had not protested. "Thank you, I shall dry myself."

Deacon waited until Annabelle finished and was dry before holding out a white, fine linen nightgown. Annabelle took it from her, put it on, and dismissed the woman.

Deacon hesitated, a slight frown on her forehead. "Begging your pardon, Madam, but may I ask if I'm the first lady's maid to serve you?"

Annabelle raised her eyebrows instead of replying.

"If I am, may I remark that it's my duty to plait your hair, put your nightcap on your head, and tie its ribbons?"

She accepted the woman's service and, after some hesitation, settled in bed.

As soon as Deacon left the bedchamber, Roland, wearing a crimson heavy silk dressing gown embroidered with a pair of fearsome black and gold dragons, entered the room. She glanced at him, and then squeezed her eyes shut, shyer than she had been at the inn when he saw her partially clad.

"Annabelle, look at me, there is no need to be frightened. When you made your vows, you gave me every right over you, but I will do nothing without your consent."

She opened her eyes and saw his delightful but crooked smile that somehow seemed rueful. With trepidation she watched him take off his splendid dressing gown. Clad only in a white nightshirt, he approached the bed. What would happen to her on this night, possibly the most important one of her life? What if she did not like married life?

His raised eyebrows posed a question.

Annabelle looked down at the quilt. Even if her life depended on it, she could not speak.

"With your permission." Roland got into bed and lay back against the plump bolster and pillows.

Self-conscious and flustered, she turned her face away from him.

"Look at me, Belle," he said for the second time.

How could she look at him, a man who was little more than a complete stranger, lying so close to her? Why, oh why did she marry him? She drew the sheet up to her chin.

"Belle, there is no need for awkwardness, we are man and wife and I promise any…er…discomfort you experience will be brief—"

Annabelle sat up and stared down at him. "Discomfort?" she squeaked. Oh how she wished she had paid more attention to the other girls' gossip and whispered confidences at The Beeches. Fanny had told her some families refused to send their daughters to school because it would lead to them being too knowing on their wedding nights. Now she wished she knew more than the little Miss Chalfont's mother had once told her with heightened colour in her cheeks and much hesitation.

"Stop looking at me as though I am going to gobble you up like an ogre in a child's tale." His hand smoothed the length of her plait. "Be kind to me. Kiss me, Belle."

"K-kiss you?"

"Yes."

If that was all he wanted in return for his many kindnesses, it was not too bad a prospect. Emboldened, she bent her head and kissed his smooth-shaven cheek. His hand slipped underneath her plait and stroked her back.

"Kiss my mouth."

By candlelight, sparks burned in the depths of his eyes. What was he thinking? A tremor ran through her as she kissed him briefly. Bashful, although she shivered with pleasure as his artful hands caressed her, she lay down and pressed her head back against the pillows. He half turned, and through her nightdress, his hands traced patterns of fire along her body until, with an impatient exclamation, he pushed back the bedcovers, removed his nightshirt and unfastened the ties at the throat of her nightgown.

Her breath came very fast. At first she was much too shocked by the sight of his naked body to speak, and she hastily looked away from the strange shape at the juncture of his thighs. Her breath came very fast and she managed to voice some of her thoughts. "This is extraordinary. A week ago I did not know you existed, and even now I know so little about you and...and—"

"Shush, Belle, like many other couples married after a brief acquaintance, we have the rest of our lives to exchange confidences. When we do so, always remember I want to be your friend as well as your husband and lover."

Roland propped himself on one elbow and bent his head to kiss her on the mouth, evoking thrilling sensations she had never imagined. He raised her nightgown.

"No!" she protested, her face on fire with embarrassment as she covered the junction of her legs with her hands.

Roland raised his head and looked deep into her eyes. "Do you want me to return to my bedchamber?"

Torn between apprehension, shock and desire for more of his thrilling kisses, she could not answer him.

"Belle, if you want me to go, I will not think the worse of you."

In her innocence, she had never imagined a man could thus delight her senses. "You may stay," she whispered.

He tugged her nightgown over her head. "You are more beautiful than I could have imagined," her bridegroom said in a hoarse voice, before her consent for him to remain with her was rewarded by his lips kissing the hollow of her neck, and then her breasts, until she moaned with ever increasing desire for she knew not what.

"Don't be afraid," Roland whispered.

* * *

"Did I please you?" Roland asked much later and after he had made love to her for the second time.

Annabelle nodded conscious of her blushes. Pleasure had overwhelmed a lingering discomfort in a part she did not know the name for—although she still found the sight of his nakedness shocking. "N-nothing w-will ever be the same again," she whispered.

"But did I please you?" he repeated. "I never want to be an inconsiderate husband who only seeks his own satisfaction."

What did he mean by "inconsiderate" and "his own satisfaction"?

"Belle?"

"Yes, you pleased me," she murmured, "but did I…that is…did you—"

"Did you please me? Oh yes, you did. As I said when I removed your nightgown, you are beautiful. So very beautiful," he emphasised, "and so…responsive. And now that our marriage has been consummated, it cannot be annulled."

Annulled? What did he mean? His touch made the questions seem unimportant. One hand stroked her hair and the other drew her closer to him. Being a wife entailed this intimacy, the delightful sharing of a bed and so much more besides. Her eyes closed and she drifted off to sleep with her cheek on his chest, still torn between embarrassment and pleasure.

* * *

Annabelle stretched and yawned. She turned over and opened her eyes. Was she dreaming? No, she was not. She was married. Roland, who lay next to her—his face relaxed in sleep—proved it. Annabelle rubbed her eyes, scarcely able to believe her bridegroom had given her such intense pleasure the night before.

Where was her nightgown? She did not like the sight of the intimate parts of his nakedness and, in spite of their love making, the thought of him seeing her naked body disturbed her. She fumbled under the covers to retrieve the abandoned nightgown. She sat, drew it over her head, and smoothed it down over her body.

What should she do? She glanced at Roland. The half-moons of his lashes guarded his eyes and his breath came evenly. Should she wake him with a kiss? If she did, what would he say? She smiled and flushed, remembering the tenderness with which he made love to her three times during the long night. Was it shameless of her to want him to take her in his arms again?

As soon as her feet touched the floor, Roland's hand reached out to detain her. "Juliet, my sweet, come back to bed," he mumbled, his eyes closed.

Juliet! Annabelle twisted round to look at her bridegroom. Why had he called her Juliet? Could he already be married? Be a bigamist? No, she could not, would not, believe that of him. If it were true, it would be dreadful. Juliet must be the name of his mistress. How dare he address her by another woman's name? What a fool she had been to believe him when he assured her he would not consort with a mistress after their marriage. If Juliet meant so much to him that he awoke with her name on his lips, more than likely he intended to continue consorting with her.

Anger welled up in Annabelle. Not entirely ignorant of the ways of the world, she might be able to forgive him for having a mistress, but she would never forgive him for calling her by his mistress's name. It was as though there were three people in their bed. Yet, when Roland fully awoke, she would not have the courage to question him, for what was his response when he asked her to marry him and she questioned him? He had implied, in the strongest terms, that no lady should raise the subject of a gentleman's mistress, even if that lady was the gentleman's wife.

Roland blinked several times, opened his eyes. His smile reminded her of a contented tomcat. "Good morning, Belle, how are you? I hope you are in the best of spirits." He reached up to draw her face down to his.

She turned her face aside from him. He released her. "Have I displeased you?" he asked, his drawl exaggerated.

Without the least idea as to how he would react if she dared to question him about Juliet, she did not know what to say.

After a short pause, during which Roland watched her as though he was the cat at The Beeches and she was a dove, his expression hardened. "My apologies. I should not have forced my attentions on you. My only excuse is that at the time you did not seem reluctant to return my ardour. And, as I told you, it was necessary for us to consummate the marriage."

Distrustful, she wanted to question him about Juliet, be taken in his arms and reassured that the woman was of no importance to him.

How should a bride behave with her bridegroom? Nothing in her education had prepared her for this moment.

"Well, Madam Wife," her husband said in a cold tone of voice, "we are now man and wife in the flesh as well as in the eyes of God."

His exquisite courtesy, in painful contrast to the night's passion, tormented her. He paid homage to her by raising her hand to his lips and pressing a kiss on it. Annabelle tensed. She should tell Roland he had no need to apologise for the consummation of their marriage, but could not—due to her jealousy of Juliet, a woman who was surely of great importance to her bridegroom—so she remained silent.

Roland's breath rasped. He dropped her hand onto the bed. Without speaking again, he swung his legs over the edge. Oh no, she could not look at the bush of hair between his legs and his most private part that nestled there: a part that had given her incredible pleasure.

Her husband pulled on his magnificent dressing gown and strode out of the bedchamber.

Before Annabelle could gather her thoughts, Deacon entered followed by maids carrying brass cans of water. They put them down by the washstand, around which her dresser put a red lacquered screen. A maid brought a pot of hot chocolate. Deacon dismissed all the maids and Annabelle watched her dresser select a white morning gown sprigged with forget-me-nots.

"Will you wear this, Madam?"

Forget-me-nots! How appropriate, she would never forget last night's ecstasy followed by cruel disillusionment.

"Madam?"

Annabelle looked at the elegant gown and nodded, her feverish mind teeming with questions. What did Juliet look like? How did she dress? Did she wear wispy silks?

"Will you breakfast in your parlour or with Major Sarrat in the breakfast room, Madam?"

Where did Roland and Juliet partake of breakfast? On a balcony in sunny Portugal, or Spain when he was in the army?

"Where is my parlour?"

Deacon pointed across the bedchamber. "Through that door, Madam."

"I thought it led to the major's bedchamber."

"No, it leads to your parlour on the other side of which is the major's apartment," Deacon explained.

"I see. I will eat with the major in the breakfast room," she said and ignored Deacon's sly look.

* * *

Head held high, Annabelle followed a servant to the breakfast room where she glimpsed herself in a mirror. With satisfaction, she noted both her hairstyle and her new gown enhanced her appearance and made her look older than eighteen.

Roland stood and bowed to acknowledge her presence. He opened his mouth to speak but she forestalled him. "May I join you for breakfast, sir?"

"You are mistress of this house and may do whatsoever you please," he replied and smiled that crooked smile which, so far, had not failed to melt her heart.

A footman drew back her chair. Annabelle sat. Another footman put the silver coffeepot, cream jug, and sugar basin on her right and asked for permission to serve her buttered eggs.

"No, I will serve myself. You and the other servants may leave," she replied and glanced at her bridegroom. "May I pour you some coffee, sir?"

Roland cleared his throat. A crease appeared on his forehead. "No, thank you, and please continue to call me Roland when we are in private."

Ill-at-ease, she poured coffee.

"Belle, I fear you will consider me churlish."

Churlish! That was not a word she would use to describe a man who spoke another woman's name on the first day of his marriage. She struggled to think of a suitable one. Although she had little appetite, she put a slice of ham and some eggs onto her plate.

Roland broke his roll apart and scanned her face. "Yes, churlish, for I regret I must leave you. Devilish is it not, to be obliged to leave my bride?"

Annabelle blinked to prevent tears of frustration forming and rolling down her cheeks. How had she displeased him? Last night, he thrilled her. How had she failed him? If she pleased him, as he said she had, surely he would not leave her. Could he be leaving her to visit Juliet?

"Wh-when will you return, Major Sarrat?"

"Roland, not Major."

"When will you return, Roland?" she asked, in better control of her emotions.

"Well, Belle, it seems you are as cool as the proverbial cucumber, so you will not mind if I am gone for a week, will you?"

Would it embarrass him if she pleaded with him not to leave, not to go to another's woman's bed? "How will I occupy myself while you are away?"

"Do as you please, but if you ride, take a groom with you and do not go further than Michenden village. Should you wish to go elsewhere, please go in the carriage. It is an old fashioned one that belonged to the previous owner of the manor, but it will serve its purpose until I purchase a new one." He put a bulging purse on the table. "This is for you. It should be sufficient until we go up to London where you may buy whatsoever you need."

"You are generous," she murmured.

"I endowed you with all my worldly goods. What is more, have I not told you I will look after you for as long as I live?"

Yes, he had and he had also promised to make her happy, but he had already broken that promise. Annabelle picked up her knife and fork. Despite her jealous outrage, irrational fear of some evil befalling him gripped her. She could not eat.

"You should have more than enough for your needs," Roland said. "But do not forget, ladies never handle money. Deacon must pay for your purchases." He smiled. "I beg your pardon for sounding like a schoolmaster, but you neither have a female relative nor any other lady to advise you, so I must do so. I should have arranged for you to have a companion. Now, Belle, I must hurry."

Roland ate hastily, wiped his mouth with a napkin, and stood. "Madam Wife," he said, his tone of voice like a tender caress. "Are you not going to bid me farewell?"

"Suppose…suppose there is an emergency. I will not know how to contact you."

Roland stood and opened the door. "This way, Belle."

She walked by his side to the book room where he sat and penned an address on a piece of paper. "In an emergency, either Viscount Hampton or his steward will know where to find me." He handed her the paper.

"Fanny's brother! I have often mentioned her. Why did you not tell me you knew him?" she asked, sensing a mystery, but unable to imagine what it was.

He shrugged. "At the time my…er…acquaintance with him did not seem important. Now, I must leave, for I do not care to keep the horses waiting. I shall not kiss you farewell because it seems you would not welcome my kisses."

Oh, he was wrong. She would welcome them if she could be sure that she would not share them with another woman.

"Don't fret," Roland said, "All will be well, and I doubt you will miss me." He hesitated before he spoke again. "As I told you, Belle. I believe I can make you happy if you will allow me to."

Before she could so much as wish him Godspeed, he left the library.

* * *

Seated in his comfortable chaise, Roland cursed himself for a fool. Instead of claiming his bride, he should have waited until they knew each other better. However, the consummation prevented any challenge to the marriage and a possible attempt by Annabelle's guardian to have it annulled. Moreover, a long delay before he bedded Annabelle might have created an unnatural awkwardness. He had made love to his bride with all the skill and tenderness at his command. At no point had Annabelle indicated his attentions were unwelcome. To the contrary, she clung to him like mistletoe on an apple tree that bore delicious fruit. Yet, when he awoke, enchanted by her beauty, she rejected him. A bitter laugh escaped him. It seemed he was not as skilled a lover as he had believed.

Roland cursed himself, this time for playing a knight-errant and marrying his adorable bride. Well, at least he had kept his promise to his wily grandmamma to wed without delay. What was the old saying? Ah yes. "Marry in haste, repent at leisure." Devil take it, her rejection made him wonder if he had mistaken Annabelle for an unworldly girl when, in fact, she was a young harpy whose reason for marrying him was his obvious wealth? He clutched his head in his hands. What a coil. Already she behaved coldly toward him. What would she say when he revealed the full truth? Women were so unpredictable that no man could be expected to understand them. How suspicious she had looked when he mentioned the name Viscount Hampton.

If Annabelle had not behaved so coldly when he woke this morning, he would have confided in her. Roland sighed and closed his eyes. It had been a long night and he was tired.

Chapter Ten

Annabelle had no time to brood over her bridegroom's sudden departure. Within moments, the housekeeper joined her and curtsied respectfully.

"Excuse me for interrupting you, Madam, but I would like to know when it will be convenient for you to let me conduct you round the house?"

Annabelle put down her empty coffee cup. "You may show me round now." Annabelle replied, curious about her new home.

By the time nuncheon was served, never again did Annabelle want to observe linen sheets and pillowcases being counted, or listen to a cook's plan to pickle and preserve fruits and vegetables from the kitchen garden. Indeed, listening to descriptions of such industry had given her a headache.

Fresh air! She needed fresh air.

After nuncheon, Deacon helped Annabelle into a kingfisher blue pelisse, and put a close-fitting bonnet with a wide brim, trimmed with a curled ostrich feather, on her head, tied the ribbons under her chin in a charming bow, and buttoned her gloves.

"The gloves are too big for you, Madam."

"I will give them to you when I have some that fit properly," Annabelle said, not so ignorant that she did not know her cast offs were the woman's perquisites.

Deacon's eyes glittered and Annabelle guessed she would get a good price for second-hand apparel. She shuddered and looked away from Deacon. In spite of the woman's competency and polite manner, something indefinable about the dresser made her uncomfortable.

"If you will be good enough to wait for me, Madam, I shall follow you in a moment."

Why did she not like Deacon and most definitely not want to spend a moment more than was necessary with her? She shook her head. "Don't accompany me. I will not leave the grounds." During Roland's absence, she preferred solitude.

* * *

In the garden, the warm sun shone on clumps of daffodils swaying in the balmy breeze and on a few early tulips with unfurled satin-like petals. Leaving the flowerbeds behind, Annabelle entered the walled kitchen garden and laughed at a pert robin perched amongst the winter cabbages while his observant, beady eyes watched a gnarled gardener planting early peas. From a distance, she admired a glasshouse and then went through an arched door to lawns leading away from the manor house.

After a pleasant walk, Annabelle reached the farthest end of the grounds and stood at the brink of an ornamental lake. In the centre of it was an island, on which stood a dilapidated, but picturesque, stone pavilion. She sauntered around the water's edge in search of an angle from which the view could be sketched most effectively. Charcoal and watercolours would occupy her until Roland's return and divert unwelcome speculation about Juliet. She would go to Guildford and buy whatever she needed.

* * *

Three days after her wedding, dressed in a cream carriage gown, worn under a cherry red pelisse, Annabelle, accompanied by Deacon, took her place in the carriage.

Deacon folded her hands on her lap. "If I may say so, Madam, you look well, very well indeed."

"Thank you," Annabelle said and thought of Roland. Would he also think she looked very well? She hoped he would not be absent for more than a week and, God willing, that he might return earlier. Moreover, when he did come home, she would lure him from the unknown Juliet forever. How she could influence a man of her husband's years and experience she did not know, but she was determined to try her best to do so.

Deacon startled her by leaning forward and tweaking the cherry red satin bow under her chin. "Be careful not to crush your ribbons, Madam."

"Yes, yes, I will be careful," she muttered, distracted by the idea of Roland in Juliet's arms.

She could not bear the thought of Roland making love to another woman. No, she should not imagine he was with Juliet. Instead of fretting, she should trust him to keep his marriage vow to forsake all others and cleave only unto her. Sad, she shook her head. If she was naïve, Fanny was not, and Fanny had told her most married men kept a mistress.

She heaved a sigh while the carriage proceeded along a country road bordered by trees, which flaunted new spring greenery, until it drew to a halt in Guildford. Annabelle alighted and looked at the cobbled High Street lined with half-timbered houses, taverns, and bow-fronted shops with glass panes glittering in the spring sunshine.

With Deacon close behind her, Annabelle entered a haberdasher and purchased some forget-me-not blue ribbon to trim the gown she wore on the morning after her wedding night. She examined the wares, exclaiming and fingering them and then, unable to resist, purchased a length of cobweb fine lace.

While Deacon paid for the items, a ridiculous young man approached her. With astonishment, she eyed his padded coat, which made his chest look like a wood pigeon's plump breast. She restrained a giggle before she looked away.

"May I have the honour of assisting you?" the impertinent gentleman asked.

Annabelle ignored him. "Come, Deacon."

"Fotherhaugh at your service, Madam. Fotherhaugh of Fotherhaugh Hall. Ask anyone in these parts about me. Everyone knows me," the ridiculous gentleman said.

Annabelle repressed another wayward giggle. Indeed, everyone must know him. Who could plead ignorance of a man who chose garments such as his pea green coat, canary yellow inexpressibles, and a waistcoat striped with all the colours of the rainbow?

The shopkeeper came forward, escorted Annabelle to the door of his small shop, and bowed so low that his nose was almost level with his knees.

Followed by Deacon, Annabelle went into the street without as much as a glance at Fotherhaugh.

Unabashed, the ridiculous young dandy followed them and asked Deacon to introduce him to the "young lady whose beauty eclipsed the sun and moon's."

Annabelle looked away from him. How dare he commit such a breach of etiquette after she had declined his acquaintance with a direct cut?

Although Deacon also ignored him, the young dandypratt dabbed his lips with his scented handkerchief and followed them.

"Who are you? Could you be the runaway schoolgirl reported in The Chronicle?" he bleated.

Deacon looked thoughtfully at Annabelle before she spoke. "What has a married lady such as my mistress to do with a schoolroom miss?" Deacon looked away from Fotherhaugh and followed Annabelle into a cobbler's, leaving the young man in the street.

After a brief discussion with him, Annabelle sat and raised her skirt above her ankles for the man to measure her foot.

"There are gentlemen peering through the windows," Deacon said. "Do you not have a private room for my mistress's use?"

"Yes, yes, I do." The cobbler ushered them through a door into a tiny room furnished with no more than a chair and a stool.

The cobbler measured her feet to make a last. Annabelle instructed him to make a pair of slippers, two pairs of shoes, a pair of half-boots, and riding boots as soon as possible. Having placed her order and receiving the cobbler's assurances that her footwear would be of the finest quality, Annabelle stepped into High Street. To her discomfiture, the group of gossiping gentlemen, who had peered at her through the window, drew close.

"Yes, you are right, Fotherhaugh, the lady does match the description of the runaway," a dandified youth said.

"We should lodge information with the Bow Street Runners," an older gentleman drawled. "The newspaper reported they are after her."

Head held high, but unable to control her flushes caused by the unwelcome attention, Annabelle returned to her carriage. When seated, she rested her head against the squab and closed her eyes. Why must people be so curious? Should she forward a letter addressed to Roland at Viscount Hampton's town house? No, Roland would soon return and in the meantime he might read the reports about her—if indeed they were about her.

The most sensible thing would be to write to Miss Chalfont. She would tell her she was safe and ask her to stop the hue and cry. Annabelle relaxed and decided also to write to Fanny, who must be in a fever to know where she was.

* * *

Accompanied by a groom on the following afternoon, Annabelle was determined not to be put out of countenance if she met any of the rude gentlemen who haunted Guildford's High Street on the previous day. Her letters in the saddlebag, she rode along a pretty country road bordered with self-sown shrubs and wild daffodils, to Michenden Village.

After she gave her letters to the postmistress and came out onto the street again, a ruddy-faced country gentleman approached her. Judging by his dress, he seemed respectable so Annabelle did not turn aside from him.

"Not the thing to introduce myself, Madam, but everyone hereabouts knows me and the servants have spread news about you."

Annabelle raised her eyebrows and wondered what had been said. "Indeed," she responded for the want of anything better to say.

The gentleman bowed. "I am Squire Weatherby. Good to know there is new blood in the neighbourhood. This afternoon, m'wife and I will call on you with our son."

"You and your family will be welcome, sir," she responded. After all, sooner or later she must become acquainted with the local gentry.

* * *

Two days after Annabelle posted her letter in Michenden Village, the squire and his family had waited on Annabelle, and her paints and other paraphernalia had arrived.

The fair weather continued, so, warmly dressed, Annabelle settled herself on a chair by the lake and sketched a graceful willow tree with branches that trailed in the water.

After a short time, loud male voices disturbed her. She turned around and puckered her brow at the sight of the squire's son and four other young dandies, amongst whom was Mr Fotherhaugh. Her frown deepened when they walked across the lawn toward her, the spring sunshine heightening the colour of their fashionable blue coats with shiny buttons.

"Hope we are not disturbing you, Ma'am," the Squire's son called. "We spied you from the house," he continued with the air of a conceited young gentleman convinced of a warm welcome. "Allow me to introduce my friends, my cousin Mr Theakstone, my good friend Mr Sutton and Mr Hammond, the rector's son."

Each gentleman bowed unnecessarily low. "Hammond, Theakstone, Sutton, I told you Mrs Sarrat is a beauty."

"Good day," Annabelle said. She did not wish to offend a neighbour so she resisted the temptation to dismiss young Mr Weatherby and his friends.

The gentlemen crowded around her, the combined scent of their pomade and cologne overpowering. Four pairs of eyes scrutinised her sketch.

"Splendid," said Fotherhaugh. "Mrs Sarrat, I shall kiss your hand in honour of your muse."

Annabelle clasped her hands together. "No, you will not, sir."

"'Pon my word, ma'am, you draw better than either of my sisters or their governess," Mr Theakstone said.

Their comments about her sketch, with which she was not yet satisfied, irritated her. She stood. "Shall we go to the house for refreshments?"

Mr Weatherby seized her easel. His friends, who picked up various items, amused her. In comparison to Roland, whom she thought of constantly, they resembled awkward children.

"Please don't inconvenience yourselves, gentlemen. The servants will fetch them."

Irritated by her visitors, Annabelle led them toward the house. When they drew closer, she looked across the immaculate greensward to the broad flight of steps that led to a veranda and saw her husband. At the sight of Roland standing motionless, arms by his side and a scowl on his face, Annabelle caught her breath. Why did he look so cross? She smiled and waved at him.

"Who is that ferocious looking man?" Mr Weatherby asked in response to her husband's glare.

"My husband, Major Sarrat," she replied and continued to walk ahead of her admirers.

"Major Sarrat?" queried Mr Theakstone. "My older brother has mentioned him. Is he not—?"

"What would I not give to tie my neck cloth like the major's?" Fotherhaugh interrupted as though awestruck. He recovered himself sufficiently to speak again. "The Waterfall is a devilishly tricky style."

Hands outstretched to Roland, Annabelle hurried up the steps. "How glad I am to see you, I did not expect you to return so soon."

"I see you have amused yourself in my absence, Madam," Roland said in clipped tones.

What was amiss with her husband? "Yes, I went to Guildford, bought an easel and was sketching when these gentlemen called on me," she began and lowered her hands.

Mr Weatherby bowed, straightened, and wiped a film of perspiration from his brow with his monogrammed handkerchief. "We are helping Mrs Sarrat, sir."

"With what are you helping my wife?" Roland asked in the same clipped tone, as he scrutinised the young man.

The squire's son looked away. "Perfectly respectable, I assure you, sir. I waited on Mrs Sarrat with my parents and have now brought some of my particular friends to meet her."

The explanation did not soften her husband's expression.

"M-my father is the squire of Michenden," Mr Weatherby explained and ran a finger around the edge of his cravat. "All of us live near here, except for my cousin who is visiting me and my parents." He cleared his throat. "I am sure my mother will wait on Mrs Sarrat again."

"Indeed, I have been overseas for so long that I have not had the opportunity to acquaint myself with my neighbours since I inherited this manor." He turned toward Annabelle and tucked her hand into the crook of his arm.

"You are hurt," she said and reached up to touch an ugly bruise on his jaw, previously concealed by the height of his starched shirt collar.

"Nothing to concern yourself with."

Mrs Knowles bustled out of the house. "Refreshments are served in the blue parlour, Madam."

"A glass of wine, gentlemen," Roland suggested and then murmured in Annabelle's ear. "Do not feel obliged to join us."

Annabelle went upstairs to her apartment. If only her bridegroom's eyes had not resembled chips of ice when she greeted him.

Much later, when she ventured downstairs, Roland sat alone in the book room. He did not look up from the volume he held in his hand. She coughed to attract his attention.

Roland stood and inclined his head. "Did you come in search of a book to while away the time?"

"Who hit you?" she asked in a fever of anxiety.

He fingered his jaw.

"I had a disagreement with de Beauchamp. Please don't worry about it. I have already put the altercation out of my mind."

She could not help being concerned. "What was the disagreement about?"

"I warned him not to spread gossip about you."

"Oh," she said, satisfied with the explanation and rather pleased because he had defended her honour. "Was it necessary for you to come to fisticuffs?"

Roland raised his eyebrows.

Annabelle scrutinised the harsh lines of his tanned face and decided not to question him. "Our guests have left?" she asked, for want of anything else to say.

"As you see, but should I apologise for ridding you of their company?" he asked in even tones.

She laughed. "No, it was not of my seeking."

His eyes warmed and he smiled at her for the first time since his return. "Is that so?"

"Yes. I went shopping in Guildford. I trust you will not censure me for being extravagant. The shoes you bought for me did not fit, so, although the quality is inferior to them, I ordered shoes, half boots, and riding boots. And I ordered paintbrushes and other materials. There was so little to do during your absence that I wanted to pass the time sketching and painting. Well,"—she took a deep breath—"the thing is, while I was in Michenden, I met that foolish young gentleman who introduced himself to me as 'Fotherhaugh of Fotherhaugh Hall.'" She giggled. "A ridiculous name for a ridiculous fop." She eyed Roland. Thank goodness, he had stopped frowning.

"How impertinent of that puppy to introduce his friends to you. Should I challenge him to a duel for his insolence?"

"No, we have already agreed that duelling is illegal. Apart from that, if you engaged him, I would be terrified because you might be wounded."

"Come here, Belle," Roland said, his voice gentle.

Without hesitation, she approached him. When she drew near, he reached out to clasp her hands.

"My dear, there is no lady to keep you company, so you should not be at home to gentlemen in my absence."

"I know and assure you I instructed the servants to say I was not at home if young Mr Fotherhaugh called on me without his parents." Hot colour rushed into her cheeks. "I hope you will not think me vain for saying I think he admires me." She eyed Roland anxiously. "I confess that I suspected he might call, although I did not anticipate him bringing any friends."

His eyes watched her as intently as that tomcat's at school when he lurked in the bushes intent on his prey. "Are you as innocent as you seem? Yes, I believe you are. Please forgive your jealous old husband."

Annabelle pealed with laughter before she pressed a finger to his lips. "Jealous? Of those nincompoops? And you are not old…at least not so very old."

"Thank you for those crumbs from your bountiful table," Roland said dryly.

She gazed at him for a moment, uncertain of his meaning. "I must change before we dine."

Chapter Eleven

Deacon dressed Annabelle in a blue silk gown that complemented her forget-me-not blue eyes. In silence, she sat and looked in the mirror while Deacon arranged her hair with deft hands.

"The hairstyle increases your height, Madam." Deacon tucked an artificial cornflower into the hair arranged high on the crown of Annabelle's head and put the comb down.

"Do you think I am too short, Deacon?" She hoped Roland did not think she lacked in any way.

"No, but the extra height adds to your consequence."

Annabelle chuckled. "I suspect you think more of my consequence than I do."

She stood and examined her reflection in a long mirror. Pleased, she fingered the short, pomaded curls round her face. No longer did they escape. Her hair was carefully controlled. "You are right, Deacon, the style adds inches to my height." Her face bright with laughter, she curtsied to her image. "I hope my major will admire me," she told her reflection and hoped she was more beautiful than Juliet.

* * *

In the old-fashioned drawing room, with dark linen fold panelling, Annabelle paused to admire Roland's single-breasted black coat and matching pantaloons, buttoned close to his ankles above his shiny coal-black slippers.

"How fine you look, Roland."

He put his book down on a low inlaid table beside his chair, stood, and walked across the room to her.

"I am not as fine as you are. Belle, I have no doubt you are the most beautiful bride in the world."

She dipped a low curtsey. "You flatter me."

"When you know me better, you will know I never pay empty compliments. All you need are some baubles. You will grace the sapphires my father bought for my mother."

"You are a flatterer."

"No such thing. I promise you will be the centre of attraction in London."

She lowered her eyes and smiled hesitantly. "Nonsense, but if I am, I promise not to flirt with anyone other than you and hope you will not flirt with any other lady."

"Belle," he breathed and reached out to her.

If Mrs Knowles had not announced dinner at that moment, she suspected he would have kissed her, careless of her fashionable hairstyle and the risk of crushing her immaculate gown.

* * *

Some time after they dined when a maid brought the tea tray in, Annabelle yawned and yawned again. "How rude of me, Roland, please forgive me."

"No need to apologise, Belle." His eyes gleamed. "Go to bed. Shall I come and sing you a lullaby?"

She laughed and retired to her bedroom where Deacon awaited her.

"Have you read the newspapers today, madam?" Deacon asked, her dark eyes gleaming.

"No," Annabelle replied, surprised by a servant initiating a conversation. She caught her lower lip between her teeth. Why was the woman trembling with some suppressed emotion?

"The missing schoolgirl has not been found, madam."

Deacon helped her to remove her clothes and put on her nightgown. Thoughtful, Annabelle sat at her dressing table and waited for Deacon to unpin her hair and brush it before she plaited it for the night.

"Do you think she eloped, madam?"

Annabelle shivered. In the mirror, she saw a hard glint in Deacon's eyes. She caught her breath before speaking. "I doubt the girl eloped. Runaway brides are more common in novels than in real life."

The woman must have guessed she was the missing schoolgirl. If she had not, she would not have dared to address her with such familiarity.

Annabelle stood and shook her head to reject the pretty lace-trimmed dressing gown, which the dresser held out ready for her to slip her arms into. "Put it away. I am going straight to bed."

The woman's eyes glittered. "If she's run off with a gentleman, and if they didn't marry in Gretna Green, the bridegroom will be sorry for wedding such a young lady."

"Why?" Annabelle shivered, almost afraid to hear the reply.

Colour high in her usually pale cheeks, Deacon spoke. "Well, madam, if he don't—I mean doesn't have permission to wed, from her parents or guardian, the marriage is illegal. What's more, the girl's ruined and the man faces criminal charges for abducting a minor."

Her heart beating too fast, Annabelle got into bed. She must not allow the woman to sense her fear. "That will be all for tonight, Deacon," she said, proud of her even tone.

"Will it, madam?" Deacon asked in a honey-sweet tone of voice.

Although Annabelle ignored her, Deacon hovered beside the bed. Her long shadow stretched across the floor. Her viper-like eyes were unnerving.

"Mark my words, madam, sooner or later the couple will be discovered and information will be laid for the reward of, maybe, as much as one hundred guineas."

Annabelle's first impulse was to confide in Roland, her second was to protect him from the possibility of imprisonment. Would a hundred guineas silence her dresser? She trembled for she did not have that much money to give the woman. What should she do? Could she ask Roland for such a large sum?

Deacon broke the lengthy silence. "I am sure someone will make shift to claim a hundred guineas and, perhaps, a little bit more."

Appalled by Deacon's indirect demand, Annabelle lay down and stared up at the thin, black clad figure of her servant.

"If I found the runaways, madam, surely you couldn't blame me for reporting them."

Annabelle could not prevent her lower lip quivering but managed to keep herself well in hand.

"I only earn twelve pounds a year," the odious woman continued. "A hundred guineas add up to more than eight years' wages. I call that a handsome nest egg, and so would you in my circumstances. And a little more than that amount would be very welcome." A slight smile curved Deacon's thin lips.

Before Annabelle could reply, Roland entered the bedroom and gestured for Deacon to leave.

As soon as they were alone, he got into bed, lay down, and gently drew her into his arms.

What possible explanation could she give Roland for needing a hundred guineas; she fretted, and tried to welcome his kisses. At the moment, she could not find an excuse for asking him for so much money.

Roland untied the ribbons at her throat.

Annabelle frowned. If their marriage was illegal where could she go and what could she do? What a dreadful situation.

Roland propped himself up on one elbow and looked at her. "What is wrong?"

"I am…am very tired. I am sorry."

"Belle, you need not make excuses. I have already told you that I will never force myself on you." Roland stroked her cheek with his forefinger, left her bed, and strode out of the bedchamber.

Alone, Annabelle lay still, the only sound, that of the fire's irregular crackle and the accelerated pumping of her heart. "I wish I could go home," she whispered into the shadows in the furthest corner of the room.

"Home!" she exclaimed with the realisation that she thought of The Beeches as home. There she could discuss her problems with Miss Chalfont and her mother. They would know what to do about detestable Deacon.

She sighed. Tears welled in her eyes. Angry with herself for such weakness, she wiped them away. Of one thing she was certain, she could not remain here and risk being responsible for her husband's imprisonment.

Throughout the seemingly endless night, Annabelle fretted over Deacon's demand for one hundred guineas. At first light, too tired to think clearly, she packed some necessities and distributed the remainder of the money Roland had given her about her person. With the fervent hope that no one would hear, she cursed Deacon, the cause of her flight, and tiptoed down the main stairs to the entrance hall.

In spite of the hurt caused by Roland speaking Juliet's name when he woke after making love to her on their wedding night, how could she bear the separation from him? It was cruel to be forced to separate from the first person whose life she shared. Annabelle summoned her courage. For her husband's sake, she must be brave enough to protect him from the law. She would not allow Roland to be imprisoned.

Distraught, Annabelle went to the stables and called quietly but insistently to James.

Rubbing his eyes, the elderly groom descended the ladder from his sleeping quarters above the stables.

"Harness the horses to the chaise," Annabelle ordered.

The man buttoned up his waistcoat and hesitated.

"Make haste. I have received bad news and must leave as soon as possible. If you do not hurry, your master will be angry with you."

"A moment, Madam, I'll fetch the head groom, and—"

"No. Do not disturb him," she interrupted. "Wake the coachman and tell him that he is to drive me to London."

James rubbed his eyes. "To London, Madam?" he asked and pursed his lips.

"Yes," she said firmly, afraid he would refuse to obey her.

* * *

Shortly before ten of the clock, the chaise drew to a halt in the stable yard of the famous coaching inn, The Angel, by St Clements Church in the Strand.

For the second time she had run away by dawn's early light, this time with a sad heart. Miserable, Annabelle sighed. If only circumstances had not forced her to leave Roland.

James opened the door of the chaise and let down the steps.

Annabelle alighted and, as she stepped across the cobbles in the direction of the inn, a mail coach clattered into the busy yard.

With a pang of regret, she remembered the gentleness with which Roland handed her down from the chaise when they first met. She sighed and agonised over her necessary separation from him. The only two good things were that she would save him from being charged with her abduction, and that she was now free to carry out the plan she had in mind when she ran away from the academy. Yet, since she married Roland, her plan seemed less urgent. Oh, how she hoped Deacon would suffer one day as she now suffered. No, she should not harbour so unchristian a thought.

"Madam," said James, who had followed her.

She took some money out of her reticule. "I do not require you and the coachman any longer. I think there is enough here to stable the horses for the night and for you to put up here. Now, please hand me my bandbox and then go and refresh yourselves."

James tugged his forelock. "Thank you, madam. A tankard of ale and a tasty cold cut of meat with some fresh bread will be very welcome."

After he went into the taproom with the coachman, Annabelle purchased an inside ticket on The Mail to Dover—pleased not to have to endure the discomfort of being an outside passenger, seated on the roof at the mercy of the weather. Next, she asked the landlord if he could provide an abigail to chaperone her.

"I'm sorry to say I can't, but a reverend gentleman and his wife will be travelling to Dover with you. If you wish, partake of some coffee while I ask them to keep an eye on you during your journey."

"Thank you, landlord, I am much obliged to you." As soon as she finished the hot drink and went back into the busy stable yard, a round-faced reverend and a plain-faced woman, who Annabelle assumed was his wife, approached her.

"Good day, ma'am," the gentleman said, smiling before he continued. "Please allow me to introduce us. The landlord suggested we should be at your service. I am Doctor Courtney and this lady is my dear wife."

Annabelle curtsied in response to his bow. "Good day."

She looked at The Mail, with its black painted upper body, mauve lower body, scarlet wheels, and yellow undercarriage. "Allow me to introduce myself. I am Miss Black."

The name Miss Black was preferable to Miss Mauve, Miss Scarlet, or Miss Yellow, and she was too distraught over her decision to leave her husband to give further consideration to surnames. She blinked her eyes to prevent tears forming. In the unlikely event of Roland making enquiries here, the pseudonym would complicate his search. She sniffed. Perhaps her husband would be too angry to chase after her. For his own sake she hoped he would be.

After Dr Courtney ensured the luggage was loaded, he helped his wife into the coach, in which a gentleman of cadaverous appearance sat, and then turned to assist Annabelle.

Seated next to Mrs Courtney, Annabelle shut her eyes. What would Roland say and do when he realised she had left? Perhaps he would laugh low in the manner that caused tingles to run up and down her spine and decide he regretted marrying a lady who made a habit of running away.

She squeezed her eyes shut to check her tears and made plans to study the art of drawing and painting, and then seek commissions. After all, her art master had praised her talent and said her work surpassed that of many professional artists who made their living painting portraits. Her money would not last long. Self-modesty about her artistic skills would not serve her—she knew she possessed exceptional talent. She swallowed to suppress a sigh. If her husband ever found out about her decision to earn her living as an artist, what would he think?

Annabelle peered through the window. She must be brave, now that she had foiled the odious Deacon's plans. Her mouth quivered. By now Roland would have discovered her flight. How ungrateful he must think her. What would he do when the chaise returned without her? Would he be so angry that he would never want to see her again? She would not blame him if he was. After all, when he returned home and found her with the Squire's son and the other young gentleman, she knew he was angry and suspected he had reined in his temper. What would it be like if he ever lost it with her? Her thoughts darted hither and thither. Even if Roland wanted her back and traced her to Dover, he would not know where to look, but if he did manage to find her, she suspected he would unleash his temper.

Ill-at-ease, she dozed until The Mail made its first stop and all of the passengers got out.

After the cadaverous gentleman grunted farewell, Annabelle went inside with the Courtneys to partake of steaming hot coffee, bread, and cold meat. By the time they returned to the coach, a plump infant in a buxom woman's arms was crying too loudly for her to converse with her temporary chaperons.

* * *

Outside the coaching inn in Dover—glad that the journey had been uneventful—Annabelle descended from The Mail and turned to thank the Courtneys for their escort. To her surprise, Mrs Courtney gripped her arm so tightly that it hurt. "Do you have lodgings, Miss Black?"

Despite the dark, she hoped to reach her destination without delay. "Yes, I do," she replied and tugged herself free from Mrs Courtney's clutch with the intention of collecting her bag and entering the inn. Dr Courtney stepped forward and grabbed hold of her arm. "My dear young lady, at this hour of the night I cannot allow you to walk the streets of Dover alone."

Annabelle's temper rose. What right had he to prevent her from doing anything? "Thank you for your concern, sir, but it is unnecessary," she replied with no intention of leaving any further clue concerning her destination.

Mrs Courtney seized her other arm. "Indeed, my husband is right, Miss Black. When our son collects us, we'll be pleased to escort you to your lodgings."

Of course, she should not be out and about on her own after dark. However, if the couple had not seized hold of her, she would have been grateful for their concern. "That is very good of you," she said, alarmed by their insistence on taking full charge of her, "but there is no need to take me to my lodgings." On the one hand, she wanted to free herself from them; on the other hand she did not want to engage in an undignified struggle.

Faced with the resolute couple, angered by Deacon's attempt to blackmail her and determined to carry out her plan, she wanted to be rid of the strong-minded reverend and his equally resolute wife. She must free herself, remain calm, and leave no trail for Roland to find her and, as a result, suffer the consequences of the law.

The guard came to her rescue. "Unhand the young lady, sir. There's no need to fret over 'er. If she ain't got anywhere to put up, I knows a respectable widow what'll lodge 'er for the night."

Annabelle looked at him gratefully. She should have appealed to him when the Courtneys first laid hands on her, for the guards on The Mail were trusted not only because they carried out their duties to ensure the mailbags arrived safely but also because they saw to the passengers' wellbeing. Grateful to the man, she decided she was too tired to continue her journey in the dark. "Thank you for your help," she said to the guard and faced the reverend gentleman whose behaviour astonished her.

"Release Miss Black," the reverend gentleman said to his wife.

Mrs Courtney released her and followed her husband into the inn.

"You wants to be careful who you takes up with, Miss," the guard admonished. "Be warned, I've heard of young girls what was abducted and forced into a shameful life."

"But surely a clergyman would not be party to anything disgraceful."

"'Ow do you know 'e's who 'e says 'e is? For all you know 'e's the owner of an 'ouse of ill repute seeking out pretty young misses like you what travels unprotected."

Annabelle did not know what a "house of ill repute" was, but she did not like the sound of such a place. She smiled at the guard. "Thank you for coming to my aid and please direct me to the lodgings which you mentioned."

With a swirl of his full-skirted, dark green coat, the guard bent to pick up her bag and called to the coachman. "Be back in five minutes. I'm taking the lady to Mrs Jenkins."

"Five minutes," the coachman replied.

Much shocked by the guard's conjecture about the Courtneys, Annabelle gathered up her skirts to keep them clear of any dirt and followed him along a cobbled street to a row of prim, terraced houses picked out by moonlight.

* * *

On the morning after Annabelle's arrival in Dover, still astonished by the guard's suspicion that the Courtneys were not as they seemed, and not wishing to be accosted either by the likes of them or men such as foolish Fotherhaugh, Annabelle engaged Martha, a middle-aged giantess recommended by her landlady.

Well before noon, Annabelle and Martha set out in a hired vehicle, but not before the driver asked. "Be you sure you want to go there, Miss?"

Annabelle raised her eyebrows in haughty imitation of Miss Chalfont at her most severe. "Yes, why do you ask?"

With an apologetic glance at her, the man opened his mouth to speak. "Begging your pardon, I wouldn't have thought a lady like you would be wanting to go there."

How kind strangers could be: the guard, Mrs Jenkins, and now this man. Mr Courtney's pale, plump face came to mind. Whether or not the guard had been right about the man, in future, she must be more wary.

"Thank you for your warning," she said to the driver, "but in spite of your caution, I do want to go there."

Within a half hour, Annabelle reached her destination on the outskirts of Dover. She left Martha in the carriage and stood on a narrow track looking at the familiar row of cottages on one side. She took a deep breath and gazed at the stretch of turf above white chalk cliffs, beyond which little waves sparkled beneath the clear blue sky.

Annabelle walked along a short path made of crushed seashells leading to one of the cottages and rapped on the door. No one answered. She peered through a window, on the inner sill of which stood a pot of daffodils in bud but not yet in flower. The door opened. Startled and guilty of prying, she turned away from the window.

"Yes," said a wiry young woman, to whose skirts a tubby toddler clung.

Annabelle peered past her into the dim, well-remembered interior.

"Good day, I have come to see Mrs Delaney."

The young mother's eyes narrowed. "She doesn't live here any more."

"But she replies to the letters I send to this address."

The mother's face softened. "Be you Miss Annabelle?"

"Yes, I am. Where is Mrs Delaney? Why did she not write and give me her new direction? And who are you?"

"I don't know why she didn't. As for me, I'm Kitty Jones."

How foolish of her to have assumed her former nurse would still be at the cottage. Yet, in her imagination, her childhood home had remained unchanged. She had anticipated Nurse greeting her with a smiling face and outstretched arms, before she accompanied her to London where she intended to pursue her vocation as an artist.

"Mind you, Miss Annabelle, Mrs Delaney said you was to be made welcome if you ever came here. Would you like to come in?"

"No thank you. If you will give me Mrs Delaney's address, I will not trouble you further," Annabelle replied, looking forward to seeing her nurse again.

"I haven't got it," Kitty said, without the least trace of curiosity on her face, now that her earlier suspicion of a stranger had been dispelled.

Annabelle frowned over the secrecy, which made no sense. "But you must have it. She replies to the letters I send to this cottage."

Kitty stroked her fractious child's head. "A foreign man collects the letters, and it's no use asking me who he is, for I don't know. Do you want to come in and write to Mrs Delaney?"

"Yes." Annabelle stepped into the cottage. Memories returned her to childhood, but without Nurse's familiar and comforting presence nothing was the same.

Kitty led her into the small, clean parlour, simply furnished with two wing chairs, a footstool padded and covered with faded tapestry, several framed watercolours, and a small desk with a straight-backed chair behind it.

Annabelle looked at the familiar candlesticks wreathed with pink china roses on the mantelpiece and at the clock that had stopped at five minutes past the hour of twelve. She sat behind the desk and smiled her thanks at

Kitty, who fetched a quill and pointed to the ink well.

"There's ink in it because the foreign gentleman sometimes needs it," Kitty explained.

"Thank you."

"Ring for me when you've written your letter, Miss."

Annabelle stroked the brass hand bell—another reminder of her childhood. How often had she toyed with it, fascinated by the clapper shaped like a tiny coiled snake?

It took half an hour or more to describe everything that had happened since she ran away from the academy and to announce her marriage without divulging Roland's name. Satisfied there was nothing more to add, she lit a candle, and then folded and sealed her letter with wax before ringing the bell.

Kitty pushed open the door and bobbed a curtsey. "I've given your coachman and your woman some ale. If you'd care to step into the other room, Miss Annabelle, I'll fetch some cordial for you."

"That is kind of you, thank you, Kitty."

Annabelle stepped into the small dining room where she had played with her beloved doll, learned some of her lessons, and taken her meals.

"I'm following orders," Kitty explained. "Mrs Delaney said, 'If Miss Annabelle ever comes here, make her welcome.'"

Annabelle sat down and looked through the window across the neat garden planted with cabbages, carrots, and daffodils not yet in bloom, and out over the cliffs toward the tranquil sea, turquoise near the coastline and emerald green beyond. In a few moments, Kitty returned with a tray set with a glass of blackberry cordial and freshly baked bread, butter, and strawberry preserve.

"Has my nurse retired or is she taking care of another child?" Annabelle asked with a pang of jealousy at the thought of Nurse's affection being lavished on someone else.

"I don't know, but I do know she thinks the world of you, Miss. She's kept your room as it was on the day you left."

Where was her nurse? Whose children was she looking after now? How could she afford to pay Kitty? With her acceptance that Kitty either could not—or would not—reveal Nurse's whereabouts, Annabelle drank and ate prior to visiting her childhood bedroom.

As far as she remembered, everything in it, from the crisp white counterpane and curtains, and her row of books in neat array on a shelf, was unchanged.

With the realisation that she had thought little about money until she married Roland, and subsequently spent more in a day than the odious Deacon earned in a year, her brow creased. Had her mysterious guardian maintained the cottage and paid Kitty's wages since she went to Miss Chalfont's academy for young ladies? Surely a nurse, such as Mrs Delaney, could not afford to do so. Puzzled, she frowned. Mrs Delaney must be acquainted with her guardian if that was the person who had maintained the cottage. After Mrs Delaney received the letter Annabelle had penned downstairs, would Mrs Delaney reveal the news of her marriage? Would her guardian be very angry? Annabelle's eyes widened. She had always imagined her guardian was a man not a woman. If the lady who took her to The Beeches, thirteen years ago, was not her guardian, could *Mrs Delaney* be her guardian? It did not seem likely, but everything about her situation would seem incredible to those whose lives held no secrets.

Annabelle shrugged and suspected a search of the cottage and garden would give no clue to her unknown guardian's identity. She returned downstairs to the front door and called out to Kitty.

Her child in her arms, Kitty hurried into the room.

"I am leaving now, Kitty. I will send a letter with my new address to the cottage so that Mrs Delaney can reply to me. Thank you for the cordial and the delicious bread and preserve."

"No need to thank me, the cottage is for you, Miss. If you want to, you may stay here until you get a reply."

If she stayed, Roland might trace her; so she smiled, shook her head, and returned to the carriage, eager to set out on the next part of her journey.

On her way back to her lodgings, Annabelle questioned Martha. "You speak well, tell me something about yourself."

"I'm from London, Miss. My father was a valet who insisted I spoke correctly. After he married, he opened an ale house here, in Dover, but when my mother died, he lost heart and six months later he rowed out to sea never to be seen again."

"Suicide? How terrible." Annabelle restrained her impulse to pat Martha's hand. After all, it was not advisable to become familiar with servants.

"Some said it was suicide, others said he went fishing and his boat capsized."

Annabelle looked thoughtfully at Martha. As soon as she met Martha, she had liked her; so she reached a decision during the short drive.

"Would you like to be my dresser?"

Martha's eyes glowed. "You mean you want me to be your abigail?"

"Yes."

"I'd be pleased to work for you, Miss Black, but I don't know anything about being a dresser."

Martha's honesty pleased her. "It is more important for you to act as my companion and protect me from strangers than it is to dress me, arrange my hair, and look after my clothes, all of which you can learn."

"I can keep men away from you, if that's what you mean."

"Very well, if you work for me, you shall receive four pounds a quarter, your board, and the usual perquisites," Annabelle said, confident of her ability to earn a living as an artist.

"Sixteen pounds a year," breathed Martha, her eyes rounded and then she chuckled. "But your cast offs won't fit me. Do you mean I may sell them?"

"Yes," Annabelle said, convinced the giantess would serve her better than the despicable Deacon.

Annabelle closed her eyes and wondered what Roland was about in her absence. She hoped he was not visiting Juliet. In response to that thought, misery flooded through her.

Chapter Twelve

Accustomed to waking early while serving under Wellington, Roland opened his eyes when dawn yielded to a new day. He yawned, stretched, and hoped his bride had slept well. His eyes narrowed. Had Annabelle spoken the truth last night when she said she was tired, or did his wife lie because she was indifferent to him? He swung his legs over the edge of the bed, stood, and crossed the room to the door leading into Annabelle's bedchamber with the intention of waking her with a kiss.

It took a moment or two for his eyes to adjust to the dim light before he approached the tester bed and drew back the curtains. Surprised, he stared at the rumpled bedcovers. Where was his bride at this early hour of the morning?

He knocked on the door of her dressing room. No reply. He opened it. She was not there. Frowning, he entered her parlour. No sign of her. Where could she be? His heart beating a little faster, he searched the summer and winter parlours. Sweat dampened his forehead. He wanted to shout out her name until it echoed throughout the manor, but he refrained to avoid arousing the servants' curiosity.

After he finished searching the house, it was as though a nightmare had become reality. In fact, a nightmare would be preferable to this reality, for one could awaken from a bad dream and shrug off its terrors. He could not dismiss the horror of imagining what evil might befall his beautiful, naïve wife, whom he would protect even at the cost of his life.

"Why did Annabelle not confide in me instead of running away?" he asked himself after searching the house for her. He ran to the stables, careless of the heavy rain, and after he realised the horses and chaise were missing, woke David, his head groom.

"I am shocked, sir," the man began, "the coachman and James took the chaise without informing me."

Conscious of his drenched dressing gown and wet slippers, Roland thought quickly and cleared his throat. "Mrs Sarrat was called away in the night. I daresay that out of consideration, she told them not to wake you."

David had looked at him with palpable disbelief, but no other convincing explanation came to Roland's mind. *Damn it*, when the coachman and groom returned he would dismiss them. Roland thought again and decided, *no*, he would not for two reasons. First, that would confirm the head groom's suspicions that something was amiss. Second, it was more than likely they had not dared to disobey their mistress. *Why did Annabelle run away?* To escape his lovemaking? Although he would have sworn in a court of law she enjoyed it on that first night. *Where the devil could she be?* To find out, he must wait for the chaise to return—if it returned. Surely it would. He doubted his wife had the means to stable the horses and pay the coachman and groom.

Roland hurried back to his bedroom. He took off his slippers, pulled off his dressing gown, and put on a dry one before he relayed an order for Deacon to come to the parlour.

"No, I don't know where Madam went and I don't know why she's left unexpectedly," Deacon replied in response to his question. She smirked. "Some ladies don't find marriage to their taste."

"You are impertinent," he snapped as though he dealt with a junior officer who had displeased him.

Deacon curtsied and for the first time, Roland noticed her viper-like eyes and sinuous, thin body garbed in black. Why had he employed such a disagreeable woman with secretive eyes? Could she have anything to do with his bride's disappearance? No, he was being fanciful. Annabelle would not have run away because of a servant. Servants could be dismissed if they were not satisfactory.

"You may go," he said in a military tone of command.

After the woman slithered out of the parlour, Roland asked himself why he had allowed his grandmother to trick him into promising to marry with the least possible delay. No, he should not blame her. No one forced him to marry Annabelle.

Roland paced up and down the parlour. Damn it, after that cad, de Beauchamp, saw him with Annabelle at the inn, he could not have risked her reputation being ruined. His decision to wed on the slightest acquaintance was not unusual. Such was the case with many members of the ton, and the majority of marriages seemed to do well enough. Yet he wanted more than that with Annabelle. Had he not pledged his word to ensure her happiness? To his chagrin, he had failed. As Deacon said, marriage was not to every lady's taste. In spite of Annabelle's assurances that his passion did not alarm her, he could think of no other explanation for her to have run away from him. Bemused by the situation, he shook his head. If she came to harm, he would reproach himself for the rest of his life.

He could not turn his thoughts away from the subject uppermost in his mind. Had their marriage bed been the reason Annabelle ran away? He could have sworn she did not shrink from him in his arms. Would he ever understand the fair sex? Roland sank onto a chair. He recalled the moment he first saw Annabelle and decided she was both adorable and brave, even if she was too impulsive and outspoken. He ran his hands through his disordered hair. Why should any lady with an indulgent husband run away?

Could Annabelle be nursing a grudge because he did not reveal his identity when they first met? He groaned. If he found her, what would she say when he revealed the entire truth?

No other morning had ever seemed to pass so slowly. Where was the chaise? He had assumed it would return. Was he mistaken? Perhaps she would keep it, but what of James and his coachman? Did she have the wherewithal to employ them? *Curse it*, where had Annabelle gone? Over and over again, questions plagued him.

At noon, when Roland sat to partake of cold meats, pickles, some cheese with bread and butter, a syllabub and hothouse fruit, his appetite deserted him.

"A lady's come to see you, sir," a maid announced.

Hope flared. "Is my wife with her?"

"No sir."

"What is her name?" he demanded, aware of the maid's eyes betraying a not unnatural curiosity. Doubtless they were gossiping in the kitchens and elsewhere about Annabelle's disappearance. A hideous thought entered his mind. Did they think he played any part in it? Would their imagination lead them to accuse him of murder?

The maid proffered a silver salver on which lay Miss Chalfont's visiting card. Roland stood so fast that, as though he was once again a clumsy youth, he knocked his chair over. "Where is she?"

"In the east parlour, sir. The maid picked up the chair.

"Bring wine there."

* * *

"Major Sarrat?" asked a lady of mature years, dressed in dove grey relieved by lilac trimming and a white ruff at the throat of her gown.

Had she brought news of his wife?

Expressionless, he watched Miss Chalfont rise from her curtsey.

"Major Sarrat at your service, madam," he said, unsmiling, although he accorded her a bow.

"Major Sarrat." Her eyes glittered with unshed tears. She dabbed them away with a handkerchief. "Forgive me, Major, my sensibilities overcome me. I took care of Mrs Sarrat for thirteen years and, although it is impertinent of me to say so, no daughter could be dearer to me."

"Very commendable, madam."

The maid, who carried a silver tray, entered, and put it down on a table.

"Pour a glass of Madeira wine for the lady, then you may go."

The maid bobbed a curtsey and then poured the wine into a glass and handed it to Miss Chalfont.

The glass shook in Miss Chalfont's hand. Drops of wine fell onto the richly patterned Oriental rug. "I beg your pardon," Miss Chalfont said.

"Don't distress yourself, madam, I doubt the wine will show on those dark reds and blues. Now, please be seated and explain why you have come here."

The lady sat without allowing her spine to touch the back of the chair. "I am here, sir, because, according to Miss Allan's letter to me, you abducted her."

His eyebrows shot up. "Harsh words madam. May I ask why you are not at your school tending your lambs before another one strays, instead of accusing me of committing a crime?"

Miss Chalfont's lips twitched and she smoothed her gown over her knees. "Major, you cannot deny you abducted an innocent."

Confound it; the lady spoke as though she trod the boards on stage. He tried to conceal his irritation. "I did not kidnap my wife. I rescued a runaway from a fate which you ladies describe as one 'worse than death' at the lecherous hands of Baron de Beauchamp."

"Major!" Miss Chalfont protested, her eyes startled.

Heaven save him from prudish middle-aged spinsters. "Forgive my plain speaking, madam, and admit you should not have urged my wife to marry a fat fop with a bad reputation."

Miss Chalfont squirmed on her chair. "I had no choice. Her guardian chose the gentleman."

"If the motherly feelings you claim to have for my wife are genuine, I cannot believe you wanted her to marry a reprobate," Roland snapped through tight lips.

The lady looked at him with a militant light in her eyes. "Do you know it is illegal to marry a minor without her guardian's consent?"

Roland folded his arms and made no reply.

"May I see Mrs Sarrat?" Miss Chalfont put her empty glass down on a low rosewood table.

He could almost hear his childhood nurse saying, *"Always tell the truth and shame the devil, Master Roland."* He clenched his fists.

"Miss Chalfont, the thing is, my wife ran away from you and has now run away from me. Damnable, is it not?"

The lady stood and glared at him as though he was a monster. "What did you do to her?"

His lips twitched with amusement. "I hope you are not implying I am the sort of dastardly husband described in those shocking gothic novels you allowed my wife to read."

An angry flash appeared and went as quickly as it came into the schoolmistress's eyes. "Indeed, sir, your wife did not read them with my permission. Unfortunately, some of the young ladies smuggle such works into school and lend them to their friends."

"Just so. Now, shall we be practical? Where could my wife have gone?"

"The poor child—"

Even more irritated than before, he lowered his eyebrows while regarding Miss Chalfont. "My wife is not a child. She is a married lady past her eighteenth birthday. Once upon a time, she would have wed and had a child or two by her age. I repeat my question, where could she have gone?"

"To Dover."

"Why?"

"To the cottage in which she spent her early years with her nurse, Mrs Delaney, with whom she still corresponds."

He narrowed his eyes. "Did you say Mrs Delaney?"

Miss Chalfont nodded.

He sprang to his feet. "Give me the direction. I shall go there and bring my wife home."

"Both of us shall go to Dover," Miss Chalfont corrected him, her determination matching his own.

He was about to say he preferred to travel alone when he remembered his chaise, his only vehicle, had not returned with his only horses. He must travel with Miss Chalfont. *By Jove.* After he found Annabelle, he would bring an end to all false pretence on his part and set up with her in style.

* * *

Seated in Miss Chalfont's hired vehicle, Roland cross-questioned her. "How did you know where to find my wife?"

"She gave me her address when she wrote to me."

"What do you know about Mrs Delaney?"

"Nothing other than she writes affectionately to Mrs Sarrat."

"My wife told me her bosom bow is a young lady called Fanny. What did she have to say about my wife…er…eloping?"

"Ah, dear Fanny, she is Viscount Hampton's stepsister. If you are acquainted with his lordship, please remind him of Fanny's existence. It is time for her to take her place in society."

Roland winced while the lady settled back in her seat. "His lordship is a particular acquaintance of mine, but it is impossible for me to drop a word in his ear about his sister."

"Please do so. Truth to tell, now that the viscount is in England, I hope he will remove the dear girl from my care. Fanny and Mrs Sarrat were inseparable and poor Fanny has been in low spirits since Mrs Sarrat's departure. Besides, it really is time for Fanny to make her curtsey to the ton."

Roland did not wish to discuss his wife's bosom bow. He sought for another subject of conversation. "It seems my wife is an artist."

"Yes, Mrs Sarrat is very talented. She painted her grey mare so realistically that I wanted to reach out and stroke its glossy coat. Of course, she received excellent instruction from the art master." Miss Chalfont smiled as though taking the credit for Annabelle's skill.

He yearned to hold Annabelle in his arms and make her happy. "When I find her, if she wishes to pursue her art, I shall encourage her to do so."

Miss Chalfont smiled at him as though her opinion of him had improved. "I am pleased. In this case, Fanny was wrong."

"What was she wrong about, Madam?"

"Dear Fanny was always telling Mrs Sarrat not to be so serious, because gentlemen cannot abide blue stockings."

To avoid hearing more about Fanny, Roland closed his eyes and pretended to sleep.

* * *

Soaked by heavy rain, Roland stood on the doorstep of the cottage where he had hoped to find his wife. "But you must know where my wife is," he insisted.

"I've told you twice that I don't know, sir," Kitty repeated and put her hand on the latch with the obvious intention of shutting the door.

Roland put his booted foot across the threshold. "Tell me the truth."

Kitty thrust her jaw forward. "I have."

"Would this prompt your memory?" he asked and held out a coin.

With incredible speed Kitty grabbed it and put it down the front of her gown.

"No, it wouldn't. Thank you and good day to you, sir."

Infuriated by the young woman's audacity, Roland returned to the carriage.

"Well?" Miss Chalfont demanded when he sat opposite her.

He shrugged. "Never fear, I will find her."

"How?" she asked and narrowed her eyes. "Now, tell me exactly what you did to make Annabelle run away."

Chapter Thirteen

A week after the runaway bride and her abigail left Dover, Annabelle waited while Martha knocked on the wide, white-painted door of a tall, narrow house in the City of London.

"I don't think anyone's at home, Miss," Martha said after a minute or two.

"We will return later." Vexed, Annabelle nibbled her lower lip.

Her abigail's forehead wrinkled. "Are you sure this is the right house?"

Annabelle nodded. "Yes, I am."

Martha's shoulders sagged. "I'll knock again."

A small, wizened man dressed in black from head to toe opened the door. "*Oui,* what is it you're wanting?" he demanded.

Annabelle eyed him with vulgar curiosity before she spoke. "I am here to see Monsieur Cavalierre."

"My master, he is not at home," snapped the disagreeable little man.

"But he is expecting me."

His eyes bright, and with the utmost impertinence, the servant surveyed her from head to foot. "Your name?"

"Miss Allan. Miss Annabelle Allan," she replied, for she had not broken the news of her marriage in her letter to the monsieur.

His eyes suspicious, the bad-tempered little man glared at her. "I know nothing, but nothing of you."

"I will wait."

With Martha close behind her, Annabelle stepped onto the black and white chequered floor of the shadowy reception hall.

"Me, I protest," le monsieur's servant squeaked. He gesticulated so wildly that Annabelle forced back a gurgle of laughter.

The servant grunted, turned, and hurried away with a speed surprising in such an old man.

Annabelle sank onto an ancient, high-backed, oak chair and smoothed her glove.

"I don't think much of the housekeeper," Martha remarked.

"I beg your pardon."

"Dirty old place," Martha muttered. "The floor needs washing."

"If it is your wish to scrub my floors, I grant it," an amused voice said.

Martha gulped and curtsied.

Annabelle looked toward the bottom of the stairs at a tall, slim gentleman garbed in severe black, relieved by his old-fashioned white wig tied back with a broad, black ribbon bow at the nape of his neck.

She stood, advanced to the centre of the hall, and halted in a pool of light cast through the semi-circular fanlight.

"*Mon dieu,* you are the picture of—" the gentleman broke off. His sensitive face contorted as though he struggled with emotion.

Annabelle took a step forward. "A picture of? Do I remind you of someone, sir?" she asked eagerly. Was it possible, could it be that she reminded him of her mother or some other female relative? Surely not, for if she did, why would he not say so?

"A million apologies, my English, it is poor. I should have said you present a picture of beauty."

What had he been going to say before he broke off with the words *"you are the picture of"*? "Monsieur, as I explained in my letter, I have waited on you in the hope that you will accept me as your pupil," she said in English, for his command of the language was too good to necessitate a reply in French. "My drawing master, Monsieur de Loches, once said I would benefit from your instruction. Now that my circumstances have changed, I hope you will teach me."

She handed her gloves to Martha.

"Your real name, *ma petite*?"

She had no objection to being called the monsieur's little one, although she had objected to Roland referring to her as a child.

"Miss Allan." He looked at her right hand.

How foolish of her not to have removed her wedding ring.

"Do you think to deceive me, child?" He raised an imperious eyebrow. "Recently, my good friend, de Loches, wrote about a runaway school girl who married unexpectedly and then left her husband." He ignored her confusion. "As he only informed me of one pupil whose talent would justify my accepting her as my student, I conclude you are Mrs Sarrat. So, it is true, is it not, that you want me to teach you?"

"Mrs Sarrat!" Martha exclaimed.

"Yes, Martha, but you must not tell anyone what my real name is."

Martha put her hands on her hips. "Why not?"

"I presume you are Mrs Sarrat's servant," said the monsieur.

Martha bobbed a curtsey. "Yes sir."

"Then you should know it is impertinent to speak if you have not been spoken to, and to question your mistress."

Martha snorted. "The black-hearted devil," Martha said to Annabelle. "What did he do to you?"

"What?" Annabelle exclaimed.

Martha glowered. "What did your husband do to make you run away?"

"Nothing, the major is all kindness."

"If he is a good man, why did you leave him?"

"Really, Martha, monsieur is right, you should not question me."

"Come, *ma petite,* we shall enjoy some wine."

"I am sorry for speaking out, madam." Martha stared at the floor. "I did warn you I am not a proper lady's maid."

"So you did." Annabelle smiled at Martha before she accompanied Monsieur Cavalierre into a large reception room.

Despite Annabelle's trepidation, the artist in her noticed the room was dusty but furnished in rich colours.

"Please be seated, Mrs Sarrat," Cavalierre said and flicked his fingers at his manservant. "Some wine for us, Henri."

Annabelle chewed her lower lip and glanced at the little man.

"Do not concern yourself with Henri's sour face, *ma petite Madame,* my excellent Henri is of the most discreet."

In spite of his master's praise, Henri thrust his lower lip forward while he poured wine for them before withdrawing with Martha.

"Now, Madame Sarrat, please tell me why you want to become an artist instead of remaining with your husband for whom it is obvious you have some tender consideration?"

Annabelle looked away from him, asking herself how it was obvious.

To prevent her trembling hand from spilling wine, she put her glass down on an ivory inlaid table. "Monsieur, of course I have, as you put it, some…um…tender consideration for my husband, but I do not want to discuss him either with you or anyone else." Her eyes opened wide. "But how did you guess how I regard him?"

Cavalierre chuckled. "I am an artist. Observation is part of my art. Do not be surprised by it. Although you have left him, your concern for him is obvious."

She looked down her nose and wished Monsieur was not so percipient.

Cavalierre put his wine glass down. "Stand in the middle of the room."

She looked into his large hazel eyes and hesitated.

"If you wish to be my pupil, you must learn to obey me without question. Good. Now, please stand in the middle of the room." He raised a haughty, pencilled eyebrow and sauntered round her. "One hopes your husband has told you how beautiful you are. Rest tranquil. There is no need to colour up. Even if it is an old man, such as I, who offers homage, a lady should accept it without embarrassment. Now, please sit down."

Paralysed by unfamiliar shyness, she remained in the centre of the room.

Monsieur took her by the elbow and guided her to a chair covered by an exquisite paisley shawl. He frowned at her. His arched eyebrows almost met in the middle of his forehead. "Good, I believe my friend's assurance that you are gifted and, on one condition, I will accept you as my pupil."

Annabelle sat on the comfortable wing chair. "Condition, Monsieur?"

He laughed before he spoke. "You are a charming child. One understands why your major married you. It is a long time since I had the pleasure of being with a lady young enough to write her thoughts on her face."

For a fleeting second, pain contorted his handsome countenance.

"What is your condition, Monsieur?" she asked again, too tactful to ask him about his pain.

"You may call me Cavalierre, for I was a cavalier in my former life," he said in the deep, rich voice she was already coming to know so well.

"Very well, Cavalierre." She smiled. "But must I beg you to tell me what your condition is."

"To paint you in the costume once worn at court in the days of my queen."

"Your queen?"

Grief flickered across his face. "Yes, my queen, Marie Antoinette. May the good God have mercy on her soul."

"I am sorry to see you so sad." Annabelle sat quite still with her hands on her lap. "Were you one of her courtiers?"

He turned aside. "Yes."

"Is your real name Cavalierre?"

"No, and it is unnecessary for you to know what it is."

"Please forgive me. I did not intend to pry."

He turned to face her. "I know you did not."

Henri entered the room. "Will Mademoiselle partake of nuncheon with you, Monsieur?"

"Yes," Cavalierre replied in English.

"And will the female, built like a boxer, eat with your servants?" Henri asked in French.

Annabelle controlled her amusement over Henri's excellent description of Martha.

"Yes, she will eat here, Henri, and you will be civil to her," le monsieur replied. "Ask the lady boxer—as you so aptly but unkindly describe her—for her mistress's address. Send for their baggage and have the green room prepared for mademoiselle. Also, make the small room next to it ready for her maid."

"Henri, my female boxer and I will try to cause you as little disturbance as possible," Annabelle said in French with a perfect accent.

"But you speak like a born Frenchwoman, mademoiselle. Who taught you?" Henri's wrinkles deepened when he smiled, as though he was unaccustomed to doing so.

"I don't know. I wish I did, but my nurse and I always spoke French, so maybe she taught me," Annabelle replied.

* * *

At noon, Annabelle and Cavalierre ate at a round table set before the fire, not in the dining room but in a cosy parlour. After the simple meal consisting of a selection of cheeses, ham, salad, and rolls as well as fruit, all partaken with excellent wine, Cavalierre suggested Annabelle occupy herself in the library while he retired for a *siesta*.

Annabelle schooled her face not to show surprise at the idea of a gentleman sleeping in the afternoon. "Seigneur, may I write a letter?"

"Seigneur?" he queried, and once more raised a haughty eyebrow.

"Yes, for I suspect the title is appropriate."

Cavalierre bowed with the grace of a young man. "If it pleases you, you may address me thus. As for your request, you will find everything you need to write a letter in the library, *ma petite*."

Annabelle smiled. For some reason or other, she really did like it when he addressed her as his little one.

* * *

The paintings, the *objets d'art* and the careful choice of colour—or lack of it in each room Annabelle either entered or glimpsed in Cavalierre's large house—entranced her. Now at ease with Cavalierre in spite of her earlier trepidation, she admired the dining room with its high moulded ceiling, rich colours, and opulent display of silverware.

"So," Cavalierre said, after they had enjoyed an excellent dinner with more succulent dishes than Annabelle had the capacity to taste, "you like my house?"

"Very much," she replied, although she would have appreciated it even more if Roland had been there to share her enjoyment.

"My house is one to inspire artists, is it not?" he asked with frank pleasure.

She gave him her full attention instead of thinking about Roland.

"I beg your pardon, Seigneur."

With a languid wave of his hand, he indicated some of his treasures. "My house is designed to encourage my muse and intrigue my patrons, whom I allow to pay well for the privilege of being painted by me."

"What do they commission you to paint?" she asked, looking forward to her first lesson.

"Their portraits, their families, horses, and dogs, but there are subjects I paint for my own pleasure."

She rested her elbows on the table, from which the cloth had been removed—prior to a bowl of shelled nuts being placed on the highly polished mahogany surface—and observed him.

"If you are in the habit of propping your elbows on tables, they will become wrinkled," Cavalierre chided.

Annabelle warmed to Cavalierre. He spoke as if he scolded a favourite grandchild, but his smile took the sting from his reprimand. She removed her elbows from the table.

"*Ma petite,* first I will paint you, and then you shall paint something of your choice to show me what you are capable of. Now, to bed with you. Tomorrow morning, Henri will serve your hot chocolate at five-thirty."

"Five-thirty?" Surely he did not expect her to rise even earlier than she had at school.

"Yes, I shall sketch you before breakfast by the light of candles, many candles. Now, bid me goodnight."

"Goodnight, Seigneur."

* * *

When Martha woke her in the morning, Annabelle groaned and buried her head in the soft feather pillow. "Go away," she muttered.

"Time to wake up, madam," Martha insisted.

Annabelle pressed her face deeper into the comfort of the soft pillow. "No, it cannot be, please go away," she protested in a muffled voice.

Martha sniffed. "Very well, madam, but don't expect me to leave my bed at five o'clock."

Annabelle sympathised with her. Five-thirty was bad enough. "So early!"

"Yes. Frenchie Henry banged on my door at that ungodly hour. Now, if you want the other Frenchie to paint you, sit up and drink your chocolate while I fetch the gown you're to wear."

Her eyes half closed, Annabelle sipped the hot, sweet liquid and wished Roland's head rested on a pillow beside her. What would she not give at this moment to hear his voice? She must be resolute. Not for anything would she be the cause of her husband's arrest for kidnap.

Chapter Fourteen

The mirror told Annabelle that the old-fashioned cream silk bodice and wide skirts complemented her fair complexion. Painfully tight lacing emphasised her small waist and drew attention to the swell of her bosom. She was not vain but knew the low cut bodice edged with a froth of priceless lace and the elbow-length flounced sleeves increased her feminine allure. What would Roland think of her if he could see her now? She fingered a knot of satin ribbons as blue as her eyes. "Martha, I do not look like myself."

"No y-you don't, though you are still beautiful. Now, hurry up, your Frenchie's waiting for you," Martha said.

"He is not my Frenchie." Annabelle slipped her feet into high-heeled red shoes ornamented with diamond centred rosettes and then slid her feet out of them. "They are too big."

Martha picked them up. "I'll carry them for you. Come along, madam, you don't want that there Frenchie to get cross." She shrugged. "As for that Henry, he's a bad-tempered creature."

"Henri," Annabelle interrupted.

"I can't twist my tongue round foreign names. As I was saying, Henry told me that there Cavalier's got a nasty temper. If you ask me, the two of them deserve each other."

Annabelle ignored her henchwoman's forthright comments and did not attempt to correct her pronunciation. "Indeed," she replied, and cautiously circumnavigated the bedroom furniture.

Annabelle went through the door sideways. If only Roland could see her now, she thought, as her wide skirts brushed against the wall while she made her way upstairs. With a mental picture of her handsome husband in mind, Annabelle entered the studio. Dressed like this, would Roland think she looked beautiful or ridiculous?

"You are as ravishing as—" Cavalierre broke off and stared at her before he came forward to take her hand.

"Who do I remind you of? My mother?"

"I was going to say, 'as beautiful as one of the ladies at Marie Antoinette's court.'"

"Which lady?"

"Any one of a number of charming ladies, *petite*."

She was not sure whether she believed him but understood he would not satisfy her curiosity if she put more questions to him.

Cavalierre bowed and led her to a raised platform on which stood a gilded chair upholstered in salmon pink. "Be seated, *Petite*." He turned to face the servants. "Henri, light all the candles. Martha, tie up your mistress's hair and put the wig on her head."

Annabelle allowed Martha to plait her hair and arrange it around the crown of her head before she put the elaborate wig that towered above her head in place.

"Perfect," Cavalierre murmured, but came forward to arrange several long, white powdered curls that fell over one shoulder to her breast, a part of which was revealed by the low-cut neckline.

"Seigneur, the wig and gown are so heavy that I cannot move."

"Good, I do not want you to move."

Annabelle tried to remain still until the costume, the wig, the odour of wax candles, and the airless room, combined to make her protest that she would faint.

Cavalierre chuckled. "Not if you straighten your back and think of your husband."

Unable to bear the pain of thinking about Roland, she would have shaken her head if the wig did not weigh so much. Instead, she posed while Cavalierre painted until Henri served breakfast.

Annabelle stretched and tottered to her feet. "Henri, please call Martha. I want the wig removed while I eat."

"No, no, no, absolutely no," Cavalierre insisted. "You must not spoil the illusion."

"The illusion?" Annabelle descended from the platform, afraid her cramped legs would not bear her weight.

"To do you justice, in my mind's eye, you must be one of Marie Antoinette's ladies," Cavalierre explained.

"But I am not. I am Major Sarrat's wife."

Cavalierre held out a wrapper that would keep her valuable gown clean while she ate.

"Do not be obtuse, *Cherie*. As an artist, surely it is not difficult to understand that when I paint you, I see a lady of the French nobility."

Annabelle slid her arms into the wide calico sleeves. "I do not understand why you want to paint me in this costume."

"*Cherie*, like your formidable Martha, you have too many questions."

A steely glint in his eye prevented her from asking another one. Instead, she sat at the round, paint-smeared table Henri had spread with a cloth before he fetched coffee, conserves, butter, plain and sweet rolls, and iced cakes.

Annabelle's tummy rumbled in anticipation. "A French breakfast, delicious, but my husband told me how much he appreciated English breakfasts when he returned to England." She frowned. How did she know the French ate such breakfasts, which were never served at The Beeches? A snippet from her past, when she was a very young child?

A slight expression of distaste appeared in Cavalierre's eyes. He made no comment, but in all probability, he would not care for steak, ham, kidneys, or other such fare so early in the day. "Now the war is over, will you return to France, Seigneur?"

He shook his head, regret filling his large eyes.

"Why not?"

"I prefer my friends in England to ghosts of the past. No, no, no, *ma petite,* do not look so…what is the word…struck?"

"Stricken."

"Thank you. Stricken." Cavalierre spread butter on a roll. "You are an intelligent lady who can comprehend that the past is done with." He patted her hand. "Please finish your breakfast. It is getting late and the light will change."

She opened her mouth to question him, but Cavalierre spoke before she could do so. "After nuncheon, you will be free for the rest of the day."

* * *

On that first day he painted her, Cavalierre spoke little, but by the fifth day he became more communicative.

"Good," he said and stepped back to scrutinise the portrait he refused to allow Annabelle to view. "I have painted your flesh."

"My flesh?"

"Yes, your face, your neck, your shoulders, your arms and your hands, so I will not need to inconvenience you further. From tomorrow, I will pay a girl to pose dressed in the oh-so-uncomfortable clothes and wig, which you complain about."

Annabelle stretched her stiff limbs. "When will my lessons begin?"

"Tomorrow, if you do not want to return to your husband—something I strongly recommend."

She shook her head. "I have good reasons for not taking your advice."

"Very well, you shall paint for me and if your work is good enough, I will accept you as my pupil. But tell me, what is so dreadful that you cannot return to Major Sarrat?"

Her fingers curled on her lap. "I cannot."

"Why not?"

She sighed and blinked her eyes to prevent tears forming. "Please believe I have a compelling reason."

"You believe you do," Cavalierre murmured. The brush wavered in his hand. "Me, I speak from experience." The brush slipped out of his hand. "*Petite,* we never know when cruel death will snatch our dear ones. We should treasure every moment with them."

Faced with his grief, what could she say? It would be impertinent and insensitive to question him.

"I apologise. You are too young to understand an old man's meanderings."

She removed the burdensome wig. "How can you say that? You do not meander. Although I have not suffered as you must have done, I know grief. I am tortured because I do not know who my parents are and because circumstances forced me to leave my husband."

Cavalierre put aside his brush. "Confide in me."

Could she trust him? She resisted the temptation to tell him about Deacon and the threat of Roland's imprisonment. Oh, how she wished she could be reunited with her husband. Tears filled her eyes. Was Roland very angry with her for running away? Perhaps he would not want her back. But to go back? What was she thinking of? She could never return and lie safe in his strong arms.

"Ah, *Cherie,* do not cry. Life is too short for sorrow. I shall take you to a masquerade where you will smile and enjoy yourself."

Chapter Fifteen

After spending a night in London—where Roland purchased a carriage and several horses, and gave instructions for their delivery—he and Miss Chalfont returned to his manor in her chaise.

"Will you dine with me, ma'am?" Roland asked, hoping she would decline, for he had endured enough of her speculations about his wife's whereabouts.

"You are very kind, Major Sarrat, but no thank you. If I leave without delay, I shall reach home before dark. I do not care to leave my pupils for a moment longer than necessary."

"I shall send two armed men with you to protect you from highwaymen."

"I am sure that is unnecessary. My coachman is armed. But thank you for your kind offer."

"I insist. I would never forgive myself if you came to harm," Roland said, scarcely able to conceal his impatience to find out if a message had arrived from Annabelle during his absence.

"Very well. Thank you, Major, you are very considerate."

He inclined his head.

Miss Chalfont clasped her hands to her breast. "What will you do next?"

"I shall go to London and employ the Bow Street Runners in the hope that they can find my wife."

"May I have your direction in London?" Miss Chalfont straightened her hat and the purple ostrich plume that curled around the brim into place.

He hesitated for a couple of moments. "I shall stay with Viscount Hampton."

"Dear Fanny's brother," Miss Chalfont murmured.

"Just so," Roland drawled.

"If you are to stay with him, you must know the viscount very well."

"Yes, I do, ma'am," he replied and failed to repress an amused smile.

Miss Chalfont raised her eyebrows. "Please be good enough to tell the viscount that it is time for Fanny to leave school."

"If I can," he prevaricated and restrained a chuckle before he spoke again. "I cannot allow you to leave without partaking of some refreshments. I am thirsty and hungry and am sure that you are."

"Thank you," she said, "but I must not delay my departure for long."

"You shall be served as quickly as possible."

Roland extended his arm to the lady as she stepped out of the chaise and then escorted her inside. "You must excuse the state of the manor. It has been neglected while I was in the army.

"Ah, my housekeeper. Mrs Knowles, are there any messages for me?"

She bobbed a curtsey. "No sir."

"I see," he said curtly. "Mrs Knowles, please see to Miss Chalfont's needs and have refreshments sent to the blue parlour immediately." He bowed to his guest. "Excuse me, ma'am, I must arrange for two men to escort you."

Within fifteen minutes, he and Miss Chalfont sat at a small table by a window that gave a view of a neglected knot garden. Beyond it could be seen the ha-ha that prevented deer from encroaching on the gardens. Trying to conceal his disappointment at the information that his chaise, coachman, and one of his grooms, not to mention his valuable horses, had not returned, he gazed at the lawns leading down to the lake.

"Shall I pour a dish of tea for you?" Miss Chalfont asked.

"Yes, if you would be so kind." He stared at the spread of cold meats, cheese, and bread and butter. "Some ham? Some roast beef, Miss Chalfont?"

"Ham, if you would be so good."

Instead of torturing himself with thoughts of Annabelle, he concentrated on serving the lady, who completed her repast in less than a half hour.

Mrs Knowles entered the parlour and curtsied. "The lady's chaise is ready, and so are the men who will escort her."

Miss Chalfont dabbed her lips with a napkin and stood. "I shall not waste any more time Major."

Roland escorted her to the carriage and handed her in. "Good day to you, ma'am."

"Good day, Major. When, or if, you hear news of your wife, do not forget to notify me." She reached out to pat his hand. "I shall write to you to enquire whether or not you have found any clue to her whereabouts."

"Rest assured you will be the first to know when I find my wife. Thank you for your help."

"Although it was not fruitful, I am pleased to have assisted you in your search. Now, I really must be on my way if I am to be home before dark."

Roland returned to the manor without a backward glance. Infuriated by the undignified necessity of being forced to question servants about his wife and knowing there was no way out, he summoned Mrs Knowles. "Are you sure there have been no messages for me?" Roland caught sight of his compressed lips and blazing eyes in a mirror and modified his expression.

Mrs Knowles hands trembled. She bobbed a curtsey. "No, Major, but your coachman and James returned while you were in the blue parlour with Miss Chalfont."

"Why the devil didn't you tell me at once? Send for them immediately!"

She pursed her lips, obviously annoyed because he swore. "Very good, Major."

* * *

Roland eyed Bob, his coachman, and James, who, still dusty from their journey, entered the hall where he awaited them, and made clumsy bows. There was no point in beating around the proverbial bush so he came straight to the point, his heart thudding in eager expectation. "Where is your mistress?"

Bob shrugged and looked at him with obvious curiosity. "I don't know, sir."

"Where did you take her?"

Bit by bit, he dragged information from the men and then dismissed them, cursing inwardly, with a hollow sensation in his stomach, because he had learned little of use.

While he ate his evening meal, with far less gusto than usual, he wanted to go to London to search for his wife immediately. Common sense prevailed. He chose to wait and travel by daylight instead of risking the hazards of travelling by night.

After the tablecloth was removed, he drank his port and fretted about Annabelle. Where was she? Was she safe? Had she gone to meet someone?

Mrs Knowles opened the door. "Begging your pardon, Major," she said, "there are two men here to see you."

He glanced at her. "Who are they?"

"Bow Street Runners, sir," the woman said, her eyes bulging with curiosity.

"Where are they?"

"Well, I didn't rightly know how to receive them, so I left them in the hall."

Roland hurried out of the dining room to the hall and led the men into the library. He sat down at his desk and neither offered them refreshment nor invited them to sit on any of the high-backed chairs. "Why are you here?" he enquired after he sat, his mind filled with horrid pictures of Annabelle in distress.

The younger man shifted from one foot to the other.

"I think you know our business, Major, and if I may say so, it is a serious matter, a very serious matter," the older man said.

"No use beating about the bush, come to the point, man," Roland snapped.

"Acting on information received, we understand you abducted and married a minor without her guardian's consent."

"Did I?" A harsh laugh escaped him.

The Bow Street Runners exchanged glances and the young man whispered to his senior, but not low enough to prevent Roland overhearing him. "He don't look like a guilty one and Lord knows we've seen enough of them."

The older man glanced at Roland and looked away again. "Shush," he cautioned his junior.

Not wishing to prolong matters, Roland came straight to the point. "Your companion is correct. I am innocent of wrongdoing. My wife's guardian consented to our marriage."

Roland wrote a brief note, waited for the ink to dry, and handed it to the older man. "Show this to your superiors at Bow Street."

The younger one peered over his associate's shoulder. "Well, well, well," he murmured, "that alters the case."

"Tell me who set you on my wife's trail."

The whip crack of his voice startled the Bow Street Runners. They looked at each other, cleared their throats, and went toward the door. "Can't divulge a client's name," they chorused.

"De Beauchamp! I wager he is behind this outrage. His pockets are to let, and the miserable toad wants revenge." Roland suppressed a smile as he, unintentionally, used his wife's soubriquet for the baron.

"You're a canny one, sir," the older man said before he and his colleague withdrew.

Alone, Roland slumped in his chair. Would he find his enchanting bride? *Why did she run away?* He could have sworn she enjoyed his lovemaking, so what made her flee? He asked himself yet again.

He shivered. Annabelle might be lying dead in a ditch. God, suppose an unscrupulous person had taken advantage of her. He would never forgive himself if she came to harm. And if he found her, would she forgive him for his *current* deceptions? As yet she did not know the truth about him. He had deceived her once. Would she be generous enough to forgive him for the second time?

Roland sighed. He knew how much she wanted to find out who her parents were, but to keep her safe, he could not reveal it.

* * *

Roland alighted from his chaise and stared at a young, fair-haired lady, who stood on the doorstep of his London mansion remonstrating with his butler, Greaves.

He cleared his throat to announce his presence. "May I be of assistance?"

The lady turned. "It has been so long, I am not sure whether I recognise you, but I think you are Hampton," Fanny faltered.

"And you, can you be my little half-sister?"

"Yes." She smiled at him uncertainly.

"Fanny, my dearest Fanny." He hugged her and then released her and held her at a small distance. "How pretty you are, my dear. But it is not the thing for a lady to create a disturbance on a gentleman's doorstep. Come inside."

Greaves opened the door wide. Roland handed his many-caped coat to Greaves and led Fanny across the peach-veined marble floor of the hall, conscious of his booted heels clicking on its surface. He led her up the broad flight of wooden stairs, cupped her elbow with his hand, and guided her along the corridor, into a sunny parlour decorated in hyacinth blue and primrose yellow.

"Greaves," he said to his butler, who had followed them, "a glass of Canary wine for me and some cordial for my sister."

After Roland dismissed Greaves he eyed Fanny. "Tell, me," he began after he heard the door close, "does Miss Chalfont make a habit of, shall I say, mislaying her pupils?" he asked in a level tone that concealed his annoyance at her absconding from school and her unanticipated arrival.

"Is that all you have to say to me?" Fanny produced a wisp of lace-edged handkerchief from a pocket and dabbed her eyes. "You are unkind, sir. Since your return to England you have ignored me."

"That is not so. I wrote to you twice and was on my way to fetch you when fate intervened."

She eyed him suspiciously. "Fate? Whatever can you mean?"

"First, tell me why you have run away from The Beeches."

"I came here in the hope that you will help my dearest friend."

Had Annabelle not explained Fanny was her dearest friend? Did Fanny know where his wife was? His hand shook. "How can I help her?" he asked in an unsteady tone.

Fanny put the tiny handkerchief in her pocket and smiled at him. "I know you will assist her. The thing is, she is a year older than I am and Lord knows we have been confined for too long at school. Yet, although it is time to make our curtseys at court, she was not desperate enough to marry Baron de Beauchamp. To avoid doing so, she ran away and married another gentleman, but I don't know who he is," Fanny gabbled and plopped down onto a chair.

The door opened. Greaves entered and proffered a plate of thin caraway seed biscuits. "Cook thought the young lady might be hungry after her journey." He lingered to adjust the long damask curtains in the obvious hope of hearing something interesting.

"Leave us," Roland ordered.

"What an odious creature your butler is," Fanny commented after the door closed behind Greaves. "He is curious enough for his ears to drop off."

"If it is in my power, of course I will help your friend," Roland said, too anxious about his wife to laugh at Fanny's joke about the butler.

"Thank you." Fanny rose and crossed the floor to perch on the arm of his chair and kiss his cheek.

He slipped an arm round her waist. "What am I going to do with you?"

"You will not return me to The Beeches."

"No, although it was wrong of you to run away. Miss Chalfont must be very worried and—" His lips tightened. "I would not entrust you to her again. This is the second time her pupils have managed to leave The Beeches without permission. She is not worthy to be in charge of young ladies."

"You are not to be nasty about her. She has always been very kind to me, and it is not her fault that I ran away. I laid my plans very carefully." Fanny pouted before she continued. "I hope she is not worried. I left a letter for her."

Roland frowned. If he told Fanny he had married Annabelle, could he depend on her not to gossip? He doubted it, for as a child she had been a prattler and all her letters to him were filled with innocent gossip. He could not trust her to be discreet. "Have you no clue to your friend's new identity?" he asked in a hollow tone.

"Annabelle did not mention her married name in her letter to me. She is incognito and refers to herself as Miss Black. Read the letter, Hampton. It explains everything. You will understand how noble and self-sacrificing she is. All her anxieties are for her husband."

"For her husband?" His voice seemed to come from a great distance. "Continue."

Fanny nodded emphatically. "Yes, she left him for fear he would be imprisoned for abducting her. Is that not noble?"

Roland mastered his emotion. "Don't talk like a play actress, Fanny," he teased. "Noble and self-sacrificing! Her poor husband must be demented with anxiety."

"Hampton, your hand is trembling. Are you very angry with me for running away?"

"I admire your spirit, Fanny, but you should not have done so. Who knows what harm might have befallen you," he said, the memory of the footpad who held up Annabelle still fresh in his mind.

Fanny fluttered her long eyelashes. Lord, what a beauty his little sister had turned into. After she spread her wings in society, there would be no difficulty in finding her a suitable husband. Gentlemen would be queuing up to ask him for her hand in marriage, and he would be rejecting unacceptable fortune hunters.

Fanny slipped her warm hand into his. "I hope you will not scold me, and also hope you will help me to find Annabelle."

"I *should* scold you, but I shall not. Instead, I will try to help you find your friend."

Fanny squealed and kissed his cheek. "You are the best of brothers and the kindest creature."

Roland tried to look severe. "How did you fund your trip to London?"

"I hitched a ride with a carter who helped me to buy a ticket on the stage. When I arrived this morning, I hired a sedan to come here. As for funds—" She hung her head. "Annabelle had a large allowance and she shared some of it with me."

"Very generous, but she could have done you a disservice. A young lady travelling alone! Anything could have happened to you."

"I doubt it. I armed myself with a carving knife—the sharpest one in Miss Chalfont's kitchen."

"Fanny, you are—"

"If you promise not to scold me, I will forgive you."

"Forgive me?"

She smiled at him. "Although you abandoned me, I believe you have a heart. Bring my dearest friend safe to me and I will forgive you everything."

"Minx!" He looked into his young half-sister's amused eyes.

"Truly, I will forgive you for ignoring me for so many years."

"My pet, I never forgot you, but I was an army officer and did my duty to the best of my ability. What was I to do when you were orphaned? Put you in the care of Grandmamma or one of the elderly aunts? I thought you would do better with companions of your own age. Was I wrong?"

"No, and I will plague you no more." She gurgled with laughter. "All is forgiven."

"I appreciate it," he drawled and kissed her cheek. "Greaves shall have a room prepared for you, and I will tell him to send to the agency for a dresser. For the time being, she can also act as your companion."

For the first time since Annabelle left him, he relaxed. He now knew where to find her, thanks to the letter she sent Fanny.

Chapter Sixteen

For the masquerade, Cavalierre wore a silver brocade, full-skirted coat, a long pale grey waistcoat embroidered with silver, and grey knee breeches. Diamonds glittered in the folds of his lacy cravat, on the buckles of his high-heeled shoes, and on his long fingers. Annabelle looked at him admiringly and thought that he presented an image of one of Louis Sixteenth's tragic courtiers.

"You are magnificent, Seigneur."

"And you, *Cherie*, will be the most beautiful lady at the masquerade." He bowed and raised her hand to his lips.

She looked down at the gown shed wore when he painted her. Her cream silk skirts were wide enough to have been worn by Marie Antoinette.

"You are too kind, Seigneur," Annabelle murmured and twitched the lace-edged ruffles of her sleeves into place.

He adjusted his mask and became a stranger who wore a white wig.

Annabelle put on her bejewelled mask. "I am ready, Monseigneur.

"So, I am elevated from Seigneur to Monseigneur." He chuckled.

"Yes. Although I do not know your real name, I am sure you are entitled to be addressed as my lord."

"*Mon dieu,* how charming you are. If you were not married, and if I were forty years younger, who knows what you would do to my heart?"

* * *

"Mademoiselle Black is not at home," a small manservant told Roland.

"I assure you she will be at home to me."

The little man's dark eyes gleamed. "And me, I assure you, she is not 'ere."

"Where is she?" Roland took a step forward.

The servant took a step backward. "At Monsieur de Longterre's masquerade. She 'as gone to a masquerade with my master, Monsieur Cavalierre."

Roland glowered. While he had been half out of his mind with fear for his wife's safety, she had not only found a comfortable home but she was gallivanting with a stranger. "'Pon my word, a masquerade." His breath whistled between his tight lips.

"Yes, at the Marquis de Longterre's, Monsieur."

An hour later, clad in his dress uniform and a black mask he had worn at previous balls covering part of his face, Roland presented himself at the Marquis's spacious house.

A footman in green and gold livery held out his hand for an invitation card.

Roland pretended to search for it in his capacious pocket. "I have mislaid it," he said in a perfect French accent.

A gentleman dressed as a cardinal came to his aid. "You fool, admit Monsieur, can you not hear he is as French as I am?"

"Thank you for your timely assistance Monsieur Cardinal," Roland said, every nerve concentrated on his errant wife.

The obliging gentleman laughed merrily and patted Roland's back. "A splendid jest."

"I beg your pardon."

"The wearing of the costume of an English officer to a French masquerade. The ladies will adore you for your bravado."

Roland inclined his head while his eyes searched the throng for Annabelle.

"Come, de Longterre is still receiving his guests," his scarlet-robed companion urged.

They stood at the end of the queue on the wide stairs lit with wall sconces and crystal chandeliers in which tall wax candles burned.

Where was Annabelle? He spied a lady who carried a pail and a tiny three-legged stool. Dressed as a milkmaid, she wore blue skirts bunched up over a red and white striped petticoat. Could she be his wife? No, she was too short and not as graceful as his wife.

He bowed to his host, murmured a few words to his hostess, and moved through the crowd to the ballroom.

***

Concealed by a miniature jungle of potted plants, Roland stood by a fountain that cascaded into an artificial pond populated by goldfish. From his vantage point, he heard the distinctive, high-pitched laughter of de Beauchamp's well-known aunt, Madame Valencay.

The young lady who sat next to Madame with her back to him laughed. It was Annabelle's unmistakable, melodious laughter. He would recognise the sound anywhere. Roland tensed while he regarded the French noblewoman, who sat straight and watched Annabelle as though she were a matchmaking mamma or a watchful *duenna*. He took a deep breath, and made his way to his wife.

Dash it, Annabelle seemed happy and at ease. Since she ran away for fear he would be blackmailed, had she spared a thought for him? He doubted it. His indignation rose. He had been prey of his imagination concerning her safety while she enjoyed London society.

Before he could reach his wife, a red-haired man in the gorgeous garb of a seventeenth century courtier bowed and claimed her as his partner for the minuet.

Roland's breath hissed like an angry snake's when threatened by a stick. He strode across the ballroom floor, regardless of anyone in his path, and tapped the man on the shoulder.

"If I am not mistaken this is my dance with the lady."

"Monsieur, I protest, my name is on ze lady's card, you 'ave no right to demand she dance with you," the gentleman fired up.

It seemed the Frenchman's temper matched his fiery hair. "I have every right," Roland said, his words clipped.

The Frenchman bowed low. "Monsieur, I demand satisfaction. Name your seconds."

"Mine is the right of a husband, but if you insist on satisfaction I will be pleased to oblige."

The gentleman blanched and bowed. "In that case, I cede the lady's hand to you."

Her right hand pressed to her mouth, Annabelle remained seated on her chair as though frozen.

"My dear, had you told me you would be here this evening, I would have accompanied you, for your charms are superior to those of my club." Although Roland forced himself to speak in a pleasant tone, his immediate instinct was to either rage at her because he had been so worried or to cover her beautiful face with kisses. However, fool that he was, in the grip of emotion, he had forgotten to speak French.

"An Englishman. I thought de Longterre invited no foreigners," said an elegant gentleman dressed in medieval costume.

"You are mistaken, sir, although I pride myself on my English pronunciation," Roland said. The last thing he wanted was a confrontation with annoyed Frenchmen buzzing like angry bees. He gripped Annabelle's elbow—but not firmly enough to hurt her—and led her out onto a balcony overlooking a garden that led down to the banks of the Thames. "Madam, are you determined to make a mockery of our marriage?"

"I can explain," she said in a low tone, her face pale by moonlight.

"Can you? I know you fled because Deacon tried to blackmail you."

"How do you know? Surely she did not confess."

"You are right." He glared at her. "Little fool, you should have confided in me. You are too impetuous. You fled from The Beeches instead of refusing to marry de Beauchamp and then, as though that did not lead you into enough trouble, you ran away from me. Such behaviour is inexcusable."

A flicker of fear in Annabelle's eyes reproached him. What was he doing? Her youth, beauty, courage, and charm had stolen his heart and now he was acting and scolding like a possessive husband in a bad play. Ashamed of his severity, he opened his mouth to reassure her, but before he could say a word, a gentleman approached him.

"'Ampton, you are 'ampton, are you not? The brave officer who captured one of Napoleon's eagles."

He had been recognised and there was no point in denying it to the man, who was obviously a royalist. Roland tried to say that fortune favoured him when he captured the eagle but the gentleman waved him to silence. "You 'onour us, milord."

Roland bowed. "Thank you, but please allow me a moment's privacy with this lady."

"As you please, milord." The gentleman turned and stepped back into the ballroom.

Annabelle stared after the Frenchman for a moment that seemed to last interminably before she tried to jerk her arm away from Roland. "Hampton, are you Fanny's ogre of a brother?" Colour flooded her cheeks. "Oh, I cannot believe you deceived me about your identity not once but twice. And you scolded me for running away from you. Is it any wonder that I did so? My sixth sense must have warned me not to stay with a…fraud, a liar, and—"

"I beg your pardon, madam," Roland interpolated. "I have many failings but I am not an ogre." He held onto her arm more tightly to prevent her dashing away from him, thus creating the scandal he hoped to avoid.

Annabelle's eyes glared at him through the slits in her mask. "Fanny said her half-brother is heartless. She is right. I will never forgive you for bamboozling me."

"My dear, please do not make fools of us. If you deny knowing who I am, you will become the butt of every gossip in town," he whispered in her ear. He drew her close and put his arm round her. Moonlight revealed the pain in her eyes.

"Do you think that by calling me your *dear* you will placate me?" Her eyes widened. "Am I your legal wife?"

"Yes, of course you are."

"Why did you conceal your real identity?"

"For safety's sake."

"I don't understand."

"Come." He guided her through the ballroom and into the hall, where his stormy-faced wife waited for a maid to bring her cloak from the ladies' withdrawing room, and for a footman to fetch his shako, cape, and gloves.

* * *

In the street outside Longterre's spacious house, Annabelle beckoned to a footman. "Summon Monsieur Cavalierre's coach and send word to him that his...ward has left the masquerade. Let him know I will send his coach back for him."

"No need, we can leave in my chaise," Roland said.

Pain knotted itself round Annabelle's heart. She straightened her back to maintain her dignity. "I doubt my gown would fit into a chaise."

"Very well, his coachman may drive us to my London house."

"No."

His eyes fierce, Roland took a step toward her. "Belle, you are my wife. Your place is by my side."

The coach drew up. A groom let down the steps. "Because I am your wife, I shall permit you to accompany me to Monsieur Cavalierre's house." Rage replaced pain. Had she married a monster? First he insulted her by calling her Juliet and now circumstance had forced him to reveal his true identity. Why had he not told her he was Fanny's half-brother?

She settled herself opposite Roland and glared at him. If he thought he could placate her by calling her Belle, he was mistaken. "Why did you pretend to be Major Sarrat?" she asked, with no intention of ever forgiving him.

Chapter Seventeen

Roland fully understood Annabelle's anger and her bewilderment that, when they first met, he had not introduced himself as Viscount Hampton, her friend's brother. At least they would have an opportunity to discuss matters on their way to Cavalierre's house. Of course, the law regarded a wife as a husband's property and he could compel her to accompany him to his house, but that would not bode well for their marriage. He would try to persuade her to return to him. "To answer your question, I did not pretend to be Major Sarrat. I served under Wellington's command," he said, aware that Annabelle was still glaring at him as he spoke.

"Do not prevaricate, my lord. You are an abominable trickster. First you pretended to be de Beauchamp and then you concealed your title from me. Why didn't you tell me the truth? What else have you lied about?"

With heightened colour in her cheeks, and her blue eyes blazing by the light of two small lanterns that illuminated the interior of the chaise, his wife looked more beautiful than ever. "I am at a loss," he began. "You are my stepsister's best friend. Can you honestly say you did not know I am Viscount Hampton?"

"Yes, I can. Fanny never referred to you as Sarrat, she always called you Hampton. Are you so vain that you think we had nothing better to talk about than you and your surname?"

Roland's sense of humour surfaced. "Perhaps I am, when I am not thinking about dear Fanny calling me The Ogre," he murmured.

The fury in Annabelle's lovely eyes lessened. "I agree it was unfair of her to call you an ogre." The expression in her eyes hardened again. "My lord, does Fanny know you married me?" she asked, and drew her lips into a thin, mutinous line.

"Not yet, but, after she received your letter—in which you referred to yourself as Miss Black—she came to London to ask me to help you to find out who your parents are." He chose his words carefully well-aware that he must be cautious because their situation had the makings of either a mutual comedy or a tragedy.

Annabelle clapped her hands. "Dear Fanny has a very kind heart. You are fortunate to have such a sister."

"Stepsister," he corrected her as the coach came to a halt.

Annabelle peered out of the window at the dark street. "Where are we, my lord?"

"We have arrived at my town house which I hope you will agree to occupy."

Annabelle shook her head. "My lord, you said you would return me to Cavalierre's house. Please direct the coachman to take me there."

"We agreed that you would call me Roland," he ventured.

"I can think of many other names for you," Annabelle purred. "Now, my lord, please do as I ask."

"If you insist on staying with Cavalierre, I will see you safely there."

His wife frowned. "I shall not force you out of the coach," he said and then opened the door to tell the coachman to proceed to Cavalierre's house before he shut it and faced Annabelle. "Do you really want to live in that Frenchman's house, where a disagreeable, shrivelled little man told me you had gone to the masquerade?"

"Yes, I do, my lord." Annabelle heaved a sigh so deep that the swell of her breasts increased. "Well," she continued in a disparaging tone, "you have found me and it might be better for both of us if you had not. Besides, I have great affection for *that Frenchman*, as you so rudely call him."

"Why do you wish I had not found you?"

"You know why. You deserve to suffer for lying to me, but I do not want you to be imprisoned for marrying me without my guardian's consent. Oh, Roland, I should not have married you, it was very wrong of me."

Every muscle in his body stilled, and he studied her face by the lantern light. "Do you truly mean that you regret marrying me?"

When Annabelle looked down at her lap and did not answer, he deemed it unwise to try to force a response from her.

"Belle," he said, falling back on his pet name for her, "when I read your letter to Fanny,

I wondered why you did not tell me Deacon tried to blackmail you."

Her cheeks flamed. "How many times must I tell you why? How could I risk you being brought to trial and suffering the full consequences of the law?'

It really seemed she did care for him.

"My dear child—" he began. *Damnation*, it was a mistake to have called her a child. It would only serve to annoy her.

Annabelle drummed her fingers on her knee. "I am not a child."

"A figure of speech," he said gently, for he did not want to cause her the slightest distress.

The coach halted, the door opened, and a groom lowered the steps. Roland got out and reached up to help Annabelle who had difficulty manoeuvring her full skirts worn over panniers. "Steady." He put his hands on either side of her waist and, in spite of her rigid corset, felt her tremble. He hoped she trembled with desire and not nervousness. When she stood on the narrow road illuminated by the full moon, Roland spread her hands wide apart. "My Belle, dressed in that pale costume, you look like a beautiful ghost from times past, yet you are warm flesh and blood and tremble at my touch. You have no need to do so. I will never harm you."

Annabelle shook her head as though bereft of speech, while the groom rapped on the front door of Cavalierre's house.

* * *

Henri opened the front door and squinted out into the night while Martha peered over Henri's shoulder at Roland and Annabelle. "You're not alone, miss," Martha said.

Martha stepped back and put her hands on her hips. "Who is the gentleman? Where is Cavalier?"

"Cavalierre not Cavalier," Annabelle corrected Martha yet again. She turned to Roland and indicated Martha. "My dresser."

"An impertinent one," Roland replied.

"I daresay, but unlike Deacon, who you chose to serve me, Martha is loyal, my lord." Annabelle looked at her dresser. "Martha, this gentleman is my husband, Viscount Hampton."

Martha glared at Roland. "So, he's the black-hearted devil who made you run away."

"Black-hearted devil," Annabelle muttered savouring the false description of her husband with amusement.

"Where can we speak privately?" Roland asked.

"In the small salon." Annabelle led her husband into a room adjacent to the octagonal hall. Henri followed them and lit candles. Roland stood in their soft light by the fireplace while she sat opposite him on an elegant couch and sank back against one of the plump cushions edged with a gold fringe.

"Some wine?" Henri asked.

The little man was surly but he knew his duty.

Roland shook his head.

"No thank you, Henri," Annabelle said. "If we want some later, we will serve ourselves. You may go." Annabelle toyed with a cream silk rose that ornamented the lowered point of her pearl encrusted bodice.

"Your questions were not unreasonable," Roland said after Henri left the salon.

"Which ones?" She bent her head as though nothing interested her more than the rose.

"You asked why I married you and why I did not tell you I am Viscount Hampton. The truth is simple. My grandmamma pretended to be on her deathbed and extracted my promise to marry without delay. I did not want to marry a spoiled miss whose only interest in me was my name and fortune, so I chose *you* to be my bride."

Startled, Annabelle peered at her husband and waited for him to express his reasons for choosing her in more tender terms. When he did not, she pressed her lips together. Over and over again, she had imagined the threat from Deacon being miraculously removed and a happy reunion with Roland. Now, in spite of her suspicions about Juliet and his trickery, she wanted him to…what?

She shrugged. To compensate for not being a cherished wife, she would become one of the most elegant ladies in society, no matter how many extravagant bills Roland had to pay.

A silk petal came adrift and fluttered to the parquet floor. She sighed softly.

* * *

Roland assumed his wife would understand his promise to his grandmother was not the only reason for making Annabelle his viscountess. He reached his hand out toward her. "Will you not forgive my deception, Belle?"

Annabelle discarded the fragile petal. "If I knew how to, I would."

"Why can't you?"

"I fear you will bamboozle me again."

Roland drew Annabelle to her feet and encircled her with his arms. "Please, don't be so unforgiving. You have no idea what it has been like to have been chased for my fortune and title from a young age. Yet in spite of many attempts to bring me to *Point Bon plus,* I never proposed marriage to any other lady. Does that not tell you something significant?"

"It would be unchristian of me not to forgive you," Annabelle said in a small voice and raised her face to look up at him.

The door opened. "*Damnation*," Roland swore at the sight of Cavalierre. If the Frenchman had not joined them at such an inopportune moment, Roland would have kissed his wife.

"I assume you are about to return to your husband," Cavalierre said, with a knowing look in his large, expressive eyes.

"You are mistaken, Monseigneur, I prefer to stay here."

"No black-hearted devil will force my mistress to do anything," said Martha who stood behind the monseigneur.

Annabelle restrained a grin. She suspected that while she spoke with her husband, Martha had been standing sentinel outside the door ready to rush to her defence.

"I think not, *ma petite*, your place is at your husband's side not at an old man's."

"My lessons."

"You may study with me if Monsieur the Viscount permits."

"Your lessons! Of course you may study if you wish to," Roland said.

"But, Monseigneur—"

"No arguments." Cavalierre raised her hand to his lips and kissed the air above it in a courtly gesture.

"Must I go?" she asked in a small voice.

"Yes, you must be reconciled with your husband."

On impulse, Annabelle kissed Cavalierre on the cheek and then gestured to Martha. "Fetch whatever is necessary for tonight. The remainder can be collected tomorrow." Cavalierre raised his hand as though he blessed her. "Be happy, *ma petitie.*"

* * *

"Am I forgiven?" Roland asked again on their way to the town house while the scent of her perfume, a blend or rose and other flowers, stirred his senses. With difficulty, he refrained from taking his wife into his arms and wooing her with his kisses until she overcame any objections she might have to his love-making.

Instead of replying, Annabelle nibbled her lower lip.

"Belle, in the matrimonial stakes, a viscount ranks higher than a baron, so your former guardian can have no objection to our marriage, and you need not be afraid of my going to prison." For the sake of her safety, he did not reveal that he not only knew her guardian's name but that he had obtained consent for them to marry. Heaven help him when the truth was revealed. Doubtless Annabelle would rage at him instead of being grateful for his protection. He might deplore his wife's impulsiveness but he did admire her spirit. Instead of being cowed by unfavourable circumstances, she did not flinch.

"Roland, if you ever deceive me again, I don't know if I could forgive you."

He had not shared all of his knowledge with her and that was not deception, was it? Perhaps she would forgive him when the truth was revealed, but more importantly she would be safe. He raised her hand to his lips and kissed it. "Please trust me, Belle. I have said I believe I can make you happy and am determined to keep my promise to look after you and protect you to the best of my ability. Those are not the words of a gentleman intent on deceiving his wife, but if I ever did so, it would have been for your own sake."

"I hope you will never again play me false," Annabelle said, her eyes appearing larger than usual in the light from the carriage lamps.

Roland decided to change tack, as it would be foolish to speak of falsity. "I wish you had confided in me when Deacon tried to blackmail you."

"So you said."

"But I have not yet told you that Fanny showed your letter to Miss Chalfont, who came to the manor and then, because you took my chaise, travelled to Dover with me in her coach."

"You searched for me there?" The displeasure and suspicion in his wife's eyes faded.

"Of course I searched for you. I was half out of my mind with worry." His voice throbbed with understated emotion. "When we first met, you had been attacked by a footpad. I feared all manner of unspeakable things might have befallen you. Some highwayman might have left you lying in a ditch with your throat cut."

"Do I mean so much to you?"

"What a foolish question. Of course you mean a lot to me. You are my wife. From now on, our life will be quite different. You will enjoy every comfort I can provide, be mistress of Sarrat Place, and take your proper position in society."

"Will I be in charge of your household?"

Was his wife's main consideration prestige? Had he misjudged her? Was the schoolgirl he married ambitious? "You will be mistress of your home but will have no need to exert yourself. Why should you? I have a steward, a butler and a housekeeper, and many other servants."

"What of Deacon?"

Were her hands trembling? He should not be so quick to judge her. "She left before I read your letter to Fanny. If the wretched woman had not, I would have had her arrested for attempted blackmail."

Annabelle plucked the pearls on her petticoat, revealed by the skirts of her gown, which were looped up with ribbons and pearl rosettes. "I want Martha to be my dresser."

"As you please, Belle, but why do we speak of servants?"

Annabelle looked down at her hands and stopped plucking the pearls on her petticoat.

"So," Roland said, "you intend to study with Cavalierre?"

"Yes, and I am honoured, for he is so much in demand that he may pick and choose his clients. He believes I have some talent which can be improved."

He smiled at her, prepared to indulge her. "Well, you will never need to paint for a living."

"No, but I am passionate about painting and want to continue my lessons."

"You disappoint me. I hoped you would have another passion."

Annabelle frowned. "Another passion? What do you mean? What could it be?"

If his wife had grasped his meaning, she would have blushed. "Nothing, I am content to enjoy your company," he hedged, fearing he had said too much.

She gazed at him. "You are too kind, my lord," she replied, as though she did not believe him.

Chapter Eighteen

Annabelle woke. For a moment, she did not know where she was. She stared at the hand-blocked, almond green wallpaper, patterned with Chinese pagodas, figures and bridges. Of course, she was in her husband's London mansion. She had been so weary when they reached it that Roland had guided her up the stairs and left her with Martha, who undressed her and helped her into bed. Later, Roland had returned and tucked the quilt round her neck as though she were a child.

"We will see each other in the morning," he had said and left the bedroom quietly.

She stretched on the luxurious mattress and yawned.

"You are awake," a cheerful voice said.

Startled, Annabelle looked round the bedroom and saw Fanny sitting on a chair near the large tester bed. "Fanny, is that really you, or am I dreaming?"

"It's me," Fanny said with a total disregard for elegant speech. "I am very pleased to see you. Until this morning, when Hampton told me he had married you, I had no idea you were his wife. But why didn't you tell me in your letter that you had married Hampton? My dearest Annabelle, I could not be happier. If I could have chosen his wife, I would have chosen you."

"Thank you." Annabelle sat, plumped up the pillows and arranged them behind her back.

Her friend stood and approached the bed. She sat on it and then bounced up and down. "Tell me everything. Where did you meet Hampton? Did he fall in love with you at first sight?"

Roland entered the bedroom, followed by Martha carrying a silver tray.

"Fanny, I might have known you would be here but please be good enough not to plague my wife."

"How romantic, Hampton." Fanny giggled, staring at a red hothouse rose on the tray.

Roland's cheeks coloured slightly while Annabelle smiled at him. "What time is it?"

"A little after ten of the clock," Fanny told her after she glanced at the clock on the mantelpiece.

"How lazy I am." Annabelle put her hand over her mouth to cover a yawn.

"During the season, we will sleep much later than this and I will not be surprised if we don't breakfast until past noon," Fanny said ecstatically.

Unable to imagine such a life, Annabelle shrugged and looked into the depths of her husband's quizzical eyes. Had he picked the red rose for her or had a servant decorated the tray with it?

***

Conscious of the servants' covert curiosity, Annabelle joined Roland and Fanny for nuncheon.

"Fanny," Roland said after he accepted Annabelle's offer of a second dish of coffee. "I think you are too young for a London Season."

"Hampton!" Fanny exclaimed, her eyes filling with tears. "That is not so. Some girls make their curtsey when they are sixteen, and I am seventeen."

Roland raised his eyebrows. "Yes, I do remember how old you are, but there is no need for you to be in a hurry to find a husband. In my opinion, seventeen is too young to enter London society. So, with your best interests at heart, I shall send you to Grandmother in Bath, where you can test your feet in the fashionable world before being presented at court."

To his astonishment, Fanny burst into tears and ran out of the dining room.

He half rose as though he would follow her but sank back onto his chair.

"You were a little cruel." Annabelle said.

"That was not my intention." Roland dabbed his lips with his napkin. "Belle, as you should know by now, at heart, I am as soft as a kitten."

"Don't you mean a tiger cub?"

Roland chuckled. "If my grandmamma's health permits, I hope she will present you at court."

Annabelle held her fork in midair as though she was more interested in conversation than food. "I might be unwelcome at court."

"Why?"

Her cheeks flooded with heat, she looked away from Roland. "I am a girl of unknown parentage. I will not be welcome in society."

'Don't look so worried. I promise every door will open wide for my wife."

She cleared her throat. "My lord—"

"There you go again calling me 'my lord', instead of Roland when we are in private."

"I want to be a credit to you," she replied and scrutinised his clean-shaven face.

"You will be," he drawled.

"Do you truly think so? But to do you justice I must look to my wardrobe. Monsieur Cavalierre told me I will be all the rage if I dress to perfection. Of course, I don't believe him but I do hope you will not be ashamed of me. And Madame Valencay, whom I met at the masquerade, recommended her modiste, Celeste and—"

Roland broke in. "Your desire to please me is flattering, but I must beg you not to become intimate with Madame. She is de Beauchamp's aunt."

Annabelle drew her eyebrows into a straight line. "What does that signify? I like her and she could not choose her relations."

"Of course, I am only your husband who must bow to your superior judgement, but it would be kind of you to humour me."

Puzzled, as she had expected him to argue the point, Annabelle stared at him.

"May I not choose my acquaintances?" She squared her shoulders preparing for an argument.

"You must excuse me, Belle. I have an appointment with my tailor." Her husband stood, kissed the top of her head, and left the room.

Frustrated because she had been prepared to voice her determination to further her acquaintance with Madame Valencay, she stared at the door as it closed behind Roland.

* * *

When her sister-in-law did not respond to her knock on the door, Annabelle entered the bedroom.

Fanny lay sobbing, sprawled on the bed, her face pressed into a pale green bedspread embroidered in gold that matched the curtains looped back around the bed and at the windows.

Annabelle hurried across the oak floor to her sister-in-law and patted her back with heartfelt concern. "Do stop crying, Fanny dearest, I am sure my husband wants the best for you. Besides, I don't think he is being unreasonable."

Fanny rolled over, pushed her curls back from her face, and hiccupped. "Roland is hard-hearted." She wiped her tear-stained face with the backs of her hands. "I don't believe he knows the meaning of affection, not even for his mistress, Juliet Parker, that married woman he took to the Peninsula."

"What!" Annabelle sank onto the edge of the bed and took a deep breath. "What are you saying? You did not see Roland for many years, so what can you know about him and his mistress?"

Fanny sat and hugged her knees to her chest. "If you had not been blind and deaf at school to everything other than reading and sketching, you would have heard the other girls gossip about my brother."

Annabelle's cheeks burned. She wanted to find out more about Juliet Parker but was reluctant to question Fanny.

Shame-faced Fanny looked at her. "I apologise, Annabelle. I should not have mentioned the woman to you. Please forgive me."

Breathing fast, Annabelle stood and crossed the room to the window, where she stood looking out with her back to Fanny.

"I am sorry. I should not have mentioned the woman. I am sure she means nothing to Roland," Fanny gabbled. "Annabelle, please forgive me," she repeated. "Most gentlemen have mistresses, and even if my brother has one you cannot be upset. After all, it is not as though you made a love match, is it? Grandmamma wrote to tell me Roland promised her he would marry without delay. She also explained he would not marry a spoiled society miss. So, when he met you, he must have decided you would do."

Decided I would do? Speechless, Annabelle stared out at a milkmaid leading a brown and white cow with full udders along the street. *How can Fanny be so insensitive?* Her skin prickled with heat although the room was cool. She took a deep breath and turned around to face Roland's sister. "Enough!"

Fanny wiped her face again with the backs of her hands. "Please don't be waspish, Annabelle. There is nothing to distress you. As I said, most gentlemen keep mistresses."

Annabelle snorted. She would not share her husband's favours with any other woman. "When you marry, Fanny, I hope you will be as complacent as you are now."

Annabelle marched out of the bedroom. Desperate to escape Fanny's ill-judged words, she hurried along the corridor and bumped into her husband, who steadied her and kissed her lingeringly on her mouth.

She could not bear the thought of his kissing anyone else and jerked away from him. "Please excuse me, my lord, I am in a hurry."

Roland's eyes narrowed and he clasped her upper arms. "It seems you are in haste to be rid of my attentions."

"I shall be with Celeste for the rest of the day," Annabelle said, choking back her distress.

"Very well, Belle, but this evening we shall dine together before attending the theatre."

She raised her chin. "I shall dine with you, but I cannot attend the theatre. I promised to visit Madame Valencay." That was only a little lie, for although she had promised to visit the lady, she had not specified a time.

Very gently, her husband raised her chin. "Far be it from me to disturb your social engagements."

Baffled by his affability she stared at him. She had expected him to protest over her defiance. Unable to curb her painful imagination concerning Juliet Parker in Roland's arms, Annabelle swallowed a lump in her throat. Convention demanded that no lady ever confront her husband about his mistress, so to contain her impulse to ask if it were true that Juliet was his mistress, she whirled round and hurried to her sunny bedroom where Martha waited for her.

What did she care about Roland? She would do as she pleased. She would learn to handle pistols, find someone to teach her the art of fencing, improve her riding, and purchase all the popular books. Moreover, she would be the most fashionable newcomer in town with every appearance of being a happy bride, although in her heart she was not.

Miserable, she allowed Martha to help her dress and then, determined not to give way to unhappiness, collected her designs for gowns and pelisses and went to consult Celeste.

* * *

On the morning after Fanny's departure, Roland put his broadsheet down and eyed his wife. "Thank God Fanny is on her way to Bath. We shall not be obliged to tolerate any more tears and recriminations. Now, let us put Fanny out of our minds. Will you ride in the park with me?"

From her chair set before the window in her parlour, Annabelle looked down into the square ablaze with spring colour.

"No, thank you. Celeste is waiting on me this morning."

"Ah, how can I, an insignificant husband, compete with your mantua maker? I shall look forward to you riding with me in the country."

"In the country?"

"I beg your pardon. Did I speak too softly for you to hear me? Yes, we are going to Sarrat Place for a fortnight before we go to Bath, where you will meet my grandmamma and make sure all is well with Fanny. Afterward we will return to London for the season."

So, he did care about his half-sister. Annabelle looked at him sideways. "As you please." By then, Annabelle hoped that Celeste would have delivered most of her new clothes. She also hoped the residents of Bath would admire her designs made in the finest materials.

Roland smiled, his face impassive. "Good, I am glad to hear we are in agreement about going out of town."

Baffled yet again by her husband, she stared at him. Was he taking her out of town because she defied him by furthering her friendship with Madame Valencay?

* * *

On the morning of their departure for the country, Roland watched Annabelle descend the stairs. "You look just the thing," he said as he eyed her mustard-yellow pelisse, with vertical dark brown velvet bands from throat to hem.

Annabelle inclined her head. "Thank you."

"One of Celeste's creations?"

"Not entirely. I designed the gown for Celeste to have made up. She hopes my style will be much admired and become all the rage. Of course, if it does, Celeste will take the credit, for I do not wish to be judged eccentric for designing my clothes."

Roland's breath caught in his throat. Ever since Annabelle returned to him, she had spoken little. His eyes narrowed as he noted the heightened colour in her cheeks and hoped he had not been fooled by a young lady on the catch for a titled, wealthy husband. No, that could not be the case. When they met, Annabelle had neither known his true identity nor known that he was wealthy. *Damn Fanny's nonsense.* She should not have planted the notion of his being an ogre in his wife's mind.

By now, surely he had proved he was not one. He scowled. To make matters worse there was his wife's dresser. He must either win over impertinent Martha—who seemed to delight in calling him a black-hearted devil—or dismiss her from his wife's service. He suppressed a groan. No, that would not do; Annabelle seemed inexplicably fond of the giantess.

He held out his arm in the expectation of Annabelle taking it before he led her out of the house to their chaise, which awaited them. Annabelle ignored the gesture, looked away, and fiddled with the crisp muslin ruff at her throat before stepping into the street after nodding her thanks to the footman, who held the front door open.

Appreciative of his wife's courtesy to the servants, he also nodded at the footman.

"Lord," Roland said, while he looked at the last of Annabelle's bandboxes being put into the baggage coach in which Martha and his valet would travel. "How much do you need for a month out of town?"

"Gowns for the morning and afternoon, riding habits, carriage gowns and evening gowns, as well as other *ensembles* for other occasions, such as music recitals and balls, which I presume we will attend in Bath."

So his bride intended to make her mark in the country before they went to Bath, where she had decided to take advantage of everything the town had to offer. "How ignorant I am of a lady's requirements," he drawled.

Annabelle lowered her eyebrows. "I hope you will not accuse me of extravagance and scold me."

"Have I ever scolded you?"

She shook her head and entered the chaise with a book in hand.

"What are you reading?" he asked after they were seated.

"*The Bride of Triermain,* by Walter Scott." Annabelle removed a bookmark and bent her head over Scott's novel while the chaise moved forward.

"I hope the tale is appropriate, Belle," Roland said after some minutes during which Annabelle had not turned a single page. It seemed *The Bride of Trierman* was no more than a ploy to avoid conversation with him.

Annabelle lowered the book and stared at him as though his question astonished her. "What do you mean?"

He took the novel from her. "You are still a bride."

For a moment, she gazed into his eyes. "I don't feel like one."

"Why not?"

Annabelle's cheeks coloured up again. "I cannot explain."

Roland took her hand in his. With his other hand he removed her glove, and then turned her hand over and kissed her palm. "Try to explain. I have been told I'm a sympathetic confidant."

The heightened colour in Annabelle's cheeks deepened. She snatched her hand away and reclaimed her glove. The gesture, he reflected grimly, did not bode well for their marriage.

Some three hours later, during which time Roland pretended to doze instead of making desultory conversation with Annabelle, the chaise slowed. It turned onto a country road rutted by cart wheels too uneven for Annabelle even to pretend to read. Roland broke his long silence. "If you are a devotee of Gothic novels, I think Sarrat Place will please you. My father admired Hugh Walpole's *Strawberry Hill* so much that he added battlements and turrets to his principal country house and filled it with furniture in the Gothic style."

"Indeed," Annabelle said, as though she responded to a boring acquaintance.

Roland frowned and then smiled. What had happened to change her so much? He had married a beautiful, impulsive girl with a ready smile and a confiding manner. Well, she was even more beautiful now, but where were her other attributes? Had Fanny or de Beauchamp's aunt, Madame Valencay, said something to distress her? Had he been mistaken in Annabelle's character, or was he the cause of it?

Silenced by her frigid reply, Roland looked out the window at the countryside enhanced by sunshine. He did not speak again until the chaise entered the long, tree-lined drive to Sarrat Place where, surrounded by cheering country people, the chaise drew to a halt.

Annabelle gazed out of the window. "Who are those people? What is happening?"

"I sent word of our arrival. My tenants and some of their farm workers are greeting you in their own way. They are taking the horses out of the traces and will pull the chaise to the house."

"I have never heard of such a thing."

"Every family has its own traditions."

"I did not imagine such a welcome," she said, her voice nearly drowned by the tumult.

"It's genuine," he assured her, as the wheels of the chaise rolled forward.

A few minutes later, the chaise halted again and a groom let down the steps. Roland descended before he turned and helped Annabelle to get out.

Wide-eyed, his wife looked round the forecourt. "How beautiful the house is."

"Yes, it is," Roland agreed, glad that the sun shone on the weathered grey stone, the green and white striped awnings and the glittering glass panes of the new garden room.

"Come." Accompanied by the cheers of the tenants and labourers, he escorted his wife up the steps to the house where the butler waited for them.

Chapter Nineteen

"My lady," Martha began while she helped Annabelle to change before dinner, "Who would have thought it? When the servants ate, I took precedence over the high and mighty maids and sat next to the butler in the servants' hall. I didn't guess I'd be raised up when you employed me." She grinned, revealing large even teeth. "As for his lordship, I might have been mistaken about him. The housekeeper told me everyone's as proud as can be of him, and that they're glad he's safe home from the wars. Well, my lady, you've never said why you ran away from him. And I can't understand it, for I'm telling you the master's as generous as he's handsome and kind."

Annabelle hid her amusement over her dresser's changed opinion about Roland. She raised her hand. "Martha, your tongue runs away with you."

"I beg your pardon, my lady," Martha said, but continued. "His lordship's very kind. Your apartment's been redecorated, and he insisted on the glass room being finished before your arrival."

Dejected, in spite of Martha's encouraging words, Annabelle looked around her bedroom decorated in delicate shades of peach and cream. She would find it intolerable to share it with Roland who, she had good reason to believe, slept with his mistress. Even if society expected a lady to ignore her husband's affairs, the image of Roland entwined in another woman's clinging arms squeezed her heart until she found it hard to breathe. If only she had a mother or an older lady she could turn to for advice. Madame Valencay came to mind, but how could she broach such a delicate subject on such short acquaintance?

Martha gazed at her. "My lady, you seem very unhappy."

Annabelle allowed Martha to slip her petticoat over her head and tie the strings. "Not unhappy, only tired."

Neither of them spoke again while Martha helped Annabelle into her ice blue and white striped gown before kneeling to arrange the triple row of lace edged flounces around the hem.

A knock sounded on the door. "See who it is, Martha."

Her dresser admitted Roland.

"Leave us," he instructed Martha, who smiled at him before she closed the door behind her.

"A miracle! For once, she did not call me a black-hearted devil." Roland handed Annabelle a flat, oblong box. "For you, Belle."

"What is it?" she asked as she took it from him.

He smiled at her. "Open it and see."

Annabelle raised the red leather lid and looked at the lustrous pearl necklace with a diamond clasp, gold and pearl arm clasps, and pearl earrings. "Oh! Thank you, they are beautiful."

"The jeweller, from whom I bought them before we left London, assured me they are the very thing for a young bride. Of course, I shall give you the Hampton family jewels but, in the meantime, I wanted to give you a wedding present. But if you don't like the pearls, I can return them and you may choose something else."

"Oh no, they are beautiful. I want to keep them." She looked at him with a hint of sadness in her eyes. "You are very kind to me."

The faintest sigh escaped Roland. "Husbands should be kind. Tell me what I can do to please you."

Annabelle looked down. "I am pleased, your gift is beautiful."

"Why do you speak to me like a polite child speaking to an adult?" With his thumb and forefinger he tilted Annabelle's chin and gazed at her. "What thoughts do those blue eyes of yours hide?"

"None." She jerked her chin free of him.

"We could get on better than this, Belle."

* * *

Yes, they could and if it was not for Juliet Parker, she would want nothing more than to be on the best of terms with her husband. She looked down again and blamed her sudden faintness not on the intoxicating scent of his spicy pomade or his proximity but on her tightly laced stays.

Roland took the necklace out of the box. "May I?" She nodded and he fastened it around her neck.

In response to his touch on her sensitive skin, her toes curled in their dainty slippers. His warm lips traced the line of her right shoulder, sending an almost unbearable bolt of desire through her. She shivered, remembering her delight when he carried out his vow. *With my body I thee worship.*

"Are you trembling with fear, or are you trembling for another reason?" Roland whispered into her ear and turned her to face him.

"It is close in this room. I cannot breathe. Please open a window."

Roland brushed her cheek with his fingers. "I hope my ardour—not lack of air—caused your breathlessness. Do you really want me to open the window?"

"Yes. No. Please do not trouble yourself." She put the jewel box on her dressing table, snatched up her painted fan, and employed it to cool her cheeks.

"Very well, to please you, I will not trouble myself."

Was he laughing at her? She looked at his reflection in the mirror, saw the amusement in his eyes, and snapped the fan shut before busying herself with the earrings and bracelets.

"Shall we dine?"

"As you please."

"I do please, and it pleases me to compliment you on your gown. Another one of your designs? Are the frills your idea? I have not noticed any other lady adorn her gowns with them at the hem."

Was he thinking of the way Juliet dressed? She forced herself to speak. "I am glad you like it."

They went downstairs, where instead of eating their meal in the dining room, facing each other from both ends of a table large enough to seat thirty guests, they ate in the new glass room perfumed by potted jasmine.

Roland picked up his soup spoon. "What do you think of your new home now that you have seen part of the interior?"

"It is magnificent."

"Yes, it is, and my family is very proud of it," Roland said and dipped his spoon into the chicken soup.

She wondered what his relatives would think about him taking a wife of unknown parentage. "Do you have a large family?"

"Yes, a clutch of female cousins and more distant relatives."

After they finished the soup, watched by the alert butler, the footmen offered a choice of poached smoked haddock dotted with butter, whitebait, and turbot in lobster sauce.

"The manor dates back to the mid-fourteenth century and is one of the earliest brick buildings in England," Roland explained.

Appreciative of the lobster sauce, Annabelle put some turbot onto her fork. "You are fortunate to own such a beautiful property."

"Yes, I am. After we have dined, I shall show you the Long Gallery in which there are portraits of my ancestors and—" He broke off at the sight of one of the glass doors opening and the sound of a woman's imperious voice. "What the devil?" he asked.

An agitated servant followed the intruder. "How dare you say his lordship is not at home," the voice shrilled. "Hampton will always be at home to me."

Roland stood. "You are mistaken, Juliet. I thought I had made it clear that I shall never again be at home to you. Please leave before I have you thrown out."

Annabelle stared at the dark-haired beauty and watched her unfasten the broad grey ribbons at her throat and push back the hood of her crimson velvet cloak lined with sumptuous pale grey satin.

Annabelle caught her breath. It seemed that this bold woman, with a perfect complexion and tiny ringlets framing her oval face, was no longer Roland's mistress. Relief flooded through her and a wave of happiness engulfed her.

"Hampton, after all we have shared, how can you be so cruel?" Juliet demanded.

Annabelle frowned thoughtfully. Roland had said he would never be at home to Juliet? Nevertheless, that was not to say he and Juliet did not meet elsewhere. Perhaps the woman was still his mistress. Annabelle forced herself to relax her hands that were clasped so tightly her nails dug into her flesh.

When Roland made no reply, Juliet smoothed her gown bound by a crimson, tasselled cord beneath her bosom. Eyes wild, she spoke. "I could not believe it when I heard you were married."

Roland stood. "You knew I would marry one day. Please leave."

"Since my husband died, I believed you would marry me," Juliet said in a tremulous voice, and then glared at Annabelle. "How did you catch him, child?" she asked, her cheeks sucked in and her nostrils flaring.

Roland strode forward, grabbed Juliet's arms from behind, and marched her out into the garden.

Annabelle gestured to the butler and footmen with her hand. "You may go."

Anger burned in her. As soon as Mrs Parker arrived, Roland should have sent her away. However, in all probability he did not know she knew Mrs Parker was his mistress and did not want to arouse her suspicion. Annabelle stood and went out into the garden. Her eyes became accustomed to the dark and she made out

Roland and Juliet standing beneath the spreading branches of an oak tree.

"Be reasonable, Juliet," she heard her husband say. "You have no reason to reproach me. From the day you joined me, I told you that even if you became a widow I would never marry you. Now leave. Your presence here insults my wife and you are testing my patience."

"Hampton," Juliet shrilled, "upon my word, what were you thinking of to marry a chit of a girl?"

"I have married a lady who is not in the habit of brangling," Roland said in a quiet tone.

By moonlight, Juliet's eyes flashed and she stepped back, her mouth open to speak. Before she could do so, a voice sounded from the narrow path that led past the oak tree to the house. "Juliet, I have come to take you home."

The beauty turned and faced a large gentleman. "Hampton is married," she said, as though that explained everything.

"What devil prompted you to come here?" the gentleman all but snarled. "Apart from your breach of etiquette, surely you could not have been so foolish as to expect Roland and his wife to receive you. If this becomes known, all hope of your being accepted into polite society again will vanish. Sometimes I think you are not right in the head and should be locked up." The gentleman came forward, took hold of Juliet's hand, and attempted to lead her down the path away from the house. "Please forgive my sister for her intrusion and allow me offer my good wishes."

"Hampton, you and your wife will be sorry," Juliet said. "Although I am an outcast from society, I shall make my voice heard. Everyone will agree you should have married me."

"A moment, Mrs Parker," Roland said in a voice devoid of all emotion. "If you choose to be a fool, you may speak as you please, but never again threaten me or my wife."

"Come," Juliet's brother said and led her away.

Annabelle hurried back into the glass room, tugged the bell pull for the servants to return, and took her place at the table seconds before Roland returned. "My apologies for that woman's intrusion," he said.

She inclined her head and, conscious that the servants had more than enough to gossip about, ate in silence with little appetite.

At the end of the last course, a footman cleared the table before putting out a decanter of port, a glass, and a bowl of shelled walnuts. Glad of the custom of ladies retiring when the port was served, Annabelle went to her apartment instead of waiting for Roland in the ladies' drawing room. As soon as she entered it, her eyes filled with tears.

"My lady," Martha murmured.

What right did that ill-bred, shameless woman have to force her way into Sarrat?

"Martha, don't speak to me. I'm in a rage," Annabelle said and hurled a figurine of a simpering shepherdess across the room.

"There, there, wipe your eyes," Martha said, ignoring the sound of breaking china.

Martha fetched a handkerchief and handed it to her. Without saying another word Martha unfastened a row of pearl buttons down the back of Annabelle's bodice. Annabelle stood with her fists clenched at her sides. "Leave me."

Martha ignored the order and undressed Annabelle. She helped her into a nightgown and eased her into a becoming pale pink wrap trimmed with broad lace.

"You may go, Martha."

"I'll fetch you some hot milk laced with camomile and brandy to calm you and help you sleep."

"I am calm."

Annabelle ignored Martha's mocking chuckle, went to her parlour, and slumped onto a chair. If only odious, under-bred Juliet did not make her marriage intolerable.

The door opened. "Martha, please leave the milk on the table for me to drink later."

"I have not brought any milk," Roland said.

Martha arrived with the hot drink and scowled at Roland. "Here you are, my lady, this will do you a power of good."

"Put the cup on the table, Martha. Leave us and do not return tonight. We are not to be disturbed," Roland ordered.

"Black-hearted devil to make my mistress cry," Martha muttered and withdrew from the parlour.

Roland ignored the eccentric servant and sat down opposite Annabelle, a crease between his eyebrows. "Have you been crying, Belle?" he asked, his eyes full of concern.

Any man would be furious if his mistress breached etiquette by coming to his house when his wife was in residence. She frowned. No matter how angry Roland had been with Juliet, it did not mean she was not still his mistress. Annabelle rested her head against the back of her chair and closed her eyes. She needed solitude but suspected Roland would refuse to leave if she asked him to.

Her husband reached across the small distance that separated them and took her hand in his. "I am proud of you for remaining calm in spite of our guest's shocking conduct."

That was too much to bear. Rightly or wrongly, she would not pretend she did not know about her husband's relationship with Juliet. If that shocked him, she did not care. "Your guest, Roland, not mine. A guest, it seems, you know very well. Approve of it or not, I will not be a dutiful wife who pretends she does not know about her husband's...*peccadilloes*. Fanny told me about the lady."

"What?" Roland roared. "What did she tell you?" he asked, regaining a measure of calm.

"That it is unusual for gentlemen to be faithful to their wives and that a woman called Juliet accompanied you to Spain."

Roland prowled around the room like an exotic, dangerous animal. "I apologise for my sister's shocking forthrightness and for Juliet's unforgivable behaviour. It never occurred to me that she would insult you by her presence under my roof."

How should she deal with this situation, which was not mentioned in the book of etiquette Miss Chalfont had ensured her older pupils read? "Your friendship with Juliet has nothing to do with me."

Roland flung himself into the chair by the window opposite the one she was sitting in. "My…er…friendship with that woman was terminated before I met you, and I do not have a mistress. Juliet and I—" he began.

"There is no need to explain," Annabelle broke in. "Our marriage was not a love match, so I do not expect you to pretend to have any affection for me."

"Belle, you're mistaken, I'm more than fond of you."

That sounded encouraging, she thought, as she eyed him in silence.

Roland cleared his throat. "We must be honest. If we are not, what will the rest of our lives together be like? Allow me to explain. Juliet and I grew up on adjoining estates. We knew each other well when we were children. Later, whenever I came home on holiday from

Eton, although Juliet is older than I, our friendship grew. By the time I went to Oxford, she decided she loved me."

"It is improper of you to discuss that woman with me."

"I know, but you are offended, puzzled, and cross, and if I am not frank, Juliet's shadow will prey on our marriage." Roland sighed. "Juliet is to be pitied."

"You are impertinent if you think that woman is of the least importance to me," Annabelle said untruthfully. Juliet's shadow would not merely prey on their marriage, it would ruin it.

"Annabelle, you instigated this conversation by telling me what Fanny said. So you will do me the courtesy of listening.

"Juliet is to be pitied. Her father was a poor man. He as good as sold Juliet in marriage to Parker, a wealthy man. He locked Juliet up. He half-starved her and I think he would have beaten her to death if she had not agreed to marry Parker. After the marriage, poor Juliet couldn't bear being shackled to a man more than twice her age. When I joined my regiment in Portugal, she followed me.

"Belle, I hope you will believe me. At the age of eighteen I had flirted with Juliet a little more than was proper, but I didn't love her, and never gave her cause to think I did."

He stood and picked up the silver beaker of milk and removed the lid. "Drink this before it gets cold." Annabelle shook her head. "To please me," Roland cajoled.

She accepted the beaker and stared at him. "Why did you not reject Juliet when she followed you?"

"What was I to do?" he asked. "She ruined her reputation by running away from her husband to join me. Only a cad would have sent her away."

Roland scanned her face with anxious eyes. What did he want of her? To share her bed with as little love as he shared Juliet's? But perhaps he had come to love Juliet? Maybe he welcomed Juliet into his bed.

"The rest is history," he continued. "After both Juliet's husband and father died, her brother, Edward, a good-hearted fellow, came to the Peninsula and persuaded her to return to England." He paused and wiped a mist of perspiration from his forehead. "Scandal makes it impossible for Juliet to re-enter society, so she lives in a house on the grounds of the run-down estate her brother inherited from their father." He shrugged. "I believe he is improving it with money inherited from her husband."

"My lord, please say no more. I have no interest in Mrs Parker."

"Belle, look at me, there is something I must say," Roland coaxed in a soft tone.

Unable to meet his gaze, she lowered her head, for he did not—indeed could not—know how hard she found it to be dignified.

Roland stood and drew close to her. He bent and tilted her chin to make her look up at him. "Juliet and I separated before I met you. Contrary to what Fanny said, I do not have a mistress. Now that I am fortunate enough to have you as my wife, why should I need a mistress? I intend to be a faithful husband."

Did she dare to believe him? Her breath came and went more easily. "Thank you for your reassurance."

Roland's eyes glinted. "Allow me to offer you more reassurance."

Her husband drew her to her feet and embraced her. The fragrance of his cologne and pomade filled her nostrils as he pressed her against the length of his lean body. His hand traced the curve of her spine.

Someone knocked on the door. Roland released Annabelle and turned round. "What the devil!" he exclaimed when it opened.

Her cheeks pink with embarrassment, Martha averted her eyes from them. "Begging your pardon my lady, I knocked several times."

"I told you not to disturb us. If you ever disobey me again, you will be dismissed," Roland said.

"Begging your pardon, my lord, your grandmother, Lady Caroline, has arrived and insists on seeing you."

"Do not blame the servant, Hampton. Had she refused to announce me I would have announced myself," said a distinctive voice from the corridor.

"Grandmamma, you know you should not intrude on my wife's private apartment, but when have you ever observed convention?" Roland stated.

"Surely there can be no objection to my joining you in her parlour."

"I thought you were in Bath. Why have you come here? Why did you not send someone to let us know you were coming?"

Annabelle nodded to Martha to step aside to allow Lady Caroline to enter the parlour.

Embarrassed by her *deshabille*, Annabelle stood still while a tiny figure bedecked with jewels and dressed in the colours of an exotic tropical bird advanced. "So this is *The Nobody* you married. Come here. Let me look at you, girl."

"Do not address my wife as 'girl,' Grandmamma," Roland said and then introduced them to each other.

Stung by her ladyship's reference to her as 'a nobody,' Annabelle became even more determined to discover her parents' identity. Instead of revealing her inner turmoil, she straightened her back and tilted her chin.

The old lady fingered her flame red hair. "Hampton, your wife is a beauty, but was it necessary to marry her?"

Roland frowned. "You have said more than enough, Grandmamma."

"Do not be prudish, my boy. My generation does not mince its words."

Annabelle choked back a chuckle. Roland's earlier conversation about Mrs Parker proved that he was not a prude, and shocking though it was, she liked him for it.

Roland gripped Lady Caroline's elbow and guided her to his apartment.

Annabelle caught her lower lip between her teeth and exchanged glances with Martha.

"Well, my lady, there's enough goings on in this house to fill one of those books you're so fond of."

This time Annabelle chuckled before she spoke. "You may go, Martha." Annabelle hoped Lady Caroline would not make a prolonged visit to Sarrat Place. "Goodnight, Martha," she said and then added, "I'm glad I employed you."

"So am I," Martha replied with a broad grin. "Since you employed me, everything's been as good as a play."

"Has it? I cannot imagine what the other servants are saying," Annabelle murmured.

Martha put her hands on her broad hips. "You've no need to worry, my lady. None of them will take that black-hearted devil's part."

"You told me his lordship is liked and respected by the servants, so please stop referring to him thus."

Martha curtsied. "May I go?"

Annabelle nodded. In spite of her distress, she could not stifle a giggle after she overheard her champion whisper. "Black-hearted Lucifer."

Alone, Annabelle stiffened at the sound of Lady Caroline's voice and realised the door between her parlour and Roland's apartment was ajar.

"Well, my boy, as though you did not cause enough scandal by taking up with Juliet Parker, you have now made a fool of yourself by marrying an unknown."

"Although my wife may be unknown to society, she is a lady born and bred." About to shut the door, Annabelle hesitated. She caught her breath. How fierce in her defence Roland sounded. And he had referred to her as a *lady born*. Could he know her true identity? Surely not. Only an ogre would be cruel enough to keep it secret from her. Yet Fanny had described Roland as an ogre. Could Fanny have reasons for doing so that she did not know about?

"Fanny assures me the proprietor of their school…what is her name?'

"Miss Chalfont," Roland replied.

"Ah yes. Fanny says Miss Chalfont knows your wife's true identity. Your gabble-mouthed sister also told me de Beauchamp agreed to marry Annabelle. So, as my wits have not gone wandering, I know what that means as well as you do."

"Please enlighten me, Grandmamma."

How stern Roland sounded. Annabelle peeped through the door. The expression on his face matched his tone of voice.

"Money!" Lady Caroline trilled. "Stands to reason. Everyone knows de Beauchamp's pockets are to let, so he needs to marry for money."

Annabelle's eyes opened wide. Could it be true? Could she be an heiress? Had Roland known that? Did he marry her for her money? She pressed her hand to her head because it had begun to ache.

"And why, Hampton, did you masquerade as de Beauchamp?" her ladyship shrilled.

A short silence followed before Roland spoke. "How do you know I pretended to be Beauchamp, Grandmamma?"

Lady Caroline snorted. "Did you think my housekeeper would not tell me about your charade?"

Although Annabelle despised eavesdroppers, she could not resist the temptation to continue listening.

"Grandmamma, my wife mistook me for de Beauchamp. If I had taken her back to school, she would have run away again to avoid being forced into marriage with a man she had never met. So, I decided to place her in your care. However, when we arrived at your manor house, you had gone to Bath. And I must say, Grandmamma, considering you appeared to be on your deathbed when I promised to marry without delay, you have made a miraculous recovery."

Annabelle pressed her hand to her mouth. Hearing her husband confirm Fanny's words concerning a marriage of convenience wounded her more than any other hurt she had ever suffered.

Roland's voice pierced her thoughts. "Grandmamma, don't blame my wife for running away instead of marrying de Beauchamp."

"A bad business, my boy, he might tell his story to anyone and everyone who will listen to him. That is why I have come to collect you and your wife on my way to London with Fanny."

Matters were going from bad to worse. Not only could Juliet Parker revive an old scandal, but de Beauchamp could create a fresh one. What would people say if they found out she and Roland stayed at an inn without chaperones before they married? Again, Roland's voice broke into her thoughts. "You are taking Fanny to London, Grandmamma?"

"Yes, I must make the best of a bad bargain by presenting your wife as well as Fanny. Do not raise your eyebrows and frown at me like that. I am being kind. You are a mere viscount and I am a duke's daughter."

Roland chuckled. "Peace, I agree your blue blood outranks mine."

"Well, Hampton, I shall sponsor your wife and no one will dare to reject her. We will hold a Chinese ball that people will never forget. The servants shall wear Chinese costumes and there will be pavilions and pagodas in the garden."

Annabelle closed the door and retired to her bedchamber. In bed, she lay sleepless and tried to forget that Roland married her for mere convenience.

Annabelle pressed her hands to her temples. Why could she remember nothing significant before she lived in the cottage in Dover with her nurse? She sighed and turned over. Fanny must be delighted by Lady Caroline's decision to bring her out. Still sleepless, she sat and hugged her knees, determined to win Roland's admiration by impressing the ton.

Annabelle yawned and lay back against the downy pillows. So much had happened in so few hours it seemed as though a storm had buffeted her. Sleepy, she thought about her sister-in-law. She knew she would enjoy Fanny's company, for although her sister-in-law was sometimes insensitive, they loved each other.

She lay down and considered her situation. If de Beauchamp tittle-tattled, maybe it would be written off as no more than a disappointed suitor's spite.

A light rat-a-tat-tat sounded on the door before it opened and revealed Roland. He entered the room wearing a splendid heavy silk dressing gown over his nightshirt. "Are you exhausted?"

"No, but I am tired and mortified to have been seen in such circumstances by your grandmamma. Although she intruded on my privacy in my apartment, what must she have thought of me?"

"I neither know nor care, for she should not have intruded." He smiled, the firelight bringing a warm glow to his face. "Never allow her to intimidate you, Belle, and remember that, in spite of her affected manners and plain speaking, she has a kind heart."

"If you say so." Annabelle remained tense.

Roland sat on the edge of the bed and held her hand. "Ah, you are not convinced. When you know her better, I think you will agree with me. For the time being, she will chaperone Fanny and present you at court."

"Yes, I know, the door was ajar." Heat scalded her cheeks. "I am not in the habit of eavesdropping."

"Your honesty surprises me."

"Roland, does Lady Caroline really intend to hold a Chinese Ball? I cannot imagine Martha dressed as a Chinese maiden."

Their lips twitched with mutual amusement at the prospect of outspoken Martha's forthcoming transformation.

She wanted to ask him if he knew who her parents were, but did not voice the thought. If he did not know who they were, it would only add to her pain. If he *did* know and had kept it from her, she would be even more pained because he knew how much she wanted to discover the truth.

"Why does Lady Caroline want to hold a Chinese ball?"

"To make sure the Prince Regent attends."

"To make sure His Highness will attend?" she queried, startled by the idea of the future king visiting their London house.

"Yes, the prince won't be able to resist seeing how well she carries out her plan, for he believes he is an authority on Chinese style. And even if he does not take her bait, he would probably come because they are old friends."

Annabelle yawned. Her husband regarded her for a moment. Revealed by firelight, his eyes burned like live coals. "I will not disturb you any longer. Go to sleep," he said and retired to his apartment.

More than likely, she would dream of him. Would it have embarrassed him if she had invited him to share her bed? Was she sure she really wanted him to? Was it possible he still harboured tender feelings for Mrs Parker in spite of all his protestations? And could she really believe he would be a faithful husband? Confused and bewildered, she did not check her tears. How could so many wives tolerate sharing marital beds when they knew their husbands had mistresses?

Chapter Twenty

A fortnight after their arrival in London, Annabelle entered the ladies' drawing room. She straightened her back, conscious that Lady Caroline was scrutinising her chestnut brown pelisse worn over a honey-gold gown, colours Annabelle knew flattered her hair.

"You will do well enough." Lady Caroline spoke as though she bestowed a great honour. "Fine feathers make fine birds. I shall not be ashamed to be seen with you in the park."

Annabelle resisted the temptation to say that going for a drive with Lady Caroline would not embarrass *her*. "Thank you, madam." Satisfied with her clothes and gold earrings set with amber, she wished Roland were present to admire her.

Fanny wrinkled her nose. "But Annabelle dresses so plainly, Grandmamma."

Lady Caroline stood and smoothed the skirt of her elegant Prussian-blue carriage dress. "Fanny, you should thank God for my guidance. Without me, you would look like a fireworks display. You would make a fool of yourself by adding unfashionable frills and flounces, scallops and ribbons, lace and artificial flowers, and I know not what else to your gowns."

Annabelle pressed her mouth into a thin line. Was Lady Caroline indirectly criticising her own choice of clothes?

Her sister-in-law looked as though she was about to cry. "Fanny, don't upset yourself," Annabelle began. "Your sea-green pelisse suits you." Sorry for Fanny, she wondered if any of her unknown relatives were as astringent as Lady Caroline.

Fanny's eyes widened. "Do you really think so?"

"Yes, I do. You are beautiful and the colour emphasises your eyes. You will soon have a sea of admirers round you."

"Where is my grandson?" Lady Caroline demanded.

Annabelle suppressed a sigh. "I doubt he will accompany us today."

Lady Caroline sniffed and dabbed her nose with a dainty handkerchief. "Hampton should be constantly at your side. It is his duty to help you make your mark on society."

"Shall we go?" Annabelle asked and pressed her lips into a thin line to prevent herself from expressing how indifferent she was to Lady Caroline's opinion. Yet, she had to admit she would like Hampton to spend more time at her side.

Annabelle followed Lady Caroline and Fanny outside to the landau and seated herself opposite the elderly lady.

"Annabelle, you look tired. Are you increasing?" Lady Caroline asked, squinting through the spring sunshine.

"Grandmamma, you have made Annabelle blush."

Her cheeks burning, Annabelle shook her head at Roland and Fanny's outrageous grandparent. "No, madam, I am not with child." She countered Lady Caroline's forthright speech with plain speaking instead of using the polite euphemism "increasing" for pregnancy.

"Good, although it is your duty to provide an heir, I do not want you throwing up at the beginning of your first season."

Annabelle bit her lower lip and put a gloved hand to her cheek. What would it be like to have Roland's child? She could not imagine being a mother. A smile hovered at the corners of her mouth. One day she might have a son who would inherit his father's thick dark hair and expressive eyes.

The landau proceeded down Park Lane toward Chesterfield Gate and, although the sunshine was weak, Annabelle and Fanny raised their pagoda shaped parasols to protect their complexions.

Lady Caroline prodded Annabelle with the tip of her blue parasol, fringed with emerald green, before she unfurled it. "Did you hear me, Annabelle?" she asked in a loud voice. "I remarked that you and my grandson should not be complacent. Although the curious have called on us since our arrival in town, neither you nor Hampton can afford to make mistakes."

Lost in thoughts of her enigmatic husband, she had not heard her ladyship. "No, madam, I did not hear what you said, and in future please refrain from poking me."

"Gather your wits, it is rude to be inattentive to your elders," Lady Caroline chided after she repeated what she had said.

"As you say," Annabelle agreed.

"However, I am sure you and Fanny will be successful. We are not short of invitations," Lady Caroline purred, "and I am certain Fanny will receive vouchers for Almack's. Of course, Annabelle, you will receive the vouchers because you are Hampton's wife. If you were not, you could not hope to obtain them because you do not know who your antecedents are, so you are fortunate."

Meow, meow, meow, Annabelle thought, wearied by her grandmother-by-law's ceaseless conversation. Roland had said she had a kind heart, but as yet, Annabelle had seen no evidence of it.

Annabelle asserted herself and ordered the coachman to pull up. She beckoned to Cavalierre, who guided his well-mannered black mare to the side of the landau and bowed to her from the saddle. "Monseigneur, I am delighted to see you. I feared I would not do so before our ball." She refrained from mentioning her art lessons.

Lady Caroline cleared her throat.

"My lady, may I present Monsieur Cavalierre?" Annabelle asked.

Lady Caroline nodded.

"My lady, I have the pleasure of introducing you and Lady Fanny to Monsieur Cavalierre, the famous artist. Monseigneur, Lady Caroline, my husband's grandmamma and Lady Fanny, his sister."

"Monsieur not Monseigneur."

"I have always called you Monseigneur and shall continue to do so."

Fanny smiled at him but Lady Caroline did no more than nod.

"I am pleased to make your acquaintance, Monsieur Cavalierre," said Fanny.

"And I am pleased to meet so delightful a young lady," he replied with his customary courtesy. He bowed again from the saddle, this time to Lady Caroline. "Madame, I am happy to make your acquaintance. I have often admired you from a distance and wished for the honour of painting your portrait."

Lady Caroline preened like a parrot and tweaked an unnaturally fiery curl while Annabelle repressed her amusement.

Cavalierre inclined his head to Fanny. "How charming you are, mademoiselle, I will be pleased to paint you. If you will allow me to do so, please wear green."

"Stop simpering, Fanny," Lady Caroline snapped.

While Cavalierre smiled at Fanny, Annabelle pretended not to have heard the reprimand and wondered if she was fortunate not to be burdened by relatives.

"Lady Hampton," Cavalierre said. "That fierce husband of yours, he does not ride by your carriage today?"

"Hampton is not fierce, Monseigneur."

"You are mistaken, *Cherie*, he is a very fierce gentleman. At the masquerade, he glared at your admirers. If his jealousy could have set them on fire, they would be dead."

Could Cavalierre be right? If she had an ardent admirer, would Roland be as jealous of him as she was of Juliet? Thoughtful, she smiled at Cavalierre. "We are to hold a Chinese ball. I shall send you an invitation."

Before Cavalierre could reply, Lady Caroline cleared her throat ostentatiously. "Please excuse us, Monsieur."

Cavalierre doffed his hat.

"Drive on," Lady Caroline ordered the coachman.

As the landau passed through the Chesterfield Gate into Hyde Park and then approached the Serpentine, Lady Caroline glared at Annabelle. "It will not do."

"I beg your pardon?" Annabelle scanned Rotten Row in the hope that Roland had changed his mind and was riding in the park.

Lady Caroline fingered the green ostrich plumes—dyed to match the fringe on her parasol—that curled round the brim of her poke bonnet. "My dear Annabelle, you cannot invite an artist to the ball."

"Yes, I can. French émigrés are accepted in the best circles, and I know my husband will approve."

"Folly," Lady Caroline snapped.

Annabelle ignored the elderly woman's rudeness. Where *was* Roland? She nibbled her lower lip. Juliet Parker had come to town to stay with her godmother. Of course she would not be received at court and many doors would be closed to her. Nevertheless, for her godmother's sake, some people might receive her. Were Roland's assurances concerning the odious creature no more than false pretences? Was he visiting Mrs Parker while she rode in the park with his grandmamma and sister?

"Is something wrong, Annabelle?" Fanny asked.

"What could be wrong when I am so fortunate?" she asked, her voice unintentionally bitter as she indicated members of the ton taking the air, in carriages, on horseback or on foot.

"Home," Lady Caroline ordered the coachman and looked at Annabelle and Fanny. "We have been seen and will rest before going to the opera this evening, and then attending the Duchess of Houghton's ball. This racketing will be the death of me. Fanny, I hope you appreciate my efforts on your behalf. The Duchess has a son who would be a suitable husband for you."

Instead of listening to Lady Caroline name eligible bachelors, and once more warn Fanny about undesirables, Annabelle scanned the crowd again in the hope of seeing Roland.

During the drive home, Annabelle's companions spoke little. When she alighted outside her house, she decided that in future, instead of accompanying Lady Caroline, she would ride in the park on horseback. What's more, if Fanny wanted to, she could ride with her. Thoughtful, she made her way to her parlour where Roland awaited her.

His manner languid, Roland stood. "Belle, I believe the season will be more exhausting than a military campaign."

"Do you?" She untied the brown and gold striped ribbons of her leghorn hat.

"Belle, please do not take it off, I have something to show you."

"What?" she asked, as eager as a curious child expecting a treat.

"A surprise." He tucked her hand into the crook of his arm and led her to the stables.

Annabelle squeezed Roland's arm with her free hand and stared at the horse Dan led toward her. "Empress, oh Roland, you found her."

Roland took the reins from Dan. "It is more a case of Empress finding you, Belle, for she made her way back to The Beeches and I sent Dan to bring her up to town."

The mare whinnied a welcome, nuzzled her, and stood still while Annabelle petted her. "Oh yes, clever girl, you remember me. Gently, if you nudge me like that I will fall over." She looked up, saw her husband's smile, and cast herself into his arms. "Thank you, oh thank you, Roland."

He held her close and looked down at her. Flames burned in the depths of his eyes. "Not the thing to kiss you here and now, although I am tempted to."

"No, you should not." Annabelle withdrew from his embrace.

The mare snorted and whickered for attention. "She is a beauty," Roland commented, the flames in his eyes doused. "Belle, I hope you will prefer riding in the park with me to taking the air in the landau with my grandmamma."

Of course she would. "Thank you, I would like to ride with you." She hoped he understood how happy she was to have Empress restored to her.

"Good, I thought my suggestion would please you." He removed a glove and held an apple out for Empress on the palm of his bare hand.

Annabelle patted Empress's neck. "You are so kind to me, Roland."

"As I told you once before, husbands should be kind to their wives." Roland seemed to be breathing a little faster than usual as he stared into her eyes. "Take the mare back to her stall," Roland ordered a groom and lowered his head. "If you permit me, I shall be much kinder," he whispered in Annabelle's ear.

"Of course I will permit you, but what do you mean?"

"We have not enjoyed a honeymoon," Roland replied in a voice too low to be overheard.

She stiffened. Could she be certain he was not dallying with Juliet Parker?

Before Annabelle could speak, Martha bustled across the cobbles. "My lady," she began and bobbed a curtsey, "Lady Caroline says that if you are not to look tired tonight, you must rest."

Roland's mouth curled. "It would not do for you to look tired," he growled.

Chapter Twenty-One

During the following ten days, Annabelle found few opportunities to be in private with Roland. Lady Caroline had made up her mind the ball would be the success of the season. In a whirl of activity, she issued frenzied orders to the servants, demanding perfection and even keeping the family busy. Exhausted by the eve of the ball, she retired to bed, leaving Annabelle and Fanny amazed by the transformed garden.

Blue and gold silk hangings lined blue, green, red, and yellow pavilions. Brass bells hanging in strings, from both a mock pagoda and pseudo-temple, chimed in the slightest breeze. Large ornamental Buddhas stood in positions where they could be best admired. To complete the magical effect, globular lanterns hung from the branches of every tree.

Yet, at nuncheon on the day of the ball, Lady Caroline seemed dissatisfied. "Pray," she said. "Pray as you have never prayed before."

For a moment, Annabelle wondered if Roland's grandmother had become religious. So far she had seen no sign the lady was unduly devout.

Roland sipped his wine. "For what should we pray?"

"For it not to rain! What would the Prince say if it does?"

"Shall we go indoors?" Roland answered, gesturing to the butler to pour him more coffee.

"What?" Lady Caroline asked.

"If it rains, I presume His Highness will say, 'Shall we go indoors?'"

Fanny tittered and Annabelle bent her head, wishing that if her parents lived they would attend the ball. If they could, she hoped they would be proud of her.

Lady Caroline rapped Roland's knuckles. "Yes, of course we shall go inside if it rains. The house is ready to receive our guests. No expense has been spared."

"I know." Roland raised an eyebrow. "It seems as though it's your ambition to bankrupt me, Grandmamma."

"Nonsense, you told me you wanted everything to be the best and, as one of the richest men in England, you can afford it."

Annabelle's breath caught in her throat. She had so much to learn about her husband. She had known he was wealthy, but had never guessed the extent of his fortune. Yet, if their marriage had been conventional, she would have known, because their attorneys would have drawn up marriage contracts.

Roland looked at her before he replied to his grandmother. "You are mistaken. I cannot purchase everything I want."

Head cocked to one side, Lady Caroline looked at Roland.

"Just so, Grandmamma." He smiled. "Enough of that, you are right, I do want everything to be of the best, and it would not do to stint on the wine, but was it necessary to dress every servant in Chinese costume? My butler does not like it. He tells me it is beneath his dignity."

"Nonsense, the Prince has assured me he will wear a splendid costume. If that is not beneath his Royal Highness's dignity, it cannot be beneath your butler's. His Highness will be enchanted by the costumes and, if fortune favours us, he will approve of Fanny and Annabelle."

"Who would not approve of my wife and sister?" Roland asked with an appreciative gleam in his eyes.

* * *

To Lady Caroline's relief, the weather remained balmy on the morning of the ball and a refreshing breeze played through the strings of bells causing them to tinkle melodiously. "Either God has answered my prayers," she declared, "or He had not planned rain."

In the afternoon, she ordered Annabelle and Fanny to rest, after which she bustled about, getting in the way of the servants and the caterers.

Roland put his arm around her shoulders. "I pay my butler well to perform his duties. Allow him to carry them out instead of trying his patience. Besides, I do not want my favourite grandmamma to be tired tonight. Please go and have a nap."

Laughter filled her eyes. "Flatterer, you only have one living grandmother."

Roland hugged her. "Even if my other grandmother were alive, I am sure you would be my favourite."

"Very well, I shall rest. Annabelle, off to your bedchamber. Fanny, why are you dawdling? Did I not tell you to rest?"

* * *

Annabelle woke before dusk and watched Martha, garbed in a white robe patterned with flowers and figures in various shades of blue, put a tray on a table by the bed.

"You look nice." Annabelle yawned and stretched before she sat.

Martha patted her thick sandy-coloured hair, arranged in a roll at the back of her head and ornamented with a skewer-like pin, decorated with artificial lily-of-the-valley and ribbon. "I look like a buffoon."

"Nonsense, you look dignified."

Martha pointed at the tray. "Lady Caroline wants you to eat all the bread and butter. She says it's best to eat something so you won't faint while you are receiving the guests who have been invited to dine before the ball."

Annabelle eyed the tray unenthusiastically. "Take it away, I never faint."

Martha poured some tea and handed the dish to her. "My lady, do eat a little."

Annabelle shook her head.

Her dresser sniffed as though she had been mortally offended. "And wasn't I particular about your bread being sliced very thin?"

"One slice," Annabelle agreed.

An hour later, Annabelle stared at her reflection. Her robe, which she had designed, was a masterpiece. Cream silk, with the delicate colours and patterns of Canton Rose porcelain, flowed in sinuous lines from her neck to her dainty black slippers. She was staring with amazement at her altered appearance when Roland's image in the mirror startled her. "You live up to my soubriquet for you, Belle."

She stared at her blushing reflection. "I beg your pardon," she said, looking at her black wig arranged in an oriental style.

"Does Belle not mean beauty? I shall be jealous of every gentleman who pays you a compliment."

Was he serious or was he flirting? With the hope that he was serious, she picked up her ivory fan, painted with elegant Chinese ladies and mandarins, opened the leaves, and fluttered it. "You are funny Roland."

"Am I? Can you not imagine me being jealous?"

Could Cavalierre be right about Roland having been jealous of her admirers at the masquerade?

"Yes, but I...that is, why should you be jealous? You did not marry me for love."

Even if he said she was mistaken and told a lie by saying he loved her, it would be a kindness she would treasure.

"Have you ever read a story in which the husband and wife fall in love after they are married?"

Roland raised her hand to his lips. Desire shot through her. She trembled and looked away from him.

He released her hand. "Do you like my rig?"

She put her cool hands against her overheated cheeks and admired his black silk, gold embroidered robe. "Very much, I am sure the ladies will admire you and I shall be jealous."

Roland laughed. Her eyes widened, then, embarrassed—for she did not want to reveal too much—she looked down.

Roland's arms went around her waist.

"Be careful, you will rumple my wig and my gown."

Her husband sighed, and led her by the hand into her parlour.

Annabelle noticed a flat box on a dainty inlaid mahogany table set in front of the chaise longue. She pointed at it. "Is that for me? What is it?"

"Open it, Belle."

"You spoil me."

"It is my pleasure to do so."

She opened the box.

"Allow me." Roland fastened one of his gifts, a jade hairpin with a butterfly on a spring—designed to make the wings quiver with every movement—into her hair.

"How can I thank you for such a delightful present?"

"There is no need to." He pushed back a silk fold and kissed the nape of her neck. "You smell delicious." His hands clasped her shoulders.

She anticipated his intention to kiss her. "Be careful, don't disarrange my hair." She turned to face him, trying to ignore the shivers of anticipation running up and down her spine. "Why do you stare at me so?"

"Am I staring? How impolite of me. But even an alley cat may stare at a queen." He cleared his throat and picked up the butterfly-shaped jade earrings, another of his gifts. "Ask Martha to help you. She will not dishevel you," he said in a harsh tone.

* * *

"The ball exceeded all my hopes," Lady Caroline crowed to Roland after the last guest departed. "Everyone of importance remarked on how long His Highness graced it with his presence." She shook her head. "What am I thinking of, Roland? Annabelle, you look exhausted. Fanny, you are nearly asleep on your feet."

Roland smiled at his grandmamma and beckoned to the butler. "Champagne."

Glass in hand he raised it. "A toast to you with my thanks, Grandmamma."

"Thank you, my dear boy." Lady Caroline's hand shook with obvious fatigue. Some wine spilled down the front of her plum-coloured silk robe embroidered with plum blossoms and delicate butterflies.

"Go to bed," Roland advised. "Fanny, please help Grandmamma upstairs. Come, Annabelle."

"I am not an invalid," Lady Caroline protested and shook off the hand with which Fanny held her elbow.

"Of course you're not," Fanny agreed, "but please allow me to help you."

Roland looked at his half-sister. "I was very proud of you tonight. I wish Mamma had lived to see you make your debut."

Fanny's eyes moistened as she fingered her shimmering white silk gown, embroidered in many shades of green. "I wish my papa as well as our mamma could have seen me."

Roland pinched her cheek, but not hard enough to hurt her. "Mamma's pearls suit you."

"Oh," Fanny squealed. "I am very sorry. I did not have a moment to thank you for giving them to me. Thank you very much. I shall always treasure them."

"Very suitable for a young lady," Lady Caroline said and yawned.

"Goodnight." Roland cupped Annabelle's elbow with his hand and guided her up the stairs to her private parlour. "We are rarely alone during the day and at night you are always so tired that you fall asleep as soon as your head touches the pillow." His mouth curved into a crooked smile.

"I am sure I will tonight. Moreover, my poor Martha must be exhausted. I hope she dozed while waiting to attend me."

"She may go to bed, I can play her part."

"What an…an improper suggestion."

"Yes, I suppose it is," Roland said slowly, while thinking how naïve his wife was. He sank onto a chair. "There is a problem I wish to discuss with you."

Annabelle arched her eyebrows and sat opposite him.

"During the day, gentlemen haunt the house in the hope of a kind word from you."

"Surely you are mistaken. They frequent the house in the hope of a kind word from Fanny," his wife said, with what seemed to be genuine modesty.

He ignored her remark. "And, every morning, Belle, you either get up before me, or Fanny and Martha enter your room before I do. What's more, from then on, both of us are busy until late at night when you are so tired that I sleep in my bedchamber instead of yours."

"I have never asked you to do so," Annabelle said in a small voice and looked away from him.

"But you never so much as hint that I would be welcome in your sanctum." His wife's cheeks flamed. "Forgive me, Belle, I daresay you think it ill-bred of me to speak thus."

Of course, he was the master of the house and could enter her bedchamber whenever he chose, but he had always wanted more than dutiful submission from whomever he would marry. Long ago, his mother had told him that she and his father were almost strangers when they wed but, she had explained, they soon began to love each other. "And," she had ended, "although married couples in our milieu do not expect to fall in love, it is so much more comfortable if they care for one another, as your papa and I do." He remembered the rosy colour that had tinted her cheeks, making him think she was embarrassed to speak of so personal a matter. She had then clasped his hands and gazed deeply into his eyes. "I hope that one day you will marry a lady who…makes you as happy, as I hope I have made your dear papa." He had no doubt she made his father happy, for, whenever she entered a room which Father occupied, a light appeared in Father's eyes and he spoke in the appreciative tone of voice he reserved for Mamma.

Roland sighed. If he wanted a happy marriage, forcing his presence on his wife in her bedchamber would not bode well. Whether or not they grew to love each other, surely they could be affectionate and enjoy each other's company. Well, for the moment, he would not speak of intimate matters but he must break the awkward silence between them. "Did you enjoy the ball, Belle?"

Annabelle looked at him again, her eyes glowing. "Yes, everyone, including the Prince Regent, was kind. In fact, I did not expect His Highness to be so gracious. Do you know what he said when I thanked him?"

"No, but I'm sure you're going to tell me," he teased.

"He said, 'Wellington praised your husband so I must not neglect to praise such a brave major's wife.'"

"The devil he did!" he exclaimed, much gratified but with commendable modesty. "Goodnight, Belle. Sleep well."

* * *

In spite of her fatigue, it took Annabelle some time to fall asleep. If only she could be sure that Roland no longer associated with Juliet Parker, she would welcome him to her bed. Eventually she slept well, and it was not until very late on the morning after the ball, that she visited Cavalierre, who stood as soon as she entered his drawing room.

"Are you not well, *ma petite*? After your success last night, I expected to see you flushed with triumph."

Annabelle sat, and pleated and re-pleated the skirt of her lilac carriage gown.

Cavalierre poured a glass of golden wine for her. "*Cherie*, you should be radiant instead of pale and listless."

Her nostrils flared. "If I am pale, it is because I must find out who my parents are."

Cavalierre sat facing her and sipped his wine before he spoke. "Ah, *Ma Petite*, your husband has so much influence. I suggest you ask him to trace them."

Her lips quivered. She caught them between her teeth and shook her head.

"Confide in your viscount."

She shook her head again. "I must not plague him. He knows I want to find out about Mamma and Papa."

Cavalierre's wrinkled face creased with obvious concern for her.

Glass in hand, Annabelle rose and paced up and down the drawing room. "Most people are courteous, but there are questions in their eyes. You cannot imagine how their curiosity makes me suffer. They glance suspiciously at me and then whisper to each other."

Cavalierre straightened his back. "Ignore the gossips, they will soon find someone else to talk about."

She slumped onto a chair. "No one understands how distressed I am because I cannot hold my head up high in society."

"Calm yourself, such passion does not help. Before you spill it, drink your wine. It will restore you," Cavalierre advised—although she noticed his long fingers tense round the stem of his glass.

"I shall take my leave, Monseigneur, please forgive me for troubling you with my problem."

"I hope you will always feel free to confide in me, but you should also confide in your husband," Cavalierre said, his face stern.

Thoughtful, Annabelle returned home. She descended from her carriage and looked up at the leaden sky.

Later, in spite of the unseasonable chill, Martha helped her to change into a pale pink muslin gown sprigged with posies. Satisfied with her appearance, Annabelle went into her parlour and settled on the day bed in front of a cheerful fire.

"Martha, no one is to be admitted."

After Martha arranged a paisley shawl over Annabelle's legs, she went into the dressing room.

The door between her own and her husband's apartment opened and Roland entered her parlour.

"The sun has come out, Belle. Shall we ride in the park?" He drew closer and frowned down at her. "You look distressed and tired." He bent over, took her hands in his, and drew her to her feet. "I thought you would be radiant after your success at the ball. You won everyone's heart." Her husband sat, drew her onto his lap, and cradled her in his arms.

The pit of her stomach tightened with desire. "You are very kind, Roland, but you are mistaken. People whisper about me because they don't know who my parents are." Oh, she could not bear the excitement caused by his intimate proximity. She tried to stand but Roland's arms held her too firmly.

"Ignore the whispers and they will die down."

She hesitated before deciding to take Cavalierre's advice and confide in her husband yet again. "I want to know who my parents are, who my guardian was, and why I was ordered to marry Baron de Beauchamp."

"Belle—"

She sat and stared into the depths of his dark eyes. "Are you like everyone else? Can you not imagine what it is like to be rootless in a society of people able to trace their ancestry? Can you not imagine what it is like not to know if you have parents, brothers, sisters, aunts and uncles?"

"However much I sympathise, I cannot really understand what it is like not to know about one's family, but I believe that one day you will have the answers to your questions. In the meantime, hold your head high and behave as though the bluest of blood runs through your veins."

"You should not have married me."

"Why not? You are the only lady I ever asked to become my wife."

"Truly?" Her spirits momentarily lifted before they sank again. "You really shouldn't have married me, because I do not add to your consequence."

"Fustian! What do I care for my consequence?"

If only he would indicate what his feelings were for her. Say that he liked her…say he was pleased she was his wife…something, anything to encourage her.

"Belle, has it ever occurred to you that your identity might have been kept secret to keep you out of danger?"

"How serious you look. Do you know something about me which you have not shared with me?"

He cleared his throat and looked up at the moulded ceiling. "Belle, please stop looking at me so anxiously. If you trust me, I hope all will be well."

"Can I trust you? You lied to me twice about your identity. Are you sure you are not concealing anything else from me?"

Roland looked at her. The expression in his eyes hardened and his cheeks paled as though his honour had been insulted. "Why the devil should you not trust me in spite of my trickery which, under the circumstances, you should be able to forgive?" He cleared his throat again. "I beg your pardon for swearing, Belle."

She looked down at the pretty pink carpet patterned with stylised ribbons, pastel flowers, and leaves.

"Am I never to be forgiven?"

Her answer stuck in her throat.

"Belle, I am not the sort of husband to demand obedience, but it would please me if you would ride in the park with me. The fresh air would benefit you."

Did he want her company, honestly want it? "Very well." She stood and went to her bedroom to change.

For once, her dresser remained silent while she arranged the blood-red folds of Annabelle's broadcloth riding habit, trimmed with the gold braid of an officer's uniform. The peaked hat, with a gold cockade, completed the ensemble. Martha stepped back to judge the effect. "The colour suits you, my lady, and the gold coloured buttons are dashing."

"That will do, Martha." Annabelle glanced in the mirror. Yes, her rig should make an impression on the fashionable people in the park.

"You are very clever to be able to design your own clothes," Martha said.

Annabelle smiled at Martha, picked up her gloves and riding crop, and went downstairs to the entrance hall where Roland waited for her.

He looked her up and down and smiled. "You are dressed in the military fashion," he commented with an appreciative glint in his eyes. "I like your hat, it is very fetching."

Before she could thank him for the compliment, Lady Caroline and Fanny came into the hall.

"You are losing the roses in your cheeks, Annabelle. Are you sure you do not have a happy announcement to make?" Lady Caroline asked, as deplorably forthright as ever.

Annabelle wished the servants did not overhear so much, which, in her opinion, should be private. She narrowed her eyes at her ladyship and shook her head.

"Hampton, are you not proud of your wife and your sister?" Lady Caroline rattled on. "They are acknowledged beauties. I heard Annabelle referred to as *An Incomparable* and Lady Jersey said Fanny is beautiful and her manners are charming."

"Would I dare to disagree?" asked Roland.

Lady Caroline laughed and reproved him with a tap on his arm. "Wretch!"

"Very well, Grandmamma, I admit I am very proud of them."

He offered Lady Caroline his arm and led her into the street where the landau, his horse, and Annabelle's mare, Empress, awaited them. After he ushered his grandmother and sister into the vehicle, he turned to Annabelle and helped her up into her side saddle.

With Roland beside her, Annabelle proceeded to Hyde Park, where her riding habit attracted much attention. They drew rein several times to greet those Annabelle already knew and for Roland to introduce her to several acquaintances. Then, while Roland spoke to a young captain who had served in his brigade, de Beauchamp approached them. His gooseberry eyes goggled at her. Before he could reach them, Roland bade farewell to the young captain and they guided their horses along Rotten Row.

Annabelle opened her eyes wide and gasped in response to a sudden realisation. She looked back and glimpsed de Beauchamp. Without doubt, the disagreeable toad knew her guardian's identity. How stupid of her not to have thought of that before. Her dislike of him had clouded her common sense. She must speak to him. Could she arrange a *tête-à-tête* with the toad without risking her reputation?

As soon as they returned from their ride, Annabelle penned a note to de Beauchamp and sealed it. She hurried out of her apartment and reached the stables without being intercepted by Roland, Lady Caroline, or Fanny—who would be sure to ask her where she was going.

Luck favoured her in the stable yard, where Dan was about to enter Empress's stall. "Dan," she called in a low voice and beckoned to him.

He tugged his forelock and grinned at her. "My lady."

"I want you to do something for me."

"Very good, my lady," he replied, his hazel eyes curious.

"Find out where a Frenchman called Baron de Beauchamp lives."

Dan nodded.

She handed him the note, stamped with her seal. "Take this note to him and do not mention it to anyone."

His eyes glowed more green than hazel in the sunlight. "A secret?"

"Yes." She handed him a shilling. "Dan, if the baron is at home, please wait for a reply. When you return, give it to Martha. If he is not at home, leave a message that you will return to collect his reply tomorrow."

Annabelle fretted until early evening, when Martha handed her a cream-coloured missive. Annabelle broke the green wax wafer and read the reply. A shiver ran down her spine. Tomorrow, she might know who her parents were. She pressed her hands to her cheeks. Suppose her past shamed her and, even worse, shamed Roland.

Chapter Twenty-Two

His feet on the fender, Roland leaned back in one of the large, comfortable wing chairs in his club and ordered a bottle of Madeira wine. He frowned, thinking of his enchanting wife. Roland wanted her to be happy but, to ensure her safety—until he pieced together all the facts—he would not reveal her former guardian's identity.

"Rolly!" a tall, well-built gentleman exclaimed, his voice breaking into Roland's unquiet thoughts.

"Goldilocks, when did you return?"

Roland stood, looked into his friend's sherry-brown eyes, and shook his hand. He smiled, watching his comrade in arms, Harry Markham, rumple the guinea-gold curls which, when they were both at Eton, caused him to be nick-named Goldilocks.

"Spare me the nicknames," Markham joked after he sat on the wing chair adjacent to Roland's and stretched out his long legs. "To answer your question, I returned last week. There's little to do in Paris and my father wanted me to come home, so Wellington released me as there is no longer much to do in our line of business."

After Roland ordered another bottle of wine, he settled against the back of his chair. "Will you stay in England?"

Markham rolled his eyes. "Think so. I am about to sell my commission. As you know, I'm the eldest son and my father says it is time to do my duty, both to the family and the estates and—" He rolled his eyes, "marry one of the eligible ladies, my parents favour, then produce an heir."

Roland chuckled at his friend's mock despair.

"By the way, Rolly, I hear *you* are shackled. Does being a tenant for life suit you? Am I to congratulate you or commiserate with you?"

"Both," Roland replied too quickly and castigated himself. No gentleman should discuss his marriage even with his best friend. "My wife is an angel."

"You said *both*. I do congratulate you but wonder why I should commiserate with you." Markham prompted, his eyes alert.

"Oh, no need to commiserate. I was funning about exchanging freedom for petticoat rule."

An old gentleman woke from his doze. "Shush, you young whippersnappers. Have you no respect for your elders?"

"My apology, sir," Roland replied, "and I am sure I also speak for my friend."

"Don't fret, Rolly." Markham's eyes filled with amusement. "Take my advice. If marriage is not to your liking, there are plenty of pretty birds to enjoy."

Roland's hand gripped the stem of his wineglass. "I am one of a peculiar breed, a faithful husband."

Markham cleared his throat. "Do you still see Juliet Parker?"

"No, that affair is long over."

"Did not mean to offend you, Rolly, but you did imply you do not enjoy petticoat rule at home, so I wondered."

"Oh, as for that, those petticoats are grandmother, my stepsister Fanny, and my wife's dresser, a confounded giantess of a woman with an unruly tongue who is devoted to my wife. Would you believe she has the impertinence to call me a 'black-hearted devil'?"

"Why? What have you done to her?"

"Nothing! *Lord*, was ever a man so plagued," Roland complained. "Sent my sister to my grandmother in Bath and what did they do? They turned up on our doorstep so that Grandmamma can present my wife and Fanny at court." He held his glass up to the light and squinted at it. "*Job*."

His friend looked round the room. "*Job* who? Have I met the fellow?"

"Chicken head, I mean the fellow in the Bible," Roland said, with familiarity bred by affection for his friend.

"Oh, you mean you are like that Biblical fellow, the long suffering Job." Markham's face brightened. "There is a simple solution. Get rid of the dresser."

"Can't, my wife is devoted to her."

"Thing is—and please do not take offence at my question—is your wife devoted to you?"

Roland narrowed his eyes. "Damn you, if any other man put such a question to me, I would never speak to him again if I did not call him out."

"My apologies, I should not have asked. The wine is loosening my tongue. Are you hungry?"

Roland peered fondly at his friend. "Yes, some food will put both of us to right." He stood and led his friend into the dining room with the intention of enjoying steak and kidney pudding. To avoid being disturbed by friends or acquaintances, they sat at a table in a dimly lit booth.

"Good," Roland murmured half way through the meal.

"I beg your pardon?"

"De Beauchamp and his crony have just sat down in the booth behind ours."

"No law against that, Rolly. Stands to reason a gentleman dines frequently at his club. And it stands to reason most of us visit our club every day."

Roland eyed Markham. "Gentleman! You and I know the truth about him," he snapped. "And what's more, I do not like the cut of the fellow's coat any better than I have ever done. Anyway, one of the reasons I joined this club is that he is a member and he dines here nearly every day." He stilled at the sound of the baron's voice.

"On my honour as a gentleman, I believe the lady regrets marrying Hampton instead of me." De Beauchamp spoke low, but not low enough for them not to overhear him. "She sent me a message asking me to meet her near the milk booth in Hyde Park at nine o'clock tomorrow morning, when most of the fashionables are still in their beds."

Roland sat as rigid as a tent pole before he half rose from his seat.

"Steady, Rolly. If you don't want your wife's name to be bandied about town you cannot challenge him to a duel. Think of the scandal."

A crease formed across Roland's forehead. "Damn it, you are right, Goldilocks."

"You're a lucky dog, de Beauchamp. Lady Hampton's a tasty morsel," the baron's crony said.

Markham reached across the table to restrain Roland by clutching his forearm. "Take no notice of them. I am sure there's a reasonable explanation. Stands to reason, no woman in her right mind could prefer de Beauchamp to you."

Never had he been so hot to engage in a duel, but appreciative of Markham's good advice, he restrained himself and sank back onto his seat. "Why would my wife want to meet him in private? She ran away from school rather than marry the fellow."

Markham rested his elbows on the table and propped his chin in his cupped hands. "Always happy to lend an ear and honoured to be your second if it comes to it."

"Thank you, rest assured I shall call on your services if they are necessary." He pushed the plate of half-finished food away. "For now I bid you goodnight."

On his way out of the dining room, Roland paused to stare at the scoundrel hard enough to make his cheeks pale beneath his rouge. The thought of his dainty wife with that gross man enraged him.

Furious, Roland made his way home. Should he believe what the baron said? Instinct told him he should. However, why would his wife arrange an assignation with a man she called a toad?

He turned the corner of the street and marched to his house where the first footman admitted him and helped him to remove his coat. "Have the ladies retired?"

"Yes, my lord."

"I thought so, the house is very quiet." Roland went to his bedroom where his eyes widened at the sight of his wife seated in a chair by the fireplace.

"Why are you here and where is Jones? He should be waiting for me."

"I dismissed him," Annabelle explained.

"To what do I owe the pleasure of your company?" he spoke in an unsteady voice due to the shock of "the toad's" words.

"We were engaged to dine at the Amersham's before going to the theatre. I was worried when you did not come home to escort us. I cried off, in spite of your grandmamma scolding me and saying that I cannot expect you to dance attendance on me all the time."

He eyed his wife. The sparkle of diamonds enhanced her fair skin, revealed by the low-cut neckline of her sinuous, ivory satin gown. Never had he desired her more. Nevertheless, furious over her assignation with de Beauchamp, he clasped his hands tightly behind his back. "Oh, I apologise, I thought we were to dine with them tomorrow." If she had ever showed any signs of real warmth for him since their marriage, he might enjoy dancing attendance on her more often. As things were, his desire to enjoy intimacy with her had been somewhat dampened, although he admitted to himself he did spend a lot of time thinking about her delectable body.

He scowled. Should he ask her if she had arranged an assignation with de Beauchamp? No, she might deny it and then he would never know the truth of the matter. "I am sorry I forgot our engagement to dine with Lord and Lady Amersham, but it is not for Grandmamma to tell you what you may or may not expect of me." His frame of mind was exacerbated by his wife's assignation. He flung himself onto a chair and tried not to glower at her.

"Why are you so cross?"

"I am not," Roland said with absolute honesty, for he was more than cross. He looked at her with eyes half closed, heard her quick intake of breath, and saw her breasts rise enticingly.

"Lady Caroline took Fanny to the Amersham's and when she returned, she told me she had made our excuses."

Despite her angelic face, who knew what devilish schemes might have hatched in her brain? "We cannot be expected to accept every invitation we receive."

"I know, but we accepted an invitation to dine with them, and I am told nothing is more vexatious to a hostess than the numbers at dinner falling short of those she anticipated."

He scowled again. Annabelle looked away from him as though scared. Surely she knew he would never hurt her. She stood and dipped into a graceful curtsey. "It is late, my lord, I shall see you tomorrow. I will summon Jones."

Roland stared at Annabelle as she went into her apartment and closed the door.

A few minutes passed before Jones hurried into the room, brushing crumbs from his jacket. "My lord, I apologise for not being in attendance on you, but her ladyship insisted on waiting here for you."

"Don't look so worried, Jones. It is your duty to obey your mistress, and it is not a sin to eat. Now, help me undress and wake me at seven o'clock."

Tomorrow, by hook or by crook he would find out whether de Beauchamp lied or not about meeting Annabelle.

* * *

His years in the army taught Roland to be aware of even the smallest disturbance. As soon as his valet opened the bedroom door, Roland opened his eyes. "What time is it?"

"Seven o'clock, my lord."

Roland thrust his feet over the side of the bed and stood. He would soon know if de Beauchamp had lied about having an assignation with Annabelle. After putting on a dressing gown, he knocked on the door of his wife's bedroom. No reply. "Annabelle," he said in a thunderous tone of voice.

The door opened and Martha peered at him. "My lady begs your pardon, my lord, but says it is not convenient for her to speak to you now."

How dare she deny him entry? Was he not the master of the house? He glared at Martha, suspecting she had prevaricated to hide her mistress's absence. "Stand aside," he ordered and strode across the threshold.

No sooner had he spoken, than he was ashamed. During his years of confidential service in the army, regardless of the situation, he had been calm and easy going. What was more, he had never lost his temper with any member of the fair sex, not even Juliet when she was at her most aggravating. Now he was in danger of losing it. He shrugged. Any husband with justification for harbouring suspicions about his wife's morals could be pardoned for having a short temper.

Martha scowled at him, murmured something about black-hearted devils, something she had not done for some time, and then stood aside and withdrew into the dressing room.

He swallowed. Surely he had not imbibed enough wine last night to cause hallucinations. There was definitely a slender man dressed in black in his wife's bedroom. His righteous indignation drove him forward. *By Jove and all that was wonderful,* yesterday evening he had been unable to challenge de Beauchamp, but he could and would challenge this stripling. "Name your seconds," he snarled, conscious of his wife's perfume—an elusive blend of lily-of-the-valley and a hint of something less sweet.

"If it is your wish," the figure said, and turned to face him. "But do you not recognise me?"

Shocked by his wife's voice, his mind reeled. Could he be suffering from fantasies, like some poor creature in a madhouse? "Madam, why are you dressed like a man? It is immodest."

Annabelle sat and crossed one long slim leg over the other. "I am learning to fence. These clothes are best suited to my lessons. Skirts would hamper me."

"The devil they would! I beg your pardon for swearing, but, I ask you, who is mad enough to teach you? Ladies do not engage in sword play."

"This lady does, and to answer your question, a friend of Monseigneur instructs me."

"Curse Cavalierre! What is he thinking of to aid you in such a foolhardy pursuit?"

"Don't blame him. He knew if he refused to help me, I would have sought a fencing master elsewhere."

"You will lose your reputation and Grandmamma will never forgive me."

"Lady Caroline would not be shocked. Do you not know that she knows how to fence? She learned the art in India, where she never knew if she might need to defend herself. Your grandfather was not as stuffy as you are."

"Stuffy? You think I am stuffy?" Roland roared, and then forced himself to be calm. "Besides, why are you learning the art of swordsmanship?"

His wife grinned mischievously. "I had wanted to learn since childhood, so I seized the opportunity to do so."

"It is a masculine skill," he protested, with the realisation that although he wanted to grab hold of her and strip her of those provocative garments, he preferred her in the femininity of the clothes she designed, which flowed over her well-shaped body.

"I am not the only lady to learn to fence so that she can defend herself, and I did not think you would object, my lord."

"If you thought that, you would have told me about your lessons. Moreover, what sort of husband do you think I am? Of course, I object to my wife dressing like a man. Besides, you do not need to defend yourself. You have me to defend you."

She looked at him thoughtfully. "Are you able to defend me, my lord?"

Rendered speechless for a moment by the enormity of her question, he recovered himself. "Oh, Belle, what am I to do with you?" *Love her*, an inner voice prompted in answer to his question. Harassed by the responsibility of being married to such an innocent young lady, he ran a hand through his hair and wondered why his wife looked at him so wistfully. His heart softened for a moment before he decided the unspoken entreaty was probably a wilful attempt to get her own way. "Of course I can defend you. How do you think I survived the war against Napoleon? I am more than capable of defending you, but if you must learn to fence, I shall teach you, for even if I forbid you to learn, I suspect you might defy me."

The dimples on either side of her mouth deepened. "Oh, Roland, you are the best of husbands." She stepped lightly toward him and pressed a careless kiss on his unshaven cheek.

He seized the moment to kiss her, thrilled when her lips parted. All too soon, she pressed her hands against his chest and he released her.

The colour in her cheeks heightened. "You are mistaken."

"About what?"

"I did not ask your permission to learn, because I thought you would refuse and I knew I could not defy you."

He looked into the depths of her beautiful eyes that seemed guileless. "Are you keeping any other secrets from me?"

His wife nodded.

Thank God, she would confess to the assignation with de Beauchamp and explain the reason for it.

She wriggled out of his arms. "Please sit, Roland, instead of looming over me and frowning. The thing is, a diet of only routs and balls, recitals, and other entertainments bore me, so I study art with Monseigneur and am learning to play the harp."

When his wife sat opposite him on one of the chairs near the window, he admired her legs sheathed in close fitting stockinette pantaloons. "How do you find time to do so much?"

"I rise before the rest of the household and am out and about before the family stirs. Please do not fret. Martha sees no harm comes to me."

His wife enjoyed a secret life. His temper rose, but he tried to control it. "Belle, you must observe the proprieties."

Annabelle's eyes widened. "There is no need to get cross and raise your voice. I have been careful not to allow anyone in the house, other than Martha, to see me dressed in masculine attire. Besides, even if someone did see me, I doubt they would realise my true identity."

"No wonder Grandmamma says you look worn to the bone."

"Does she? How unkind of Lady Caroline." Annabelle hurried to the mirror and examined her face in it. "Do you think I look very tired?"

He sank onto a chair. "No, but do not cut up my peace of mind by keeping secrets from me."

"That is hardly fair, you kept secrets from me. You concealed your identity."

"*Touché*, Belle, but I hope you will not make a practice of being deceitful. Besides, it does us no good to rake up that matter yet again."

Annabelle looked away from him. "Very well, I will not mention it in future, now, please excuse me. I am late for my lesson."

"It is cancelled, but when we return to the country, I will teach you how to fence."

"Are you qualified to do so?"

"Am I qualified?" he said, much affronted and in a raised voice. "There have been many occasions when my life has depended on my skill as a swordsman."

Annabelle glanced at the clock. "Well, if I am not to have a fencing lesson, I shall visit my dressmaker and discuss the design of my new gown for the Duchess of Gower's ball."

"Damn your dressmaker." Roland sprang up, drew her to her feet, caught her to him, and kissed her.

Before the kiss ended, her body trembled against his. He released her, uncertain whether she trembled with desire or fear. Colour rushed into his wife's cheeks. "Stay with me awhile," he murmured into her ear.

"You do not want me to be dowdy, do you?"

Fobbed off, he sighed. "As you wish, Belle, but by now we should have reached a better understanding than this." He did not believe she was going to consult her dressmaker. "Are you sure you are concealing nothing else from me?"

His wife's blush deepened. "What else could I have to conceal?" The clock struck the hour. "I must go if I am to have time to choose the fabric before riding in the park with you this afternoon."

Could she be innocent? Had de Beauchamp lied? He had given her every opportunity to be frank. What would he do if she were lying? Lock her up in a dismal dungeon like some knight of old, or order her to be kept under surveillance at all times?

An unwelcome thought crept into his mind. Perhaps he should not have married Annabelle. Yet what else could a gentleman have done?

* * *

Dressed in plain black, an unfashionable, broad-brimmed hat on his head in the hope he would not be recognised, Roland rode to Hyde Park little more than a half hour after his wife's question, "You do not want me to be dowdy, do you?" No, he did not, but on the other hand, he did not want her to be deceitful.

He sat at one of the tables set out near the milk booth and partially concealed his face with a broadsheet. If he was to be betrayed by his wife the sun should not shine. Dark skies should herald thunder and lightning and the placid cows should moo uneasily.

De Beauchamp arrived and Roland took a deep breath. With pleasure—for in his opinion the wretch deserved nothing of merit—he noted the fellow's showy chestnut gelding was too short in the back.

The toad took a flask from the pocket of his greatcoat and drank.

Roland watched de Beauchamp, who stood at one side of the booth until Martha descended from a hackney and approached him. With a smile on his fat face, which Roland wanted to erase with his fist, the baron entered the hackney followed by Martha.

Was his wife in the hackney? If so, at least she was not alone with the fat reprobate. He took a deep breath to calm himself. Thank God he was now a civilian, no longer bound to total secrecy—although he still wanted to settle accounts with Frenchmen such as the baron.

His mind churned. What business did his wife have with the wretch?

While he rode home, Roland considered how best to tackle Annabelle. Deep in thought, he cut several acquaintances, who had recognised him in spite of his hat.

As soon as he entered his house, he went to the library and poured a glass of wine. By the time Annabelle returned, he had decided to put her under surveillance.

Roland looked out of the window. He did not have much luck with the ladies. His father had not considered his first love to be a suitable match. His second love accepted another man's proposal of marriage. Then Juliet left her husband and foisted herself on him. Of course, he should have refused to keep her, but he had been young and chivalrous. He had believed that, as an honourable gentleman, he should be her protector. He scowled. Now, Annabelle seemed unworthy of single-minded devotion.

In spite of the circumstances, doubt nagged. From the moment she met de Beauchamp, Annabelle had declared her dislike of him. No matter what it cost him, he must carry on as usual until he reached a decision about their future. What were the options? Either banish Annabelle to a house in the country or live under the same roof under false pretences that there was nothing untoward in their marriage. On the other hand, although he could not think of one, his wife might have an innocent explanation for contacting de Beauchamp.

Chapter Twenty-Three

Annabelle blinked and put her handkerchief to her nose. Accustomed to Roland's pleasant toilet water, de Beauchamp's musky scent, heightened by the stale confines of the hackney, disgusted her.

She compared the elegant simplicity of Roland's attire to de Beauchamp's colourful garb, more suited to an actor than a nobleman. She restrained a giggle and dared not look at Martha, who was a fount of interesting information about gentlemen's dyed whiskers, padded chests, corsets, toupees, and wigs. What a shock the bride of a man using such artifices must have on her wedding night. Annabelle checked such frivolous thoughts and concentrated on the purpose of the assignation.

De Beauchamp sighed and leaned forward in an attempt to hold her hand. "Do we *need* a *duenna*?"

Annabelle shuddered and clasped her hands together. "My lord, it would be improper of me to meet you alone."

"No need to be shy, my pretty bird. Must say it doesn't surprise me to find out you regret marrying Hampton. I have never liked your husband's haughty manners."

"My lord, I am not a *pretty bird,* and not for a single moment have I regretted my marriage," she stated in a tone intended to freeze him.

Once more his lordship, who seemed to think he could charm her, tried to hold her hands. Martha's cough and bunched fists deterred him. He sat back. "Well, stands to reason you would be grateful to Hampton for saving your good name."

"Indeed!" Annabelle exclaimed, annoyed by de Beauchamp's total lack of finesse.

The baron's protuberant eyes gleamed. "No need to be so fierce, Lady Hampton. I have long expected repayment for never mentioning I saw you without a chaperon at an inn. An inn, I remind you, where you spent the night with Hampton before you married him."

Annabelle regarded the toad with acute dislike. To lose her temper would not be to her advantage. "Monsieur le baron, we are at cross purposes."

De Beauchamp smirked. "I think not. I believe you regret not accepting my hand in marriage."

She ignored Martha's derisory snort and forced herself to remain calm. "I shall come to the point."

De Beauchamp clasped his hands on his plump knees sheathed in bright blue broadcloth.

"I am sure you are gentleman enough to want to help a lady."

While he hesitated, his eyes bulged and he licked his artificially coloured lips with a white-coated tongue. "You disappoint me, my lady. Am I to understand our assignation is not of a romantic nature?" Too repulsed to speak, Annabelle nodded. The fixed regard of his peculiar eyes intensified. "Be good enough to enlighten me, child."

She did not appreciate being addressed as a child, but not wishing to antagonise him, did not protest. "I shall be very obliged if you will tell me who my former guardian was."

The baron frowned, drumming his stubby fingers on his knees, and shook his head.

"Why not tell me, Monsieur le Baron? It would be a kindness on your part." De Beauchamp's lips pursed. Must she beg him? "Monsieur?"

He cleared his throat. "I might be persuaded to tell you for a price."

"Blackmail, my lady!" Martha rapped on the roof of the hackney to instruct the driver to rein in his horses. The hackney halted and Martha grasped the door handle.

"Wait," Annabelle ordered Martha, and then turned her head to face the baron. "Monsieur, name your price."

"For a modest sum, I will tell you what you want to know."

"How much?" she drawled in a passable imitation of Roland.

"Five hundred guineas."

"I don't have five hundred guineas."

De Beauchamp flicked open his snuffbox. "You could raise it."

Roland was generous, but she did not have that much left from this quarter's pin money.

On the other hand, in order to trace her parents through her former guardian, she was prepared to do almost anything to find out who that person had been.

De Beauchamp took a pinch of snuff, sneezed, and wiped his nose. "Do not look at me as though you are about to challenge me to a duel, Lady Hampton. As for my price, I will be satisfied with jewellery worth the same amount."

"What shall I do if my husband finds out some of my jewellery is missing?"

De Beauchamp glared at her with shocking malevolence. "Say it has been stolen."

"Very well, tell me who my guardian was and I shall send the jewellery to you."

"Not so fast, my pretty bird. Send your woman with it and I shall give her the name."

"Very well," Annabelle agreed, unable to think of an alternative. "Martha shall come to you tomorrow while my husband and I attend Lady Kent's breakfast."

De Beauchamp got out of the hackney and bowed. "At which I will have the pleasure of seeing you after our transaction is completed."

"My lady—" Martha began, as soon as they were quit of the baron.

"Do not say anything," Annabelle adjured through tight lips. "The creature really is a toad, a horrible toad, but there is no other way to find out the truth which I must discover."

"If you say so," replied Martha, her back straight as an iron rod and the expression in her eyes grim.

* * *

After a restless night, during which she did not sleep soundly until dawn, Annabelle woke late. "Martha, please give me my hand mirror," she requested, when the woman brought her morning chocolate.

Martha fetched the hand mirror. Annabelle looked into it and saw her red-rimmed eyes stare back at her. She looked unwell and hoped Lady Caroline would not ask her once again, if she was about to make a happy announcement.

Annabelle accepted a dish of hot chocolate from Martha and watched the woman tidy the bedroom.

Annabelle held the dish with one hand and pinched her cheeks with the other to bring colour into them

"Will you wear your new sapphire blue gown this morning?" Martha asked.

"No, it is too sophisticated for a breakfast in the country. But why it is called breakfast when it won't begin until one of the clock, I do not know."

Martha answered a tap on the door and admitted Fanny, who greeted Annabelle with a kiss.

"Mmm, I'm hungry. May I have a slice of your bread and butter, Annabelle?"

"Of course you may," Annabelle replied as she spread cherry conserve onto a thinly cut slice of buttered bread.

Martha coughed. "My lady, you could wear either the sprigged muslin trimmed with primrose yellow ribbons, or the pink and white cambric."

What she wore today, of all days, seemed of little importance. "No, I wore the sprigged muslin on Monday and the cambric is unsuitable, so I shall wear the new pale blue muslin."

Fanny shook her head. "The blue is too plain. Why not wear your new pale grey gown embroidered with yellow and trimmed with matching ribbons? It is so unusual that it is sure to be much admired, and you can wear it with your yellow pelisse," Fanny said.

"Very well, but what does it matter what I wear?"

Fanny put down her bread and butter and poured some hot chocolate. "Annabelle, what is wrong? You are always so particular about your gowns."

Roland entered the bedchamber through the partially open door from Annabelle's parlour. "Good morning ladies."

Annabelle smiled at him and answered Fanny. "I did not sleep well."

"Shall we forgo the breakfast?" Roland asked, an unfathomable expression in his eyes.

Annabelle shook her head. "No, I am only a little tired."

Roland frowned, but before he could say more, Fanny spoke. "Annabelle, I am sure you will be a picture of perfection just like a colour plate in *La Belle Assemblee*. You are so clever. Several ladies have had your designs copied but they never achieve your elegance. Oh, I forgot why I came here. May I borrow your plaited willow hat, the one with the poke front and the high crown trimmed with artificial cherries?"

"Yes, but please accept it as a gift. You will look charming in it."

"You are very kind and generous." Fanny kissed Annabelle's cheek again. "Thank you very much. I am going to exchange the white silk ribbon on my new muslin gown for a red one which will match the cherries and make me look more dashing."

"Hurry up, Fanny, you do not want to be late," Roland advised, but Fanny ignored him. She dawdled and sipped her hot chocolate.

Annabelle contemplated Roland, handsome in his bottle-green riding coat, buff pantaloons, and black riding boots polished to perfection.

"My love," he said, with an indefinable expression in his eyes, "as you are still abed, I assume you do not intend to ride in the park with me this morning."

Sensitive to every nuance of his spoken word, she scrutinised his handsome face while Martha retreated to the dressing room. She shrank back against the pillows. He rarely called her "'his love" and never before had he spoken to her in so cold a tone while the golden lights in his eyes blazed.

"I apologise Roland, for waking too late to ride with you."

"No need to, I went earlier, but would have accompanied you if you had expressed a wish to ride." He indicated his buckskins. "I must dress for the breakfast."

Annabelle watched him leave with tears in her eyes. He had not so much as kissed her hand or cheek as was his usual custom. And she really did not want to part with her jewellery. Oh, how she hated de Beauchamp.

Annabelle shuddered. She should not be so tired and unhappy when she would soon know her former guardian's identity.

"You look very sad. What are you thinking of?" Fanny asked.

Annabelle forced herself to smile. "Nothing in particular."

* * *

Several hours later, Annabelle checked her reflection in the mirror to make sure the folds of her elegant gown were in place. "Martha, fetch my jewel case," she said, satisfied her appearance could not be improved upon.

Martha marched out of the room. Several minutes later, she returned carrying a red leather case and put it in front of Annabelle on a low occasional table.

Annabelle opened the lid. Which pieces should she choose? What would Roland say if he found out they were missing? She removed the trays and stared at the contents. It was unthinkable to give de Beauchamp the jade Roland gave her on the evening of the ball. She set aside treasured pieces, her jade, her diamonds, a sapphire suite given to her by Lady Caroline and a coral bracelet and earrings Fanny had given her.

Annabelle examined the family heirlooms. Among the pieces were two ropes of pearls. Surely one of them would not be missed. Only she and Martha had the keys to the case and should mention be made of the pearls, she could claim she received only one rope. Her cheeks burned at the thought of telling a falsehood, but what else could she do? She sighed. She took note of the emerald and diamond tiara and the matching necklace, earrings, armbands, and brooch. Surely no one would expect her to wear the old fashioned jewels.

"The emerald suite and the pearls must be worth five hundred guineas. De Beauchamp will have to be satisfied with them," Annabelle sighed.

"And so he should be, my lady." Martha replied, her face stiff with disapproval.

"Do not part with them until you obtain the name of my former guardian."

"I'm not a ninny, my lady."

"I know you are not." Annabelle smoothed her gown with a damp palm and then put on her pelisse and gloves. She checked the angle of her hat and picked up her pretty parasol. "I am ready and will not require anything else. You may go."

Without saying another word, Annabelle went downstairs to the parlour, where Roland waited to escort her to the breakfast at the Kent's mansion near Richmond.

"How well-turned out you are, my lord."

"Thank you for the bounty from your table." Her husband sat down. "You look tired, Belle."

She eyed him, and saw an indescribably intense but wary look in his eyes, which she could not interpret. "It is ungallant of you to say I am not in good looks," she teased. "To tell the truth, I did not sleep well last night."

"If I did not know you better, Belle, I would say you have something to hide from me."

As though he was omniscient, she stared at Roland in alarm. Surely he could not know about either her meeting with de Beauchamp or her agreement to hand over some of her jewellery.

"Why did you not sleep well, Belle?"

Unable to think of an answer, she looked down at the tips of her fashionable, round-toed shoes.

Roland slapped one of his fine leather gloves against the other. "Ah, last night, did you wait for me to come to your room? But, as you reminded me, husbands and wives should not be expected to live in each other's pockets, or should you have said beds?"

There was an unfamiliar note in his voice. "My head ached," she said truthfully, somewhat unnerved by his altered demeanour toward her.

"Did you flout me by having a fencing lesson today?"

"No, I keep my promises!"

Roland drew on his gloves. "You should sleep more. Early morning rendezvous are not good for you."

"Rendezvous?" she queried. Annabelle was unnerved but forced herself to be still although hot colour flooded her cheeks.

"Your art lessons with Cavalierre and who knows what else?" Roland tilted her chin with his thumb and forefinger. "One would think you are ill-at-ease, but why should you be?"

Her nervous irritation increased. Annabelle wondered if by any chance he had found out about her meeting with the baron. She dismissed the thought as too fanciful. How could he possibly know about it?

Roland inspected his gloves as though he had nothing of importance on his mind other than their perfect fit. "Shall we cancel all our engagements and return to The Priory? Country air would refresh you."

Annabelle took a deep breath. It would be torture to be secluded with him if he had no deep feelings for her. "But, Roland, how can we leave town? It is the middle of the London season and we have so many engagements."

Roland smoothed one of his gloves with the edge of his thumb. "We could leave Grandmother and Fanny in town and retreat on our own."

To avoid looking at her husband, she glanced around the elegant parlour decorated in blue and ivory and hung with gilt framed paintings of Roland's ancestors. With pleasure, she noticed the tastefully arranged vases of flowers on an escritoire and several small, low tables.

"Ah, Belle, I hope I have not embarrassed you. Perhaps you are too shy to say you would like me to devote my time to you?"

He really was playing with her like a cat with a mouse. She twirled her parasol. "You neither look nor sound devoted."

"How remiss of me. Remind me to prove I am. At some functions, so many admirers crowd round you that I cannot reach you."

Annabelle fluttered her eyelashes. "You are always welcome at my side."

"Am I? Sometimes you are as formidable as an ice queen."

She caught her lower lip between her teeth while she failed to find an acceptable response.

"But I am forgetful." Roland picked up a broadsheet from the table next to his chair. "There is something I want you to read."

Faint, Annabelle sank onto a chair, hoping against hope that it did not contain news of her tryst with de Beauchamp. Oh, she was being ridiculous, why should it be reported? A little voice said the 'doings' of the ton were eagerly written of and read. Suppose—

Roland's voice seemed to come from a distance. He stood and handed her the broadsheet. "Please read the report I have circled."

She read fast and looked up. "Deacon has been jailed. Is it your doing?"

"No, I was not the magistrate." He smiled for the first time since she joined him in the parlour. "But I do confess to having her brought to justice." Her husband stood, drew her to her feet, and held her close for a moment. "Belle, you may always share everything with me, whether it is good or bad. Do not forget that we married for better or worse."

To avoid his scrutiny, she looked down at the horizontal, green stripes of his waistcoat. "I don't have any problems," she replied, too dispirited by her web of falsity to confess. Roland gripped her shoulders.

"You are hurting me."

"I apologise."

She stared up at him, wondering why he sounded so angry.

* * *

At the breakfast, the sight of Annabelle surrounded by admirers exasperated Roland. He withdrew into a clump of trees from where he could discreetly observe her, and could not help brooding, aggrieved because she had not responded to any of the opportunities he had given her to confess about her rendezvous with de Beauchamp.

"Do not glower," a familiar voice murmured.

For a second, he looked into the depths of Juliet's dark mournful eyes but did not speak.

"Hampton, there is no need to cut me. No one can see us beneath this oak tree, and I doubt anyone else will stray in this direction."

"I did not know you had re-entered society."

"Our hostess and my mother were friends. Some people are kind," she murmured.

The thought crossed his mind that her life would have undoubtedly been very different if her mother had not died. "I am pleased she invited you, but you should leave out of respect for my wife."

Roland looked through the trees and across the crowded lawn at Annabelle, who stood near the bank of the rippling Thames sparkling in the sunshine. A parasol shaded her beautiful face as she turned to look at that young fop, Colindale.

"Yes, some people are kind to me, but you are not." Tears filled Juliet's eyes.

"Do not subject me to a fit of the vapours. I have done all I can for you. My settlement ensured you are provided for, unless you are uncommonly wasteful." He frowned. "A word of warning. In future, I shall never acknowledge you in public. And a word of advice. If you wish to re-establish yourself in society, brash behaviour will ruin any chance."

His wife stood. Where was she going? If Juliet had not caught hold of his coat sleeve, he would have returned to the lawn.

Juliet's eyes burned like a pair of sentient coals. "Do you have no tenderness for me?"

"No. Accept my advice. Ignore me as you would the sufferer of an infectious disease. Do not incite gossip by accosting me like this." He removed her hand from his coat sleeve as though it was a loathsome object and walked toward the lawn.

"What do I care about gossip when I love you?"

His temper boiled over. "No, you do not. You never loved me. You used me to escape from an intolerable marriage. Do not protest. You know, as well as I do, that you played on the chivalry of an untried, impetuous youth. Yet, I wish you well and, one day, I hope you will re-marry and be happy."

He turned his back on Juliet, who tried to cling to him like a leech. Once more he looked at his wife, who stood with her face turned in his direction. *Damnation!* Had she seen him with the woman? Curse Juliet. Never again would he be drawn into her rash web.

* * *

Annabelle laughed. She did not want anyone to suspect she had glimpsed her husband

and Mrs Parker in conversation. Even more, she did not want anyone to guess how jealous that made her. She opened her parasol. "I would like to feed the ducks," she announced, aware of the pretty picture made by her pose next to the willow tree.

While three young gentlemen rushed to fetch bread, she allowed Colindale to remain by her side and pay her compliments.

"Your eyes are incomparable," the infatuated youth said.

Annabelle stared across the broad stretch of the Thames and pretended she had not noticed Roland's approach.

His back toward Roland, Colindale stepped closer to her. "I wish you were not married."

"But the lady is married, and I have the good fortune to be her husband," Roland said.

"N-no offence, my lord," Colindale stammered.

Annabelle's other admirers returned.

"I have brought a basket of bread, Lady Hampton. Do feed the ducks," young Farringdon suggested.

"And you have brought cake for them, as well as bread," Roland drawled. "Do you know, it is rumoured that the French rioted after Marie Antoinette suggested they should eat cake if there was no bread?"

"They guillotined her," Colindale said.

"Exactly. I am glad your head is safe on your shoulders. Duels are tedious are they not?"

Annabelle shivered, but not from cold. Roland had made it plain that he would never be a complacent husband.

"Leave us," Roland said to her admirers and took the basket from Farringdon. "Come, madam, if you wish to feed the ducks, I am at your command."

She walked beside him along the riverside path. The scent of scythed grass filled the air and the river lapped lazily against the bank. "Madam," her husband's harsh tone spoiled the tranquil scene, "if we do not present a picture of harmony, people will gossip."

She halted and looked up at him. What did she care for what other people thought? "Do I count for nothing?"

"Of course you do. I have told you more than once that I want you to be happy."

"Then you should consider my sensibilities," she said in a raised voice. She knew, but did not care, that etiquette demanded she ignore the knowledge that minutes earlier her husband had disgracefully engaged in conversation in public with his former mistress.

Roland grinned. "You are jealous." With a total lack of propriety, her husband drew her into his arms. "My love."

Despite her anger, she smiled at him. The endearment thrilled her. Ripples ran up and down her spine, her parasol fell to the ground, and she pressed closer to him. His passionate kiss ended. He gazed deeply into her eyes. Self-consciously, she patted a stray ringlet back into place. "My lord, you forget yourself."

"How could I forget myself in your company, Belle?" he asked as he released her.

In silence, they strolled toward the manor with her hand resting lightly on his arm. People stared at them and someone sniggered, presumably because they saw her husband kissing her. She held her head high. If Juliet Parker approached Roland again, she would not mince words, and that would give the gossips something else to talk about.

* * *

Long after twilight, seated next to Annabelle in the carriage, Lady Caroline shook her head several times. And as soon as they reached home, Annabelle obeyed the old lady's summons to attend her in the parlour, where they would partake of refreshments before retiring for the night.

"Child, you have no mother, so it is my duty to guide you," Roland's grandmother declared as soon as Annabelle joined her.

Indignant and upset by the painful mention of her unknown parent, Annabelle strove to control her temper.

"It is not the thing to embrace your husband in public."

Annabelle squared her shoulders. "I suggest you reprimand your grandson."

"I shall, for the poor fool is so besotted by you, he is losing his sense of decorum." Annabelle's ears buzzed and her heart pounded while Lady Caroline continued. "Your admirers drive the poor man insane with jealousy."

"You are mistaken. His sentiments are engaged elsewhere."

Lady Caroline rolled her eyes as though she dealt with a lack-wit. "If you think he still has warm feelings for Mrs Parker, you are foolish beyond belief," remarked Lady Caroline, who never dissembled and believed in plain speaking.

Annabelle gripped the chair back like a drowning woman clutching a plank.

"Your love match is the talk of the season." Lady Caroline pursed her lips and flicked open her enamelled snuffbox. She put a pinch of it on the back of her wrist and sniffed it delicately.

"You cannot be serious," Annabelle whispered.

Lady Caroline looked at her incredulously, wiped her nose on a handkerchief, and closed the snuffbox. "Do you mean Hampton has not told you he loves you? No need to answer. The expression on your face tells me all I need to know." She chuckled, her eyes bright by candlelight. "Well, I must say that, although he is an intelligent man, he has made a mull of things. As for you…well, all I shall say is you and your husband are a pair of ninnies."

Annabelle stared at Lady Caroline, astounded by her forthrightness. Could it be true? Did Roland love her? No, Lady Caroline must be mistaken. Yet he had called her his love at the breakfast, and kissed her passionately, careless of onlookers. No, she would not allow herself to nurse false expectations. Roland had proved he wanted her in his arms, but she was not so naïve that she did not know there was a difference between desire and love.

Roland and Fanny entered the parlour. One footman brought in the tea tray and another, a tray on which was a plate of bread and butter and a plate of thinly cut ginger bread.

"Fanny, how happy you look," Annabelle commented while wondering about the truth of Lady Caroline's words concerning Roland.

"Has a lucky gentleman engaged your interest?" Roland teased his half-sister.

"No, my affections are not engaged," Fanny replied, her cheeks fiery red.

Lady Caroline reached up to tap Roland on the cheek with her ivory fan. "Roland, sit down and do not quiz her."

Fanny sat next to Annabelle. "Do you regret marrying before your first London Season?" she murmured.

Surprised, because her husband's family were nothing if not frank, Annabelle glanced at her sister-in-law. "Why should I regret my marriage?" she asked in a very low voice while she busied herself pouring tea.

"Please be honest, Annabelle. Do you not wish you had the opportunity to meet more gentlemen before you married?" Fanny whispered.

Annabelle gazed at her husband. "No," she breathed, "no, I do not have any regrets."

"Do you love Roland very much?" Fanny asked, her voice now loud enough for her grandmother and Roland to hear her.

"That question is in very bad taste, Fanny," Lady Caroline replied. "Come, it is time for us to be in bed."

Amused and irritated by Fanny's tactlessness, Annabelle followed them upstairs.

* * *

While Jones handed him his nightshirt, Roland's common sense told him his wife was not romantically inclined toward the baron. Heartened by Annabelle's admission that she did not regret their marriage, he looked forward to resolving their misunderstandings.

Someone knocked on Roland's bedchamber door and Jones opened it.

"May I speak to his lordship about an urgent matter?" Martha asked.

Eager to join Annabelle in her bedchamber, Roland pulled on his dressing gown. "Can you not wait until morning?"

"If you insist, my lord, but I think you'll thank me for speaking my piece tonight."

"Very well, Jones, you may go." Roland clasped his hands behind his back. "Well, what have you to say to a black-hearted devil?"

Martha scowled. "You are a black-hearted devil when you make my mistress unhappy."

Was his wife miserable, really miserable? His breath caught in his throat. That was the last thing in the world he wanted for her.

Martha clutched the package to her large bosom. "I'm not sure I'm doing what's right."

Roland sat on a chair by the hearth. "Does it have something to do with her ladyship's meeting with Baron de Beauchamp?"

Martha put the package on a table and supported her bulk on it with the flat of her hands. "You've been spying on us."

"For her ladyship's own good."

"I don't know why you spied on your wife, but I'll make a clean breast of the matter."

"Sit down, Martha, I daresay you are tired and would rather be in your bed."

The colour in her broad cheeks heightened. "Oh, no thank you, I can't sit in your presence, it wouldn't be fitting."

"Nonsense, I was too long in the army to be top-lofty."

Martha picked up the package and sat on a wing chair near the window. "My lady wants to know who her guardian was, the names of her parents, and whether she has any living relatives."

He twisted his wedding ring round his finger. "I know she does."

The abigail stroked the package as though it was a small, furry creature. "That's why she met de Beauchamp."

"Did he tell her?"

"No, but he will for a price, and that's why I'm here."

"An extortionist! Damn it, I have just dealt with one and now I have to deal with another."

"No, you don't." Martha chuckled and handed him the package. "He wanted five hundred pounds. When my lady protested she couldn't pay so much, he asked for some jewellery. Her ladyship ordered me to take it to his lodgings while both of you were at the breakfast." Martha sighed. "Even if my mistress is very angry with me when she finds out that I told you, I've done my duty as I saw fit."

"Thank you."

"You don't need to thank me, but please tell me what I'm to do when my lady discovers de Beauchamp hasn't got the jewellery."

"Let her think he is lying." He opened the package, eyed the emerald and diamond suite, and then ran the rope of pearls through his hands. "Now, go to bed."

"Thank you, my lord, I'll sleep all the better for having told you about this."

And he would sleep well now that he knew the truth.

She hesitated by the door. "My lord, please don't be too hard on my lady. She's very young. Although she thinks she's *up to the snuff*, she isn't. And what's more, she didn't mean to do wrong."

Roland's mouth twisted. What sort of a husband was he, not to have earned his wife's trust? She should have felt able to turn to him for help before seeking out de Beauchamp.

Chapter Twenty-Four

On the morning after the breakfast, Annabelle sat at her escritoire scanning invitations, letters, and bills. The door opened almost without sound. She looked across her parlour and welcomed Roland with a smile.

"You are busy, shall I go away?"

"No, I can attend to this later."

She hardly dared to hope Lady Caroline was right when she said Roland had made the love match of the London season. "Did you want something in particular, Roland?"

"Are we going to the masquerade at Berkhampstead House tonight?"

She nodded and concentrated on arranging some papers into a neat pile.

Her husband bent forward, placing his hands on the escritoire. "Will you indulge me?" he asked, his face level with hers.

"Indulge you?"

"Yes, I would like you to wear a particular gown."

His close proximity rendered her breathless. "Which one?"

"The one you wore when Cavalierre painted you."

She suspected her cheeks paled and caught her breath before she could reply. "I will pen a note to Monseigneur to ask him if I may borrow it."

Roland caressed her cheek with his forefinger before he straightened. "That is not all. I have another request."

Her cheek tingled and an excited knot formed deep within her. "What is it?"

"Amongst your jewellery are two ropes of pearls. Please wear both of them tonight. They will look well with the gown."

Annabelle blinked several times and pressed one hand over her heart, which beat faster than usual. She must not panic. She must remain calm.

"You seem concerned. Is there any reason why you should not wear them?"

Heat rushed into her cheeks. She shook her head.

Roland raised his eyebrow. "I regret I have some business to attend to, so I cannot ride in the park with you today. However, I will dine at home before the masquerade."

Nervous, she watched him leave the room and groaned.

Annabelle paced the length of the carpet. What was she going to do? Maybe de Beauchamp would return the pearls if she begged him to exchange them for some other jewellery.

Her dresser entered the parlour and handed her a letter.

After she read it, she stared at Martha in a state of shock. "That odious toad denies you gave him the jewellery."

"Does he my lady? I can't say I am surprised."

Annabelle sank onto a chair and covered her face with her hands. "His lordship expects me to wear both of the necklaces at the masquerade. What shall I do?"

Martha's eyebrows pushed up almost to her hairline. "Don't fret, my lady, things might not be as bad as they seem."

Annabelle ran her hands through her hair. "They are, indeed they are worse than they seem." She sank her head in her hands. "Oh, what a fool I am."

The expression on her face inscrutable, Martha spoke. "You could tell his lordship the truth."

"I doubt he would understand why I approached that odious man."

"Well, my lady, as my mother used to say, it's no good crying after you've spilled the milk, not that we could afford to spill any."

Annabelle tried to smooth her disordered hair. "Instead of writing to him, I shall go to Monseigneur and ask him to lend me that cumbersome gown he painted me in."

She sighed, trying to decide if she should confide in the old gentleman and ask his advice. Abstracted, she allowed Martha to help her change into a celestial blue carriage gown before they went to Cavalierre's house.

* * *

"Oh, no! Look, Martha, a groom is walking my husband's horse!" Annabelle exclaimed as she stepped out of the carriage. Her eyebrows drew together. Why had Roland decided to visit Monseigneur?

Her dresser rapped on the door. Henri opened it and scowled. "My master is not at home."

Martha ignored both Henri's frown and words, edging her way into the house. "My lady has urgent business with her husband."

Annabelle followed Martha inside and noticed Henri eying Martha with a mixture of annoyance and grudging admiration. She held out her calling card. "Martha, give Henri my card. Henri, please give it to your master while I wait in the blue salon."

"No, my lady, not the blue salon!" the little manservant exclaimed and hurried up the stairs after her. Unable to prevent her entering the room, he scurried away.

On either side of the fireplace two portraits of ladies faced them. Both of the painted figures bore a strong resemblance to her, and were dressed in the elaborate gown Annabelle had worn when she posed for Cavalierre.

Annabelle pointed at the paintings. "Look, Martha, I don't understand. Why did Monseigneur paint two portraits of me?" She examined them more closely. "But the one on the right is not of me, although it would be my mirror image, if the eyes were blue not green. And there is another difference. There is an emerald ring in the other portrait. Look at it, Martha."

"I am looking," her henchwoman said.

Is she my twin? The portrait's title is Lost Love. *Whose lost love? Monseigneur's? Could he be my father? Did I inherit my artistic abilities from him? Am I looking at my mother's portrait?*

"You're shocked. Please sit down, my lady." Martha took a tiny flask from her pocket and removed the stopper. "Sniff this, my lady. I don't want you to faint."

"I never do so," Annabelle protested and sank onto a wing chair.

How well she remembered the beautiful French lady who took her from Dover to The Beeches. Even now, she could visualise the mysterious lady's distinctive emerald ring. Why did she never hear from her again?

"Belle...." Immaculate in his navy blue coat, pale blue waistcoat, and biscuit-coloured pantaloons, sunlight illuminating his handsome face, Roland called from the doorway.

"Leave us," Roland ordered Martha. "Belle, I trust you are not spying on me."

"What an odious accusation. I did not know you were here until I saw your horse. Instead of writing to Monseigneur, I came in person to ask him to lend me the gown you want me to wear tonight." She smiled, not knowing what to say next, and then ventured, "Roland, is this the first time you have seen these two portraits?"

Before her husband could reply, Cavalierre entered the room and greeted her. "Good day, *Cherie,* I hope you are well."

Annabelle curtsied. "Yes, I am, but I am also shocked."

Cavalierre bowed and kissed her hand. "I beg you to be patient and ask no questions. Follow me." He led them to another salon furnished in sea green, gold, and white, and hung from floor to ceiling with framed paintings. "*Ma petite,* I think you have been introduced to Madame Valencay."

She frowned. Her husband had asked her not to further her acquaintance with the lady. Why was she here? With Cavalierre at her side and her husband behind them she stepped forward. "Good day, Madame."

Annabelle wiped a rush of tears from her eyes with the back of her hand and scrutinised Cavalierre's face. She could contain her questions no longer. "Monseigneur, are you my father?"

Cavalierre took her trembling hand in his warm one and raised it to the level of his heart. "I would be proud to be your father, but I regret I am not."

"The portraits," she faltered, "one of them is titled *Lost Love*."

"Monsieur, Annabelle, please be seated." Although her husband was a guest in Cavalierre's house, he had taken charge. He opened the door, which revealed Henri stationed like a small watchdog next to Martha. "Fetch Mrs Delaney."

"My lord," Annabelle cried out, "you have found my nurse. How can I thank you? Where is she? You cannot imagine how much I longed to see her."

Roland hurried to her and captured her hands in his. "I hope," he said gravely, "you will be satisfied before this day is done."

Puzzled, she looked up at him until the sound of footsteps on the wooden floor alerted her to Mrs Delaney's presence and she stared toward the door.

Garbed in a grey gown and a white apron edged with narrow lace, her former nurse was just as she remembered. If Roland's hand on her shoulder had not restrained her, she would have dashed across the room to kiss the woman's cheek as though she were still a child. "Belle, please be seated," Roland repeated.

His face set in severe lines, Cavalierre took a stance in front of the fireplace, while Roland stood near her as she sank onto a sofa.

Mrs Delaney advanced toward her. When the woman stood before her, Annabelle gazed up into a pair of strange, yellow-green eyes. "Your eyes," she said astonished, "they are—"

"Yes, they are," Roland broke in. "I wondered if you would see the resemblance."

"Am I in a mad house? Can the kindest of nurses be related to—" Annabelle began.

"Mrs Delaney, stand against the wall opposite me," Roland ordered.

The woman obeyed, her hands trembling.

"What does this mean?" Annabelle asked.

"Mrs Delaney, Madame Valencay, and Monsieur Cavalierre have all played a part in your life." Roland's face set in granite lines as he looked at Mrs Delaney. "Before I reveal their parts, let me explain how I discovered the truth. I must confess that when I served in the army, Wellington relied on me to spy on the French at home and abroad."

"You were a spy? How can that be if you were a major serving in—" Annabelle interrupted.

The lines of his face softened. "Shush, Belle, later you may ask as many questions as you wish. How I came to be a spy is too long a tale to tell now. It is enough to say, I have a talent for dialects, disguises, and languages, so my country employed me to gather vital information about the enemy."

Annabelle bent her head. How many more secrets had he kept from her?

"Belle, I became privy to both secret information and several puzzles before I met you. One of those puzzles concerned Baron de Beauchamp and his intended bride. When I met you, I could not prove your identity, so, for fear of disappointing you, I did not reveal my suspicions."

"But what has *the toad* to do with me, other than the arrangement for him to marry me?" she asked, both curious and sick with apprehension.

"Before I deal with him, I think it would be best to explain Mrs Delaney's role." He glanced balefully at the woman. "Belle, your late mother arranged for this creature to care for you no matter what happened."

So, her mother was dead. Annabelle clasped her hands so tightly together that she winced when her fingernails pressed into the fleshy pads.

"Are you ready to hear the truth?" Roland asked, his voice gentle.

"Yes." She looked up at him. "For as long as I can remember, I have wanted to know who I am."

Roland's eyes seemed to ask her to be brave before he continued. "Your poor mother did not know Mrs Delaney's real name is Madame de la Nie or, as those damnable French revolutionaries addressed her, *Citoyenne de la Nie*. Moreover, your mother did not know de la Nie is the mother of the man now presumed to be Baron de Beauchamp."

"Presumed?" she asked, astonished, containing her impatience to know the truth. "Oh, Roland, when I looked into her eyes, I guessed she must be related to him for they have the same bulging ones, the colour of overripe gooseberries.'

De la Nie glared at Roland. "Fine words, but you have no proof."

"Yes, I do."

"How could you deceive me and allow your son to try to force me to marry him?" Annabelle asked.

De la Nie ignored her, dashed to the door, and opened it. Before she could flee, Martha, who stood in the hall next to Henri, grabbed her. Roland caught up with them and seized de la Nie's arm.

"Fetch the footman," Roland ordered.

Henri scurried away, and only moments passed before two tall, muscular footmen arrived. Cavalierre beckoned to them and after a brief word, walked de la Nie out of the salon toward the stairs.

Annabelle stood. "Wait, do not hurt her. Whatever else she has done, she never mistreated me when I was a child."

The footmen came to a halt and de la Nie stumbled.

"Take her away," Roland ordered. He glanced at the doorway where Martha and Henri lingered. "Go," he ordered, "and shut the door behind you."

Annabelle nibbled her lower lip. What part did Madame Valencay and Monsieur Cavalierre play in her history?

Roland released her. "It is Madame's turn to speak, for she is your mother's sister."

"An aunt! I have an aunt?" She hurried to sit next to the lady and embrace her.

Roland smiled at them. "Madame Valencay, please tell my wife about the role you played in her affairs."

Madame returned the embrace before she released her and began. "*Oui, ma chere,* it is true I am your aunt—"

"Why did I live with de la Nie instead of you?"

"I was in Switzerland when I received a long delayed letter about you from my sister telling me that she was going to England with you to save your life from the guillotine. Soon after I read it, I set out for England to be reunited with you and my sister. However, she had returned to France, leaving you with de la Nie. To be brief—and I will answer any questions you might have on another occasion—I had to hide you from that licentious man, the false Baron de Beauchamp, a man unfit to care for a dog, the scoundrel, who pretended to be the man appointed in your father's will to be your guardian."

"I don't understand. How did de la Nie manage to foist her son on London Society? Why did I live in Dover with her? Why did you not expose him and why did you not stop him from trying to marry me?"

Madame Valencay opened her mouth, swallowed, and seemed to be in the grip of so much emotion that, for the moment, she could not speak.

With sympathy and a flood of emotions ranging from despair to relief at being told the truth, Annabelle regarded her aunt's wrinkled face and scant white hair partially revealed beneath a muslin and lace cap. Her aunt's eyes misted. "I am sorry to tell you that after your mother died, it suited de la Nie to be your nurse. She kidnapped you and took you to Dover where you lived until I rescued you."

Annabelle's head drooped. Where and when did her mother die? She glanced at Roland, always at her side, ready to smile at her encouragingly or to soothe her tangled emotions with a touch on the shoulder. "Your aunt means she found out where you were and saved you."

Annabelle stared back at her aunt, who sat so straight that her back did not touch the chair. "I told you your surname was Allan and took you to The Beeches. Ah, you will never know what it cost me to remain apart from you, my last living relative. Yet, whatever the price, I made up my mind to protect you from de la Nie. Why, I asked myself, did that woman abduct you—although I would have kept her on as your nurse in the belief that she served your family faithfully." The expression in Madame's reddened eyes hardened. "As for her son, how he traced you shortly before you ran away from school, I do not know. However, although his documents were bogus, he arranged for you to marry him. Oh, he was a clever one. Poor Miss Chalfont believed you would be cast out penniless into the world if you did not agree to the marriage."

"I feel as though I am in Bedlam," Annabelle said. "I wrote regularly to Madame de la Nie and she replied affectionately."

Madame Valencay's hands fluttered. "My poor child, she had not the least affection for you. In the hope that when you grew up you would visit the cottage, and thus put yourself in her power, de la Nie continued to rent it—although she did not live there—and she continued to rent it after you married. By the time you returned there, it was too late for her and her despicable son to carry out their plan. In the meantime, I paid my servant, Kitty, whom de la Nie never suspected, to have your letters to that evil creature forwarded to me."

Bewildered and confused, Annabelle clutched her aunt's hand. "So, you replied to my letters."

"*Oui.*"

Roland stood behind the sofa and put a hand on her shoulder. "At the moment, we cannot answer all your questions. But in due course of time, we hope to do so for, by now, the Bow Street Runners have arrested *Citoyenne de la Nie* and her son, the false Baron de Beauchamp."

Annabelle trembled as though she was near the end of an exhausting journey and did not know if her destination would be worthwhile. She turned to her aunt. "Is there a *real* Baron de Beauchamp?"

After she let go of Annabelle's hand, Madame drew her fine wool shawl close around her thin shoulders. "He is dead, but before he died, his parents first fled to Ireland and later to Louisiana, taking *Citoyenne de la Nie's* son with them, to be his companion."

"Why did they choose her son?"

"The de la Nies served the Beauchamps faithfully for several generations," Madame replied. "To continue, I assume that in Louisiana, the de la Nie boy acquired an education that later served both his mother's and his own wicked purposes." Madame's lips trembled. "The report—that I bless your husband for obtaining—explains that, before *Citoyenne de la Nie* returned to France, Baron de Beauchamp, his wife, and son died after suffering from violent stomach cramps and high fevers. I suspect de la Nie's son of poisoning them." She waved her finger at Annabelle. "Let go of my hand, you will break my bones."

Annabelle released her aunt's hand and touched the emerald ring. "Did you wear this ring when you took me to The Beeches?"

Madame patted her hand. "Yes, it is one of a perfectly matched pair. Your grandfather gave one to me and the other to your mother."

Annabelle stood and went to Cavalierre. "Did you know—?"

Roland intervened. "Monsieur le Duc, it is your turn to speak."

"So," Annabelle began, "I was right, you are entitled to be called Monseigneur."

Cavalierre nodded. "Yes, but I prefer to be an artist known as Cavalierre. My compatriots respect my wishes."

Later, she would question him about this, but at the moment other preoccupations clamoured for attention. "Was my mother your lost love, Monseigneur?"

With exquisite courtesy, Cavalierre led her back to her aunt and smiled at her. "Sit next to your aunt before I continue."

While he resumed his stance in front of the fireplace, Annabelle sank onto the sofa.

"C*herie,* I met your mother at court and fell in love with her. Alas, I was betrothed to another lady. After I married, I relinquished your mother, but not my memory of her." He closed his eyes. "Years passed and—God rest their souls—while I fought for the royalist cause, my wife and children went to the guillotine." For a moment, he shaded his eyes with his hand. When he removed it, they shone bright with unshed tears. "In England, I courted your mother, Marie-Louise. I would have married her and loved you as though you were my own, but she decided to serve the royalist cause. After she engaged *Citoyenne de la Nie*—who pretended to be an Irishman's widow—and doing all in her power to secure your future, she returned to France as a spy."

Annabelle bit her lip and lowered her head to conceal her face. "How did my mother die?"

Roland put his warm hand on her shoulder. "So far as I could ascertain, *Citoyenne de la Nie* denounced your mother."

A pain stabbed her chest, even as the enormity of de la Nie's betrayal stabbed her. And she had asked the footmen to treat the woman kindly! Hatred, which she had never experienced before, filled her.

Cavalierre crossed the room to stand in front of her. "No, no, now that justice will be served, to hate, *Cherie,* is to allow your enemies to triumph." He made the sign of the cross. "Be proud of your mother. In every sense of the word, she was a noble woman."

in my wildest imagination could I have guessed the truth. Even now I can scarcely believe it. My poor mother is dead and I am a Frenchwoman. But what of my father?"

Monseigneur glanced at her husband who nodded. "*Ma chere,* it is my misfortune to have to tell you that your father, Monsieur le Comte de Belle Isle, and both of your brothers, were murdered by a mob which stormed their chateau during your mother's absence."

She wiped away the tears that streamed down her face with the back of her hand. "Why did you paint those portraits?"

"I painted Marie-Louise's from memory. When I met you masquerading under false pretences, I guessed you were her daughter and indulged myself by painting you."

"You were cruel, Monseigneur. You remained silent although you knew how much—

how very much—I needed to know who my parents were."

Very gently, Roland put his hand on her shoulder and she reached up to clasp it.

"Like your good husband," Monseigneur continued, "I had no proof of your identity other than your resemblance to your mother. After all, people might have said you were illegitimate."

Her cheeks burned at that thought, although it had once been one of her greatest fears.

"Console yourself with this, *Cherie*. Your father loved you very much. You were christened Marie-Annabelle, and he said you were 'The Beauty of Belle Isle' and its greatest treasure." As he spoke, Cavalierre's voice grew huskier and huskier. He cleared his throat. "Although you have lost your father, I hope you will believe that, had your mother married me, I would have cherished you, for you are the daughter of my heart."

"And you," Annabelle said, overcome by her sensibilities, "are the father of *my* heart." Annabelle brushed tears away with the edge of her thumb. "If you had married her, I would have been proud to call you Father." She stood. Roland came around the sofa and stood next to her. For comfort, she held tight to her husband's hand and realised it seemed the most natural thing in the world. "The thought of being in that false pretender's power sickens me. Oh, what a tangle it is. I ran away from you, my lord, because Deacon told me you would be imprisoned for marrying me without my guardian's consent."

"You are adorable." Her husband put an arm around her waist and drew her close.

Grateful for his support, both physical and emotional, she leaned against him. "When did you discover my identity?"

"It is a long story. All I will say for now is that when your father married, he appointed Monsieur de Beauchamp as his children's guardian—in the event of his death. In return, your father agreed that, in the event of the baron's death, he would be the guardian of the unfortunate youth who died in Louisiana.

"Without doubt, the man you know as de Beauchamp is a French spy. Moreover, it suited his government to forge false documents which confirmed he was the baron and that your guardianship had passed to him." He raised Annabelle's hand to his lips and kissed it. "As for me, I saw your mother's portrait at an exhibition of Monsieur le Duc's work. When I met you, I guessed your identity immediately, but for fear of putting you in danger, could not share my suspicions with you. So, I left you at Grandmamma's manor and applied to your aunt, your only living relative, for permission to marry you."

"*Oui*, it is true, and I was pleased to give my consent. I was confident you would be happy and safe with a gentleman of your husband's calibre," Madame Valencay interpolated.

"Thank you, Madame," Roland responded and continued. "Of course, Annabelle, after securing your aunt's consent, my acquaintance with the Bishop of London enabled me to procure the licence."

"But you tried to stop me from having anything to do with my aunt."

"For fear she would not be able to resist revealing her relationship to you." He bowed to Madame Valencay, a twinkle in his eyes. "Please pardon me, I could not be certain you could keep your own counsel."

Annabelle's eyebrows rushed together. "You promised to have no secrets from me after you told me…oh, never mind about that, you know what I refer to. Yet all this time, while I was tormented by not knowing my parents' identity, you kept the truth from me. How could you? You are cruel."

"Believe me, I had no choice. I had some unfinished business to conclude for the government and as a result the de la Nies will be brought to justice for their crimes against you, your family, this country, and their own country."

"I wish you had trusted me with the truth." Her heart pounded. "Please don't put yourself in danger again. I could not bear to lose you." She turned and after a moment's hesitation, rested her hands on his shoulders.

Madame Valencay coughed. Annabelle removed her hands and faced her aunt. "Why did *Citoyenne de Nie* want me to marry her son?"

"That conniving woman knew you were the sole heiress to your English great-grandfather's vast estates and wanted them for her son," Madame explained.

"My head whirls. Tell me why my mother did not claim them on my behalf."

"Perhaps she feared one of his other descendants would become your guardian and remove you from her custody."

"That seems unlikely. After all, she chanced losing me forever when she risked her life for the Royalist cause." Sadness threatened to overcome her. "She did not love me enough to live." Annabelle extricated herself from Roland's arm around her waist. She sank onto a chair. "Extraordinary, I am a French count's daughter; I have English blood in me; I am an heiress, and you are my aunt." Torn between grief and happiness, she hesitated before speaking again. *"Madame,* God is good to have spared you. I have no words to describe how glad I am to be reunited with you."

Madame Valencay trembled, setting the fine lace at her bosom a-flutter. Annabelle hurried to sit next to her, and then kissed the delicate old woman's soft cheek and cradled her in her arms. As though a dam had burst its banks, a cry escaped from Madame's bloodless lips and tears cascaded down her cheeks.

"*Tante*, you must rest. My carriage is outside. With your permission, we will take you home and for as long as you live, you will never lack anything it is within our power to provide."

Roland nodded at Annabelle's aunt. "Madame, like my wife, I am at your service."

"Thank you, but I will return to my lodgings. I want to be with my friends."

"Very well," Annabelle agreed, "but you must go in our carriage."

She gazed hopefully at Roland. After so many years of speculation, there was only one more thing to find which her life had lacked.

Chapter Twenty-Five

Exhausted after the revelations at Cavalierre's house and shocked by the de la Nies' wickedness, Annabelle lay on the chaise lounge in her parlour, and watched Martha pick up a glove from the floor. "Go and inform his lordship that I am too ill to attend the masquerade, and then do not disturb me."

"Very good, my lady," Martha said, and bustled out of the parlour.

Bereft of her dream of a reunion with her parents, Annabelle tried to accept that she was French by birth. She should have guessed. When she arrived at The Beeches, she spoke both fluent French and English with an accent the other girls teased her about.

The door opened. Annabelle looked up, irritated by Fanny's intrusion.

"My first masquerade," Fanny declared, and sank onto a chair. "Will I be recognised? What will it be like, dancing with people one does not recognise while knowing they are acquaintances? Are you looking forward to it?"

"I am too unwell to accompany you."

"Oh, you poor creature, what can I do for you? Would you like me to bathe your forehead with lavender water?"

"No thank you."

Fanny eyed her. "You are very pale. Have you got a headache? Shall I put a cold cloth on your head?'

"You are very kind, but no thank you." She appreciated Fanny's concern, but it grated on her heightened sensibilities.

Her sister-in-law stood and twitched her muslin skirts into place. "There is no need to raise your voice. I only wanted to help."

"I am sorry." Tears, which she tried to quickly rub away, trickled down her cheeks. "I know who I am and why Miss Chalfont told me I was to marry *the toad*."

"Your parents?" Fanny handed her a handkerchief.

Annabelle blew her nose and held her sister-in-law's hand for comfort. "Guillotined, they were French."

Fanny sat next to her on the chaise lounge and hugged her. "How dreadful for you, I know how much you hoped to find them, but we never imagined the truth."

Annabelle related her complicated history and sniffed when she reached the end. "Please don't tell your brother I have been crying, he will think I am weak."

"Of course he would not. Who could blame you for crying?" Fanny continued to hold her tight. "Shall I send for Martha to undress you and help you into bed?" Annabelle shook her head. "If you are sure there is nothing I can do for you, I will go. We can talk more later." A smile illuminated Fanny's face. "A spy…Now I understand why Roland left me at The Beeches. Wellington depended on him, so he had not a moment to spare while engaged in dangerous business."

* * *

Alone, Annabelle closed her eyes. She had always believed she was English. Now that she knew the truth, it seemed as though she inhabited a stranger's body.

"Why are the curtains closed? Why are you in the dark?"

Roland's voice roused her from a troubled doze.

"I must have fallen asleep."

"Have you recovered, or are you too ill to attend the masquerade?"

She hesitated for a moment before she answered. "I am not so unwell that I cannot attend it if you wish me to."

"Good." He lit the candles and stood with his back to the fireplace. "It is time to prepare for the masquerade. Cavalierre has sent the gown I wish you to wear."

Her hands twisted the ends of the gauze ribbons tied beneath her breasts, into a tangle. "Why do you want me to wear it?"

"You look beautiful in it."

Annabelle had not anticipated her husband's shy smile. She must admit the truth about the pearls.

"I am well enough to attend but—"

"Good, I shall accompany you."

She dared not look at him. "I have a confession to make."

"How serious you seem."

Heat scalded her cheeks. "You know how much I wanted to discover the truth about my lineage," she said and glanced at him to gauge his reaction.

"Yes." Roland removed his wedding ring from his finger and held it up to the light as though nothing could be of more importance.

Annabelle went to the window and peered through the drawn curtains at the residents' private garden in the middle of the square. "I hope you will not be angry with me."

"I doubt that anything you could do would anger me."

Much encouraged, she turned to face him, even as the thought crossed her mind that he might be irritated by her. Uncertain, she hesitated, and then realised she must be brave. "I realised de la Nie's son knew who my guardian was."

Roland put the ring back on his finger and raised his eyebrows. "Since I met you, I have appreciated your intelligence."

"Thank you, but it was unintelligent of me not to have thought of that before. Please don't be annoyed with me. I met with de Beauchamp—I mean de la Nie—in private and asked him to tell me the truth."

"Most improper," he said as his mouth began losing its severe lines and his dimples started appearing.

Roland did not seem put out. In fact, he looked so pleased that she eyed him suspiciously. "Yes, I know, it was shocking of me, but I did not meet him alone. Martha accompanied me. Oh Roland, the man is worse than the most abominable toad. He is—"

Roland grinned before he spoke. "Yes, I know, but there is no need to dwell on him. Try to put him out of your mind."

Dumbfounded, Annabelle stared at him. Did he care so little about her that her lack of conduct did not disturb his peace of mind? She turned to look out of the window again. "This is so difficult. For a price he said he would tell me who my guardian was, so, in exchange for information, as well as the old-fashioned emerald and diamond suite, I gave him the pearls you want me to wear tonight."

Roland put an arm around her. "There is nothing to forgive."

She shuddered. "But you don't know the worst, he denies receiving them."

"Wait here for a moment." Her husband released her, went to his own apartment, and then returned. "Annabelle, close your eyes and put out your hands. I have a surprise for you."

She did as she was told. Something cool rested in her palms. Annabelle opened her eyes and saw the pearls. "Roland!"

He smiled that crooked smile of his. "It's my turn to confess. I knew you met the fellow near the milk booth in Hyde Park."

Astonished, she stared up at him. "How on earth did you—?" she began.

He chuckled. "Never question a spy."

Annabelle decided to change tack. "How much did you pay him for the pearls?"

"Nothing, Martha gave all the jewellery to me instead of handing it over to him."

"I shall scold her for disobeying me."

Roland put his finger to her lips. "Do something for me." His heart-winning smile charmed her, although she was still displeased with Martha. "Praise her instead of admonishing her, Belle. She served you well."

She frowned. "If you insist, but only because you are the most forbearing of husbands."

He regarded her keenly. "What is wrong, Belle? After our wedding night, you became distant from me."

Her mouth quivered. She looked away. Now, if ever, was the moment for one last confession. "If I am distant it is because, in the morning, when you were half asleep, you said Juliet Parker's name."

He looked into her eyes, wrapped his arms around her, holding her close. "Is that why you have avoided my embraces?" he asked, his voice husky. "Belle, since we met, you have been the only one who haunts my dreams."

A wave of happiness rushed through her and set every nerve on fire.

"If only you had confided in me, Belle, we would not have wasted so much time sleeping apart every night. I thought the consummation of our marriage offended you so deeply on our one and only night together that you could not bear my touch." He cleared his throat and looked down at the ground. "I cannot apologise enough for saying Juliet when, as you put it, I was half asleep. Please forgive me. On that occasion my mind must have played a trick on me. All my dreams and thoughts are of you."

Annabelle linked her hands around the back of his head, her fingers boldly entwined in his thick hair. "No, you did not offend me," she responded, gladly abandoning modesty.

"I believed you cared nothing for me and suffered on account of your admirers."

She smiled at him and sighed with contentment. Only their future mattered.

Roland's face neared hers. His lips teased her mouth. All too soon the kiss ended. She wanted more. Much more.

He kissed her cheek and released her. "It is time to prepare for the masquerade."

She held onto him. "Must we go?"

He smiled down at her and nodded. "Yes, as much as I want to make love to you, we must go because, after we unmask at midnight, your aunt, with Cavalierre at her side, will reveal your identity to the ton."

"Truly!" she exclaimed, more delighted, if anything, by his confession that he wanted to make love to her, than the forthcoming revelation, and a trifle unnerved at the idea of so many people watching her when it was made.

"Yes. And Cavalierre will be relieved to see you publicly restored to your proper place in society before he returns to France."

"But he told me there is nothing for him in France."

"The new Bourbon king demands his presence at the French court."

She wiped tears from her eyes. "I shall miss him."

"If it pleases you, we shall visit Monsieur le Duc in France, but now it is time to dress for the masquerade."

* * *

After the masquerade, on the way home in the coach with Lady Caroline and Fanny, Roland lowered his head. "Belle," he whispered, "you cannot imagine how impatient I am to be alone with you."

"What did you say?" Lady Caroline demanded from the shadows while Fanny looked at them curiously.

"Nothing of interest to you, Grandmamma."

"Roland, I am prepared to overlook your wife's French ancestry. After all, she is well born. And since she has been brought up in

England, apart from most of her blood being French, she behaves like a real Englishwoman."

"You forget to mention the fortune she has inherited from her great-grandfather," Roland murmured.

"A fortune cannot compensate for a person's inferior birth—not that Annabelle's birth is inferior—it is merely of the French nobility instead of the English nobility, which I would have preferred. Yet I am pleased because your wife is heiress to an English fortune," Lady Caroline concluded with obvious satisfaction.

"Grandmamma sounds like a cat on the verge of purring and making friendly overtures," Roland whispered.

Annabelle suppressed her giggle as the carriage drew to a halt and the four of them went to the drawing room for a glass of wine before they retired.

Lady Caroline yawned. "I am fatigued and shall seek my bed."

Roland escorted his grandmother to the door. "Goodnight, I hope you will sleep well."

As soon as the door closed Fanny giggled. "Only imagine, Grandmamma has set her cap at Lord Stanton."

"The devil she has," Roland exclaimed. "Please pardon me for swearing," he added hastily.

"I hope she will be successful, if that is what she wants," Annabelle responded before her husband could reply. She yawned. "I apologise, but it is nearly dawn. I shall retire."

"But I have something to say," Fanny said.

"Can it not wait until morning?" Roland asked.

Fanny shook her head. "No. Roland, with your permission, I want to marry Charles Luton. Grandmamma said he approached her and that he will request your permission for us to wed."

"We will talk about it in the morning. Don't look so downcast, I have nothing against the fellow. Now, I suggest you go to bed."

No sooner did Fanny leave than Martha entered. "I am sorry, my lord, but with your permission I want to have a word with my lady."

"If you must," Roland growled.

Martha ignored him, although for once she did not address him as a black-hearted devil.

"My lady, I've something to tell you. Caval...oh, I can't twist my tongue round his name...is going to France. But Henry, I mean, Henri, wants to stay in England. So, with your consent, my lady, we'll marry and both of us will serve you and his lordship."

The thought of little crosspatch Henri marrying Martha, whom Henri called a female boxer, made Annabelle's lips twitch. Aware of a strange sound escaping Roland, she did not dare look at him for fear of bursting into laughter.

"Martha," Roland said, "Marry Henri and seal the peace between our two countries. For now, please leave."

"I hoped you would be pleased," Martha said and withdrew with dignity.

"Belle!" Roland exclaimed as they collapsed into laughter, "Henri betrothed to Martha. I can scarcely believe it. However, they may do as they wish, but we shall not be here."

"Where shall we be?"

"If you agree, my dear love, we shall honeymoon apart from friends and relatives."

Roland appeared nonchalant, but his breath came much faster than usual. If he loved her, why did he not take her in his arms?

His voice echoed in the candlelit room. "I hope you are satisfied now that your devoted servant has avenged the de la Nie's villainy?"

"Roland, I do not seek revenge, I seek something my lineage and inheritance can't buy."

"What?"

"Happiness."

"My love," he said, the tender expression in his eyes revealed by the golden glow of candles, "what can I do to make you happy?"

"Be honest. You call me Belle, but I do not know if you think I am beautiful, and you have never expressed your sentiments where I am concerned." Oh, she should not have said that. Suppose Lady Caroline was mistaken. Suppose he did not love her.

Roland's irresistible dimples deepened and caught at her heart. Smiling, he advanced until he stood an inch away from her, his hands behind his back. "Is it possible?" he asked, his eyes glinting in the soft light.

"Is what possible?" she countered, the suspense unbearable.

"Goose, why do you think I married you?" Roland chuckled and put a finger to her lips. He traced their outline, sending shivers of desire through her. "No, no, please do not say I married you to save your reputation. To tell the truth, I think I fell in love with you the moment I first saw you." His eyes clouded. "And you, Belle, why did you marry me?"

She guessed he would feign indifference to her if she was coy. "I married you for love, and that is why I have forgiven all of your false pretences."

He swept her up into his arms and hurried up the stairs to her bedchamber.

"When will we go on our honeymoon?" she asked, delighted by his masculine strength.

He put her down and held his arms out to her. Joyously, she entered into his embrace. At long last she had found the loving harbour she had yearned for as long as she could remember.

Roland trembled and lowered his head. "My love, my dear, dear love, I hope you agree our honeymoon should begin now."

"With all my heart," she concurred, enveloped in a fever of love and desire.

Rosemary Morris books published by Books We Love

Historical 18th Century
The Captain and the Countess

About the Author

Rosemary Morris was born in 1940 in Sidcup Kent. As a child, when she was not making up stories, her head was 'always in a book.'

While working in a travel agency, Rosemary met her Indian husband. He encouraged her to continue her education at Westminster College.

In 1961 Rosemary and her husband, now a barrister, moved to his birthplace, Kenya, where she lived from 1961 until 1982. After an attempted coup d'état, she and four of her children lived in an ashram in France.

Back in England, Rosemary wrote historical fiction. She is now a member of the Romantic Novelists' Association, Historical Novel Society and Cassio Writers.

Apart from writing, Rosemary enjoys classical Indian literature, reading, visiting places of historical interest, vegetarian cooking, growing organic fruit, herbs and vegetables, and creative crafts.

Time spent with her five children and their families, most of whom live near her, is precious.

* * *

Did you enjoy *False Pretences?* If so, please help us spread the word:

- *Recommend the book to your family and friends*
- *Post a review*
- *Tweet and Facebook about it*